GO ALL IN
SCARLETT FINN

ISBN: 9781914517211

www.scarlettfinn.com

Also by Scarlett Finn

GO NOVELS
GO WITH IT
GO IT ALONE
GO ALL OUT
GO ALL IN
GO FULL CIRCLE

EXILE
HIDE & SEEK
KISS CHASE

WRECK & RUIN
RUIN ME
RUIN HIM

**THE BRANDED
SERIES**
BRANDED
SCARRED
MARKED

**FORBIDDEN
PREQUEL DUET**
ALL. ONLY.
ONLY YOURS

THE FORBIDDEN NOVELS
FORBIDDEN DESIRE
FORBIDDEN WANT
FORBIDDEN WISH
FORBIDDEN NEED
FORBIDDEN BOND

**BOMBSHELLS & BILLIONAIRES
(ROXIVERSE)**
NOTHING TO HIDE
NOTHING TO LOSE
NOTHING IN BETWEEN: ONE
NOTHING TO DECLARE
NOTHING TO US
NOTHING IN BETWEEN: TWO
NOTHING TO SAY
NOTHING TO GAIN
NOTHING IN BETWEEN: THREE
NOTHING TO YOU
NOTHING TO THIS PREQUEL: ONE WILD NIGHT
NOTHING TO THIS
NOTHING IN BETWEEN: FOUR
NOTHING TO DO
NOTHING TO NO ONE
NOTHING TO FEAR
NOTHING TO DENY
NOTHING TO BEAT
NOTHING TO THE WEDDING
NOTHING TO TELL
NOTHING TO IT
NOTHING TO SEE
NOTHING TO WIN
NOTHING TO OFFER
NOTHING TO PROVE

**LOVE AGAINST THE ODDS
STANDALONE COLLECTION**
SWEET SEAS
HEIR'S AFFAIR
RESCUED
MAESTRO'S MUSE
GETTING TRICKY
THIRTEEN
REMEMBER WHEN...
RELUCTANT SUSPICION
XY FACTOR

KINDRED SERIES
RAVEN
SWALLOW
CUCKOO
SWIFT
FALCON
FINCH

MISTAKE DUET
MISTAKE ME NOT
SLEIGHT MISTAKE

LOST & FOUND
LOST
FOUND

**THE EXPLICIT
SERIES**
EXPLICIT INSTRUCTION
EXPLICIT DETAIL
EXPLICIT MEMORY

TO DIE FOR...
TO DIE FOR TRUTH
TO DIE FOR HONOR
TO DIE FOR VIRTUE
TO DIE FOR DUTY
TO DIE FOR LOVE

**RISQUÉ & HARROW
INTERTWINED**
TAKE A RISK
FIGHTING FATE
RISK IT ALL
FIGHTING BACK
GAME OF RISK

ONE

"WHERE IS SHE?"

Whoever he was, he was mad. Harlow Sweeting's eyes were assaulted by blinding light, she closed them again fast.

Cutting through the white noise impeding her senses, his voice rose once more. "You don't get the fuck out my way and I'll—"

"We sedated her," a calmer male said. "She was as manic as you. What the hell were you thinking, staying in there? You could've got yourself killed. How would I have explained that to her when she woke up? Do you think she would've bought it? After what we did when you got shot?"

No, probably not. Wait... Harlow replayed that thought, then dismissed it as unimportant. *"Staying in there..."* that felt important.

Her head was groggy; her body ached. She couldn't focus. The calm guy had said something about sedation. From the way she was feeling, he must have been talking about her.

"I need to see her, Bale."

"Ryske—"

"She'll be better if you let me get to her."

The aggravated guy was trying to sound calm so that the calm one would buy his story. She wasn't buying it. Ryske was—

Sitting up fast, Harlow gasped in clarity. "Ryske," she breathed out.

With frantic haste, she threw back the covers, desperate to get out of the bed holding her prisoner.

Yanking at the wires on her chest, she pulled the tube from her nose and ripped off the tape on her hand, holding the IV in place. Machine alarms went crazy. What did she care? All she wanted was freedom. Opening her mouth in reaction to the sensation sliding beneath her skin, she eased the needle from her arm.

Someone took hold of her shoulders and tried to push her down.

"Take your hands off me," she snarled at the male, uniformed like some sort of medical professional. Taken aback by her wild, threatening words, he froze. Raising the needle she'd just pulled from her arm, she held it like a dagger. "Touch me again and I'll jam this in your fucking eye."

"Trink!"

Whipping around, she saw him fifteen feet away, blocked by Bale, trying in vain to contain his brother.

"Crash," she screamed and leaped out of bed, leaving the medical man stuttering in shock.

Dashing toward Ryske, overjoyed that he was there, safe... The world spun, bringing her to a sudden halt.

"Shit, she's going down," someone said just a fraction of a second before her knees buckled.

But she didn't go down. Two strong arms came around her, capturing her, saving her from collapse.

Although her vision was unfocused and her body weighed a ton, Harlow knew who held her. "Crash," she whispered.

"I've got you, baby," he said, sweeping her feet from under her and carrying her back to the bed.

"You tried to leave me," she mumbled. "You didn't come out... asshole."

One of his arms slid out from under her legs. Terrified he was an illusion and she might lose him again, Harlow grabbed for the arm at the back of her neck before he could pull it free.

"I am an asshole, baby. You're right." His mouth touched her forehead. "You're always right. Dover needed me."

The others. "What happened?"

Ryske eased her back down when she tried to sit up. "Everyone is fine, baby. They're all back at Bale's."

"Where you have to go too," Bale said. "Ryske, you've gotta go. You have to. Her parents are on their way. You're not supposed to be in here with her."

"Shit," Ryske hissed. "Fuck, baby, I don't want to leave you again. But if I don't—"

"Proxy," she breathed out, her head falling against his shoulder.

Bone-tired, she couldn't keep her head up. Harlow didn't know what had happened. The details were fuzzy. After collapsing on Maze, she had a vague recollection of EMTs and panic, and then… this.

"Goddamnit, you're right," Ryske said.

"Right about what?" Bale asked.

Too tired to lift her head and check, Harlow made a guess that the doctor was the one putting the wire back on her chest and the tube in her nose.

Ryske breathed out a laugh. "I'm her medical proxy. I have power of attorney," he said. "Every decision about her is mine."

Bale made a sound of disgust. "Wow, Ryske, I never thought I'd see the day you'd con Harlow." His volume lowered and his voice got closer. "Why does a perfectly healthy woman sign power of attorney and medical proxy—"

"She did it while she was in jail," Ryske said. "Yeah, that shut you up… She wanted someone on the outside who could act on her behalf."

"And she chose a con man who wasn't even her boyfriend at the time?"

"A man who would walk through hellfire for her," Ryske said, "yeah."

"Still doesn't change the fact her family are on the way… Don't they think you're engaged to someone else?

Wait, don't they think you're someone else entirely?"

"I want him here," she said, touching Ryske's chest.

The bed was angled up to a seated position. Ryske's arm was around her shoulder, so he had to be sitting next to her. The awkward twist of his upper body suggested an uncomfortable position, half-on, half-off the bed. With one leg straight to the floor keeping him supported, he couldn't be relaxed.

But she needed him close, and tried her best to open her eyes wider to see more. Harlow wanted to stay with him for as long as she could.

"She wants me here."

"Yeah, and if you're medical proxy, you're allowed to be here. How are you going to explain that to her family? Why would a man who's engaged to someone else be sitting by Harlow's bedside? What story—"

"You think I can't come up with something?" Ryske snapped. "If Harlow wants me here, I'm staying."

"Are you injured, Crash?"

Though her head was still spinning and her chest tight, she pushed away and did her best to check him for injuries. He was wearing hospital scrubs, which if she was more awake, she might consider hot.

His face was dirty, smeared with soot that was thick in his hair too. Everything he'd touched had a mark on it: her hospital gown, the bedsheets… Harlow wasn't complaining. Getting him into the scrubs was probably as much of a battle as Bale was willing to take on. A shower would've kept them apart for longer than Ryske would've tolerated.

"I'm not hurt, baby," Ryske said, attempting to guide her back down against him.

She pushed on him and sat straighter, sweeping her hair away from her face. "Where are my clothes?" she asked and coughed.

Bale leaped closer. "Harlow, you're not going anywhere," the doctor said, checking the monitors next to her bed.

"How did you know I wanted to—"

"Because I've been this crew's doctor for a long time.

I know how stubborn all of you are," Bale said. "You have to stay here. For, at least, the next forty-eight hours."

Shaking her head, she kicked at the bedcovers. Somehow, they'd found their way over her again. "I have plans on Saturday."

"Plans? Are you nuts?" Bale asked, looking to Ryske for support when her legs slipped off the edge of the bed.

The doctor caught them and tried to put them back onto the mattress.

On impulse, she kicked out. "Don't touch me!"

"Hey," Ryske said in a tone so smooth it startled her.

Leaning over, he scooped a hand around the curve of her thigh and slid it up slowly, taking her limbs from Bale and easing them back onto the bed. His hand went higher, gathering her hospital gown from her thigh to let him caress her ass. It was only when he reached the curve of her hip that he allowed his hand to move over the top of the material to continue up to her ribs.

He planted a straight arm on the bed, beneath her arm. Harlow found herself under him, her upper body trapped beneath his.

Thinking about why it was necessary for her to get up and move, Harlow opened her mouth to tell him she wanted to leave. Except she didn't get a chance to say anything. His mouth closed over hers, stealing her words. Every need she'd ever had in her life became about the twine of his tongue around hers.

He tasted dirty, or maybe it was her. There was a grittiness to their charcoal kiss. Given what they'd been through that night, she couldn't expect anything else. Skimming her hands up his arms, Harlow lost her fingers in the hair at the back of his head.

"Ryske, you've got to be careful, man. She's on oxygen."

Easing back, Ryske brushed his nose across hers. "She can have mine."

Heaviness overtook her. Using all her energy, Harlow managed to shake her head in a rocking motion on the pillow. "You're not allowed to leave me again."

"Never," Ryske said, trailing his lips across hers.

Turning her nails into his scalp, she wished she could keep him this close forever. "I want to get married," she whispered.

His surprise made him recoil a couple of inches.

As Ryske's lips curled to a smile, the doctor mumbled, "I better check her oxygen levels. She must have a low tolerance for sedation."

"If you want to get married, Trink," Ryske said, tracing the back of his fingers from her jaw down her neck. "We'll get married."

Nodding, she closed her eyes and tucked her head against his shoulder when he scooped an arm around her and twisted to rest at her side.

"I thought you guys weren't even together," she heard Bale say.

"Her guard drops when she's drained," Ryske said. "She's always been this way… Easiest time to get in her panties is when she's tired."

Slipping a hand under the end of his shirt, she dragged her nails across his tattoo. "Is this the hospital you died in?"

"Yeah, baby," Ryske said and kissed the top of her head. "Don't worry about that."

"None of the EMTs were the same," Bale said. "And you've been admitted, so you're upstairs from the ER… The idiot wasn't in the hospital long enough to make an impression. I kept everyone out of his room."

"Anyone does recognize me, I'll tell them I have a twin and get emotional about my loss."

She smiled and tipped her chin up to look at him. "I was pretty devastated when you died. Less than a year later I'm supposed to be screwing your brother?"

Ryske's attention rose to narrow on Bale somewhere behind her. "She's talking about me, doc. Don't get ideas."

Bale's quiet laugh helped to relax her. "She was pretty vulnerable… I could've slipped in there—"

"You think about slipping anything in anywhere, even after I'm dead, and I'll leave instructions for you to be gutted."

Bale's next laugh was louder. "We've already drawn straws on who gets to take over after we've wiped you out."

Sighing, she wouldn't have expected to feel so content after what transpired that night. "Sorry, doc," she murmured, skimming her nails across Ryske's torso. "If he goes, I go."

"You… you… what?"

Ryske guided her chin up, looking into her face wearing a concern she couldn't feel. "You playing?"

"Playing? No," she said, shaking her head. "If you think tonight scared you, then you have no idea… I wouldn't live through grieving you again. I wouldn't…" Her hand went to her wrist. When she didn't feel what she was expecting, her fingers clamped tight around it. "Ryske…" Panic was an understatement for what began to build. "Ryske!"

"Relax," Bale said, reaching over her shoulder to show her bracelet dangling between his fingertips. "I took it off in the ER." Swiping it from him, she looped it onto her wrist. "You're welcome… You know, you're getting as bad as him with these mood swings."

"We're passionate people," Ryske said, fingering the bracelet on her wrist.

Harlow touched her neck. "Where's my—"

Bale's hand appeared over her shoulder to show the bullet she'd looped around her neck before they ran. "You can't put this back on. We'll need another chest film… maybe a few. I'm waiting for your pregnancy test results to come back."

Groaning, she hooked the leather band over Ryske's head and settled the bullet against his chest. He'd have to keep it safe until Bale freed her.

"This man is obsessed with my uterus."

"I prefer the part adjacent to it," Ryske said.

Her eyes rolled. "Yeah, we all know that."

"You think it's not my right to protect my niece or nephew from what could be harmful radiation?" Bale asked, pulling over a chair to sit down by the bed on the opposite side to Ryske.

Shifting to get a better look at him, he was wearing

scrubs under his white doctor coat. She'd only ever seen him in the coat for a brief minute when she came to meet him for lunch. This was her first chance to really absorb the sight.

"I'm having a weird, brother doctor fantasy thing right now," she said, looking back and forth between them. She tugged on the end of Ryske's scrubs. "Can we take these home?"

"Think I have to unless you want me going home naked," he said, settling back against her pillows, locking both hands behind his head. "You have a thing for doctors?"

She shrugged. "Who knew?"

"I bring it out in a lot of women," Bale said.

She laughed. Waving her fingers back and forth between them, her head twisted left to right. "It's like you're switching personalities." Touching her head, her smile fell. "Maybe I did die."

"I think if you died, we'd be somewhere nicer than a hospital room," Ryske said, sliding a hand up her back when she sat straighter. "Like a beach… a nudist beach… a private nudist beach."

She smiled. "Now who's having a fantasy?"

"Think I'll add contraception to your med list," Bale muttered. "Have you been taking your pills? Faithfully?"

Pulling her legs up, she crossed them beneath the sheet. "What is with you?" she asked, throwing up her hands and letting them flop again. "I'm not pregnant."

"We made a deal about ten years ago," Ryske said, stroking her back and straightening his crooked leg to get more comfortable on the bed.

"What deal?"

"That he'd settle down when he became a father," Bale said. "Stop with the illegal shit; the shit that could get him killed."

Both Ryske and Bale had parental issues. Bale's adoptive parents were dead. Ryske's father had beat him. Their mother was… less than a stellar role model. Bale probably wanted to know that his niece or nephew would have a stable influence in his or her life.

"Well, I guess we should talk about that," she said,

twisting around to set her focus on Ryske who looked like he could go to sleep himself.

"You think if he goes straight, you'll lose interest?" Bale asked from behind her.

Ryske didn't look worried. Why would he? His confidence in his sex appeal was solid and with good reason.

"No," she said, struggling to maintain her smile. Toying with the tie on Ryske's pants, she kept her focus away from both of them. "Because I don't know if I want to have children."

Ryske didn't flinch, but Bale seemed upset. "Why not? Why wouldn't you want to have kids?"

"Don't stress, doc," Ryske said, slipping his hand between the tied sides of her gown to drum his fingers on her spine. "We'll work it out."

"She just said she wanted to marry you, but now she doesn't want to have your baby. You're not offended?"

"No," Ryske said, shrugging one shoulder. "These things have a way of figuring themselves out. She's already said she wouldn't get rid of my kid, so if it happens, we'll handle it… If it doesn't… we'll still be happy. All I need is my Trinket."

That made her happy, though it pissed the doctor off. Slumping back in his seat, he squeezed the arms.

Harlow lay down, nestling herself against Ryske. "Finding somewhere to live is going to be the priority," she said, resting a hand over his heart. "How's Dover?"

"Going nuts," Ryske said. "He's gonna take this hard."

He was underestimating how all the crew were going to take it. Floyd's had been their life since they were kids, and God only knew what was left of it.

"How bad is it? Is he insured?"

"Yeah," Ryske said. "'Cept if it's arson, we could have trouble…"

Sitting up again, she searched his face. "You think someone set the fire on purpose?"

"I think the alleyway staircase was an inferno… I know the hallway was impassable… What kind of fire would set in a line from the door to the den? All the way along, through the bar, to the stairwell at the opposite side of the building? The front of the building is practically untouched," Ryske said. "The firefighters are there. They'll do an investigation, we can't stop that… But this is going to be Dover's life for a while."

"And we won't be pouring drinks," she said, forlorn and a little overwhelmed by the sad situation. They'd lost what had become a staple in all their lives. "Is anything salvageable?"

"We'll have to figure out if they set the trail through the basement and how sound the foundations are… There will be a structural assessment. Good news is the fire didn't spread to the second floor. Though, I guess there will be smoke and water damage up there."

"So I wouldn't be in such a rush to get out of here if I were you," Bale said. "Everyone's squashed in like sardines at my place… Don't know how long that will work out."

"We're used to existing around each other," Harlow said, thinking about how it might be an adjustment for the doctor. "You're the one who'll be going crazy."

"You're not usually in such a small space," Bale said.

He came to the Floyd's apartment to hang out; he knew their setup. The apartment was almost the same size as the bar beneath it, so they did have some room to breathe. Privacy was non-existent. The crew shared a bathroom with a door that didn't close completely. They shared a closet, where all their things were crammed in. Their beds were in the same room. Even though it was a large one, it still led to an unusual level of forced intimacy, which had quickly become her norm.

"We'll work it out," Ryske said, not stressed. "Supporting Dover is a priority. Everything else is details. Everyone we care about is alive. That's what matters." Pulling her closer, he pressed a kiss to her hair. "Tell me my girl's gonna be okay, doc."

"I fainted," she said. "You're making a big deal of nothing. Maze said you were still inside. I was freaking out. I couldn't breathe… It was stupid, but not a big deal."

"You're being treated for smoke inhalation," Bale

said. "They thought about intubating you until you woke up in the back of the ambulance and started smashing the place up."

"They're going to bill me for that mess," Ryske said.

Harlow prodded his ribs. "They'll have to find us first."

Ryske laughed, a deep purr of appreciation. The doctor wasn't so impressed and chose not to address her impertinence.

"They sedated you and brought you here," Bale said.

"The firefighters forced us out," Ryske said. "Dover and I were trying to contain it… wasn't easy."

"You're an idiot," she said. "If you'd left me to protect bricks and mortar, even special bricks and mortar, I'd never have forgiven you."

He smirked. "Is there ever a scenario where you'd forgive me for dying on you?"

Thinking about it for a second, she came up with nothing. "No… I'll still be pissed even if you die when you're ninety."

"Yeah, I can relate," Ryske said. "I could tell something was wrong the minute I saw Maze. I asked about you. All he'd say was that Noon had taken Anwen to Bale's… That's it. That's all I could get for a minute and a half… felt like a year. When he said you'd been blue-lighted to hospital… Man, baby, I didn't know if I wanted to start shooting or throw myself off a bridge."

"Good thing you came to check on her first," Bale said. "You know, you guys always talk about being in love, but you're damn quick to think about pulling the trigger on yourselves."

Reflecting on how it had felt to lose Ryske, Harlow wondered if she'd ever be able to think back on that memory—knowing that he was alive—without feeling the chasm of emptiness. The licking flames of excruciating torture that had been her life in grief still felt as potent as they had then.

"You'll never know what it's like," she murmured, drifting. "To think you're living in the world without the other half of your whole… There are no words to describe it."

Ryske's arm slid around her to pull her closer. In a moment of respect for what she'd endured, no one said a word.

Their reverie was shattered when the door flew open and her family poured inside.

"Oh my God!" Jean Sweeting, her mother, declared. "Harlow, what have you done to yourself?"

What had happened wasn't her fault. She hadn't considered what she'd tell her parents about the fire. Regardless of which facts were shared and which were concealed, there was one thing Harlow had no intention of hiding.

Ryske tried to be subtle about sitting up and sliding his arm out from around her.

Harlow grabbed his hand as it was about to leave her shoulder and pulled it back down. "It's nice to see you too, Mom."

TWO

HER MOTHER WASN'T the only new arrival. Harlow's father, Brysen Sweeting, and her sister, Lena, were present too. All of them looked somewhat disheveled. They'd have been pulled out of their beds at this ungodly hour by whichever orderly decided it was a good idea to rat on her.

First responders had a habit of recognizing her. Especially since she'd become notorious as the kind social worker turned suspected murderess who'd wheedled her way out of felony charges.

There were probably cops on the fire scene. Given Harlow had been identified by a cop on the Hagan security tape, and she'd been arrested outside Floyd's, it wouldn't have taken long to make the connection.

In children and family services, she had worked with cops. Even if someone didn't know her personally, they'd remember her face from that damned security video. From there, her former employment, or prison records, could be accessed at the touch of a button. Her parents would've been listed on both as her official next of kin.

A lot had changed since she'd been gainfully employed. Harlow didn't know if her lawyer, Greta, had lodged the papers stating Ryske was her proxy with the court.

Everything had happened quickly after he'd signed them. Even if it was written somewhere official that Ryske was her proxy, no one would have been able to get in touch with him. He didn't have a phone.

At least he was still officially alive. That was something. Although she'd believed Ryske was dead after the shooting, he had never been legally dead. The fact that he was breathing wouldn't raise any questions for official agencies. Huntley Ryske had no death certificate. The crew had gone that far in faking Anwen's death, but Ryske's death had only been meant to fool her. Harlow hadn't demanded paperwork; none of that had been needed to convince her.

Her parents came deeper into the room, pulling Lena between them. Then came the cherry on her sundae when Rupert walked in too. Bale was getting to his feet, greeting people and shaking hands.

"Are you her doctor?" Brysen asked.

Rupert shook Bale's hand. "We've met. You're Harlow's friend."

"Doctor Bale is her boyfriend," Lena said, starting with confidence but trailing off as she caught on to what the other perplexed people seemed to have noticed.

They all knew the man sitting on the bed with her.

Her mother was the first to make the identification out loud. "Mr. Ryske?"

They were used to him being more preened. Tonight, he wasn't even clean. There was no slick suit, only hospital scrubs. Harlow didn't blame them for being confused.

"Just Ryske is fine," Ryske said, turning his face into her hair. "Want me to handle this?"

That was his way of asking if she wanted him to vamp. To conjure up some story that her family would buy as to why he was there and why he had his arm around her.

"No," Harlow said, patting his thigh. "I've got it."

"What are you going with?"

Sitting up, out of his embrace, Harlow smoothed the bedcovers over her thighs. "The truth," she said, then smiled. "Ryske and I are together."

She hadn't exactly cleared that with him. As of a few

hours ago, they hadn't been together in the strictest interpretation of the word… or maybe any interpretation of it. Yet, there she was announcing her relationship to her folks without getting the okay from her declared other half.

The panic of nearly losing him brought so much into focus. Grievances got sidelined fast when tragedy threatened. Sure, she wasn't ready to jump into full bliss. Her comment about marriage had been drug and adrenaline induced, but she was ready to call them an item and build a relationship with him.

"To… together?" Lena asked, glancing at Rupert at her side. "What do you mean together?"

"I thought he was engaged to Ophelia Hagan," Rupert said.

Harlow noted how although they stood next to each other, neither Rupert nor Lena was touching the other. There was a clear foot of awkward space between them. If they'd told her parents about the baby they were expecting together, they hadn't gone so far as to explain that Harlow knew, or if they had, her parents hadn't taken the news well.

"No," Harlow said. "He's not… and he actually never was." Ryske's hand curved around her shoulder in a show of support… That's how she chose to interpret it anyway. Maybe he was telling her to hold back, maybe not. It didn't matter; she wanted everything out there. "He's not a millionaire tycoon either."

"He's… he's not a millionaire?"

Lena's questions might be sort of dumbfounded and naïve, but at least she was managing to hazard them.

"No."

"So what does he do?" Lena asked. "And why did he—"

"We'll leave that up to your imagination," Harlow said, peeking over her shoulder at Ryske to see he was smiling. After he winked, she carried on. "We've been together for quite a while…"

"I've been on her since the minute we met," Ryske said, which was so true and so hilarious that Harlow had to laugh out loud. "What? You said truth. It's true."

"Yes, it is," she said, seeking his hand to interlace their fingers. "Our relationship has been rocky, to say the least. We broke up…" When he came back from the dead. "Ryske came to SweSec, not to trick anyone, but to get close to me… He wanted to get close to me again."

"That was months ago," Rupert said. "That was when we…"

The way he trailed off made Lena look over her shoulder. Rupert dropped his gaze.

"It's a complicated story, but I didn't lie to you," Harlow said. "I intended to do what I told you I would."

Clarity raised Rupert's chin. A straight, accusatory finger ascended too. "He's the one."

"The One?" Harlow asked, pulling Ryske's hand to her lap. "I don't know if I believe in all that soulmates stuff. He's an arrogant prick most of the time, but—"

"No, the one you said you were with in the city. You told me you were with another man."

Harlow nodded once. "Yes."

"He's the one who likes to see you with other men."

Jean and Lena both squawked.

"Uh, no," Ryske said. "That's not what she said. She said it pisses me off and that she likes pissing me off… Both of those are true." He kissed her shoulder. "This truth stuff is cool."

"Oh my God, you were listening to us," Rupert said on a gasp. "You were there in the hallway and after you… Both of you took a long time to come down the stairs."

"Yeah, she was giving me head."

Squeezing hard, Harlow dug her nails into the back of his hand. "We don't need to share every truth, honey."

If it was just Rupert, or even Rupert and Lena, she wouldn't mind so much. But it was clear her parents were in shock. Adding more illicit details wouldn't speed their recovery.

"You're together… You're with this man," Jean said. "Were you with him tonight? We… we got word you were in a bar fight, I—"

"Fire, Mom," Harlow said. "The building we were in

was on fire. They brought me here by ambulance, but I'm okay."

Rupert's finger was still pointed at Ryske until he swung it around toward Bale. "I don't understand, who is he?"

"A good friend of both of ours," Harlow said. "Bale and I were never together. He came to hang out with me after I learned Ryske had been an asshole again. It's sort of a recurring theme in our relationship."

"This is… this is shocking," her father said and clung to the end of her bed. "You were never going to invest with us."

"I'm invested in your daughter," Ryske said. "SweSec is safe from me and mine."

Harlow hadn't confirmed how Ryske made a living. From her father's pallor, she assumed he was reaching his own conclusions. Ryske had sold himself well. Brysen had been drawn in, something her father claimed would never happen to him.

"You're together," Rupert said.

"Gonna get married," Ryske said, picking up her hand to kiss the back.

"Well, we're going to talk about it."

Ryske muttered something probably along the lines of her being the one to have brought it up or being fickle.

"This is… I don't know what to say," Rupert said.

"You were in a fire?" Lena asked. At least one person was paying attention to the real drama. "In a bar… Why were you in a bar in the middle of the night?"

"We live in a bar," Ryske said.

"Oh my God, you live with him?" Rupert snapped. "You wouldn't live with me until we were engaged. Despite his claims, I don't see a ring on your finger."

Was he offended? In her worrying about her parents' reaction, it hadn't occurred to her Rupert's would be this strong. Before Harlow had learned about him and Lena, she might have been more sympathetic to indications her relationship hurt him. But the man had impregnated another woman and was planning to marry her. He couldn't claim ownership over her anymore.

Her curiosity about Rupert's reaction was tempered when Ryske sat straighter. She could feel him tense. Before her love could say anything, or act, Lena spoke up.

"Why do you care who she's marrying? You've been broken up forever… Isn't that what you told me?"

"I… I wasn't saying that I cared," Rupert said, though his reaction said it for him.

"Doctor," Jean said to Bale. "You are a doctor, aren't you?" Bale nodded. "What's wrong with her? Will she be okay?"

"We think she'll be fine. We do want to keep an eye on her for a day or two," Bale said. "The fire was intense and the smoke may have damaged her lungs. We'll want to take some more pictures of her chest, just to make sure nothing sinister develops."

"What the hell is sinister?" Ryske asked. "You never told me sinister."

"I couldn't tell you anything because you were too busy charging around like a wild animal," Bale said. "She's fine and I'm sure she'll be fine. If she follows her doctor's orders."

There was an undercurrent there that reminded her of the stars on her arm. Bale was her doctor, he was the crew doctor, and they were bound to do what he said.

"I have to be out by Saturday," she said, touching her stars.

"Baby, I'll take care of that," Ryske said.

Flipping around, she touched his jaw. "I'm in this. We're in this…"

"What about Ophelia?" Lena asked, drawing everyone's focus.

For a second, Harlow was shocked to discover her sister was aware of anything Pothos related. Then she remembered what they'd been talking about before.

"Yes," Jean said. "She stayed at our house… She said she was engaged to Mr. Ryske."

"My friendship with Ophelia was genuine," Harlow said, refraining from adding the word "once." "She and Ryske have been friends for many years."

"She perpetuated the lie?" Rupert said.

He had a real bug up his ass. "Can I have a minute alone with Rupert, please?" Harlow asked, unable to take her attention from her ex.

Her parents wouldn't think anything of her wanting to talk to a man she'd been close to for years. Especially if they didn't know about his connection to their youngest daughter. It seemed they were still ignorant. Despite an initial visible urge to object, Lena stayed quiet and let her mother put an arm around her.

"I'll see what I can do about finding a hotel for tonight," Brysen said and headed to the door with his wife and daughter in tow.

Bale stood up after they were gone. "I'll go see if your labs are back."

He took one step before she spoke. "Bale," she said, and flicked her eyes to the side toward the man on her bed.

Ryske wouldn't want to leave. The only way she'd get him out the room without a fight, and keep him out, was if someone took responsibility for him.

"Right," Bale said and came around the bed to punch Ryske's arm. "You need to call and find out how everyone else is doing."

"Later," Ryske grumbled.

Harlow pushed his thigh. "I think that's a great idea. They might need supplies."

"I'm not leaving."

"You have to," Bale said. "There's a bunch of paperwork you have to sign."

"Shouldn't her parents do that?" Rupert asked.

Ryske gritted his teeth, and something like a growl seeped out of him.

"Ryske has medical power of attorney… all power really," she said to Rupert while stroking Ryske's leg. "He makes my medical decisions. Authorizes whatever I need."

"Bet you never had that, did you, Marlowe?" Ryske snarled.

His adrenaline from the fire obviously hadn't waned just yet.

Twisting around, she stroked his stubble. "Just give

me one minute, baby… please… Crash."

"Why?" Ryske grumped, his focus zeroed in on Rupert. "I already know he fucked your little sister and knocked her up. There's nothing he can hide from me."

Rupert's shock was palpable. Bale must have felt it too because he grabbed Ryske's arm and was more forceful about pulling him off the bed. The doctor hadn't known who the father of Lena's baby was, more because she hadn't gotten around to telling him than because she didn't trust him with the secret.

Rupert wouldn't appreciate his shame being broadcast. He couldn't possibly understand how informing her crew was a formality, not a betrayal. Harlow would trust them with her life. Tonight had proven again how far they would go for each other.

"Come on," Bale said, yanking Ryske along. "We'll find some people for you to glare at in the waiting room… come on."

THREE

RYSKE KEPT HIS glare on Rupert until the very last second. He wasn't the only peeved man around either. As soon as Bale pulled Ryske out of the room and the door swung shut, Rupert marched over to drop down on the edge of her bed.

"How could you tell him?" he hissed. "We haven't even told your parents yet."

"Ryske isn't going to tell anyone," she said. "I was in shock after I found out. Ryske supported me. He supports me through everything, Rupert. Don't ever be surprised if he knows everything I know because I wouldn't hesitate to tell him anything."

"What about our deal? About your promise to come back to me, does he know about that?"

"Yes."

Assuming his question was supposed to deliver some sort of gut punch, Harlow smiled.

He flinched. "You told him that?"

"I tell Ryske everything… eventually. I trust him. More than I've ever trusted anyone."

"More than you trusted me?"

"Not at the time," she said. "At the time we were together, I thought you were the most straight up together guy

I'd ever met… I'll tell you, this thing with Lena has opened my eyes… You're just as screwed up as the rest of us, Rupert. No matter how much you try to hide it."

It surprised her that he wasn't offended. "That may be true. I don't want you to be hurt, and a man like him…"

"You loved Ryske when you and Daddy brought him back to the house… or was it just his money you loved? Great thing about him? He can be whatever you want him to be. I want him to be himself. But if it means something to you for him to put on fake airs and graces, I'll ask him to do it. We'll turn it into a game."

He sneered. "A sex game?"

Marrying a half-shrug to a half-smile, she sank back into her pillows. "Maybe… He will do pretty much anything for sex, so…"

Shaking his head, Rupert took a moment to compose himself before moistening his lips and rubbing a hand across his chin. "I don't understand this. I don't understand how you could let yourself be led by—"

"Ryske doesn't lead me," she said, rejecting the laughable notion. "If anything, I lead him… He'd do anything to make me happy. Anything in the world, Rupert."

"I would've done anything to make you happy and it wasn't enough. Why is he different?"

Harlow shook her head. "You're comparing apples and oranges," she said. "You're two very different men. I can give you an example from ten minutes ago. Ryske sat in this room and told Bale that it didn't matter whether we had children or not. He said that all he needed to make him happy was me." Harlow smiled, tracing her fingertips across the bracelet on her wrist. "I believe him, Rupert. All he wants is me. And all I want is him."

"It was about children? You left me because of children?"

"No," she said and breathed out. "We've talked about this. You and I, we weren't suited. We didn't want the same kind of life. What I have with Ryske, it's dynamic. We adapt. We change. Nothing is set in stone and nothing is a disaster… As long as we're in each other's lives, we're never alone… I felt alone with you. I felt… You had an affinity with my father. Lena was close to my mom… I always felt like I was looking at you all from the outside. I didn't get it. I never got it… With Ryske, I get it, and he gets me… He accepts me. He accepts my faults. He accepts that I might not always want to be his best friend and that I might not always bend to his will."

"I accepted you."

Shaking her head, she couldn't figure out how to make him understand. "It's not the same," Harlow said, and reached for his hand.

At the contact, an odd sensation made her withdraw.

"What is it?" Rupert asked. "He doesn't let you touch other men? We were in love before we even knew he existed."

"Rupert, you can't make this a competition," she said. "For one thing, after I made our deal, I was prepared to leave him. The delay was never because of him… We didn't even think about getting back together until I was in jail. By then, I was determined to make sure Ryske was free. I knew he loved me… I also knew it was likely I'd spend the rest of my life in prison. I wouldn't let him tie himself to me. I couldn't."

"It was him…" Rupert exhaled with new clarity. "All those times when we tried to arrange visits and you said we couldn't come. You were seeing him."

"Some of the time," she said. "Sometimes it was our friends."

If he got on his high horse about that, she'd put him in his place fast. Harlow had refused to let her family visit on just a handful of occasions. Ryske and her crew were the ones who'd gone out of their way to reshuffle schedules to accommodate Rupert and her father.

"I can't believe you kept this from me."

"Do you really want to start throwing that around?" she asked and lowered her voice. "Why haven't you told my parents about Lena? Have you told your mom?"

Rupert's mom would be over the moon to have a grandchild; she wouldn't care where it came from. After their break up, Rupert's mom had made her dislike of Harlow known to anyone who would listen. At the same time, she'd broadcast that the separation was mutual; most people saw through that half-truth.

While Harlow hadn't up and decided to break his heart for fun, she couldn't deny being the instigator of the separation. If she'd kept her mouth shut, everything would've been fine… for Rupert and their families. She'd have been the only one to suffer in a life of misery and apathy.

His aversion to the topic was understandable. "Do you think now's the time to talk about this?"

"I think this is the first time we've been alone," Harlow said. "I think this is the first time my head is on straight. And I think that as much as I'm a little creeped out by the idea you've been with both me and my sister, I have to accept that this is reality. Just like you have to accept that Ryske is now a part of your reality."

"My reality?" he objected. "I won't have anything to do with the man. He lied to me."

"Yeah? Get in line," she said. "Ryske did lie to you and you lied to me. You would never have told me about you and Lena if she hadn't gotten pregnant. What if Ryske hadn't existed? What if I wanted to come back to you? We'd have based our whole relationship on a lie."

Accepting her statement brought him down from his high horse enough to show some contrition. "I do not have to accept his lie. There's no love between him and I."

"Maybe not," she said and smiled. "But if I do have children, they'll be his, which means his children and yours will be cousins. You said you were going to marry Lena, and you always spend holidays with us. You and Ryske are going to be brothers-in-law, unofficially if nothing else. You can despise each other as much as you like, and I'll say the same thing to him. But, honey, you're family now."

The door opened again. Another person came bundling in shimmering with tension and fear.

"What is—"

"Clyde," she said, her lips settling into a smile. "Hey, honey. How you doing?"

"How am *I* doing?" he asked, rushing across the room to pull her into a hug. "What the hell happened? Where's Ryske?"

As soon as he uttered the name, he leaned back and clamped his lips, side-eying Rupert. Obviously, her friend was worried he'd just revealed a secret. As far as he knew, her family and Rupert were ignorant to her and Ryske's connection.

Harlow laughed. "It's okay. We're out now. How did you hear about the fire?"

"It's all over the neighborhood."

"Clyde, honey, you don't live in the neighborhood."

"Felipe called me. Gina did too."

"Oh, Felipe," she said.

She should get in touch to let him know the crew was okay.

The kid was close to everyone at Floyd's. He'd be devastated if any of them were hurt. She should call Costello too; she couldn't ask Ryske to do that.

"What happened?" Clyde asked, sitting on the edge of her bed facing her.

"Arson, Ryske says." Clyde's mouth opened in shock. "I know… Dover's going to be off the reservation for a while."

"Or forever."

"Who's Dover?" Rupert asked.

The man thought he knew her so well. For a time, he'd been the closest person to her. But the distance growing between them stretched every day.

Why were so many people awake at this time of night? And why did they all have questions and agendas? As if proving her point, the door opened again. The medical guy who first appeared stepped aside to reveal someone else.

Shit. She bristled at the sight of the last woman she wanted to see.

"Oh, Harlow!"

"Ophelia," she said, unable to keep the foul taste on her tongue from slipping into her tone. "What do you want?"

Ophelia came gliding across the room, assessing both Clyde and Rupert. "I just heard," Ophelia said. "Isn't it awful, Mr. Marlowe?"

Rupert was at a loss for how to respond. He would

probably agree that a fire where life was endangered was an awful thing. But he'd also just learned that this woman had been lying to him for months.

Opening her arms, Ophelia was about to thrust Clyde out of the way when Harlow noticed the sparkle on her hand. Reaching for the precious rock, she pulled Ophelia's hand down before she could think about hugging her or blocking Clyde.

"We're going to need that back," Harlow said, squeezing Ophelia's hand as she tugged the ring from it.

"Wh… what?"

Once Harlow had the ring, she admired it for a moment and then held it toward Rupert. "You're going to need the money… I don't need it anymore." Ophelia squawked. "Yeah," Harlow said, scratching her earlobe. "That was a hand-me-down."

It wasn't her intention to humiliate Ophelia; that was just a nice side benefit.

"Harlow, I don't understand why—"

"It doesn't matter, Ophelia. We're business partners," Harlow said and picked up her hand to pat it. "We're stuck with each other and that's that."

Clyde was the only one as amused as her. Rupert was holding the engagement ring, probably still trying to fathom why Ophelia had it. Figuring it out shouldn't take him too long. Rupert had been told that she and Ryske were together, and that the Ophelia engagement was fake. The engagement ring had been lying around. It was a good prop, hence why it was used.

Ophelia snatched her hand back. "Where's Ryske?" she asked, her jaw tight.

Dropping her smile, Harlow feigned solemnity. "He's dead."

Ophelia's eyes widened. Clyde's smile dropped too because he hadn't actually got an answer to his question about Ryske. Sometimes it took her friend a second or two to catch up. It should've been obvious to him that she wouldn't have been kidding around if her love had been murdered… again.

"No," Ophelia gasped.

The door at the other end of the room opened. Ryske came in with Bale.

"Hallelujah, it's another miracle," Harlow said and enjoyed her own joke with a laugh.

"What the fuck is going on?" Ryske asked, storming over to get in front of Ophelia, blocking her from the bed.

"I think Harlow's high," Clyde said, his lips contorted in a badly disguised smile.

Ryske was intent on Ophelia. "What the hell do you want, Fi?"

"She miraculously heard about our misfortune," Harlow said, extending a finger to touch his ass, drawing lines up and over the tight curve, then spreading her fingers to stroke him. "Isn't that funny? In the middle of the night when most people are asleep, Ophelia heard about a random fire all the way across town."

She could only see Ryske from behind, but guessed he was glaring. Her suspicion was confirmed when his head snapped to the side to fixate on Clyde, and she got a good look at his profile.

"What's the sap doing here?"

"Felipe called him," she said, patting his butt. "The whole neighborhood's awake. You should let him know we're okay."

"I was worried about Harlow," Clyde said, standing up like he intended to defend his presence. Only he quickly lost his nerve and his smile. Facing up to the threat probably reminded Clyde that Ryske didn't have a history of being happy to see him. Instead of backing down, he tried to fake confidence. Bad move. "All we knew was there was a fire. She could've been killed. You're supposed to keep her safe!"

Harlow winced. "Oh," she said, repeating the word over and over when Ryske grew more tense and swept Ophelia aside. "Oh. Oh. Oh…"

Grabbing for Ryske's arm, she caught his wrist and tried to pull him back. Didn't take him much effort to yank his hand away to advance on Clyde. Her friend tried to maintain his bravado while retreating.

"You think I put her in danger on purpose?" Ryske

snarled. "You fucking prick. You want your ass handed to you again? Huh? I let you get away with laying lips on my girl once. This is the fucking shit that happens when guys think you're soft."

Seizing Clyde's jacket, Ryske slammed him back against the wall. "I… I…." was all her friend could muster.

"Goddamnit," Harlow said, fighting to untangle her legs from the covers. Extricating them, she pulled the cannula out of her nose and tugged the wires from her chest again. When the machines started hollering, Ryske's head snapped around to check her, but he didn't release Clyde. "Yeah, that's right, I'm dead." Throwing her legs from the bed, she ignored her wobble and went storming over to them. "While you're over here playing macho man, I could be taking my last breath. Well done, Crash."

"Get back in bed," he barked at her and returned his attention to Clyde. "We're gonna take this outside."

"You've been desperate to beat on someone since that Costello mess," she said, grabbing his arm and pulling on it until she could duck down under his elbow and squeeze herself between him and Clyde. If nothing else, being the meat in their sandwich kept her upright. "Now all you're doing is rubbing his dick on my ass."

Tilting her head, she waited for Ryske's growl. He shoved away, thrusting Clyde against the wall.

Her man grabbed her shoulders to haul her forward. "Get away from him."

"You know there's nothing between us," she said, stroking his chest and letting him put an arm around her to guide her back to the bed.

Almost a minute later, while Ryske was tucking the covers around her hips, Bale ran in with a nurse. He took in the scene, saw she was okay, relaxed, and spoke to the nurse.

"False alarm," Bale said. The nurse slipped out. "I'm tempted to sedate you again, Sweeting."

Bale eyed Ophelia and the panting Clyde still flat against the wall. The doc only spared Rupert a brief glance. He came over and tried to push Ryske aside, but her man wasn't for budging.

"He's having a moment," she said, patting Ryske's arm.

Bale didn't ask anything else. He went around the bed to where Rupert was standing and started to reconnect her to everything.

"When you were sedated, you weren't such a difficult patient," Bale said and nodded toward his brother. "I thought he was bad."

Tension radiated from Ryske with such intensity, it almost had mass.

Leaning forward, she took his hand, knowing it was her responsibility to loosen him up. "If my doctor sedates me, will you take advantage of me?"

It took half a minute for Ryske to even blink. The various sounds of horror from Rupert, Clyde, and Ophelia broke through to him.

"Damn right I will," Ryske said, sinking down to sit on the bed again, shoving her across it to give himself more space.

"Ryske, I would like to speak to you," Ophelia said, probably assuming she was asserting herself. "Alone."

Tiredness dragged her down the bed while she pulled her covers higher.

"I want you to get the fuck out and never come back," Ryske said. "Only one of us will get our way."

"I think the patient needs to sleep now," Bale said, always trying to find the calmest way out of a fraught situation.

Grateful for the doctor's suggestion, she relied on his support. "I do," Harlow said, searching for Ryske's hand to bring his palm up to her face so she could embrace it.

"I'm going to find your parents," Rupert said. "We'll come back in the morning."

Harlow's eyes closed. Ryske growled when Rupert's lips met her head, so she held him tighter.

"Thank you for coming," she whispered and assumed Rupert left.

"I'm going to go too," Clyde said. "I just wanted to check you were okay."

Her friend didn't come near her. That was no surprise

given how Ryske reacted when Clyde tried to stand up for himself. When she was out of the hospital, she'd make a point of reconnecting with Clyde who she'd valued so much in her lowest times.

"Everyone else is getting the hint," Ryske said, probably talking to Ophelia.

"I'll wait and walk you out," Ophelia said.

Ryske scoffed and stroked Harlow's hair with the hand she wasn't embracing. "You'll be waiting a while. I'm not going anywhere."

"You can't stay here forever."

"Only until my girl leaves," Ryske said.

Harlow heard a sound like boots hitting the floor and then he took his hand away. Her whimper of disappointment was answered by him changing position to lie down to gather her against him.

"You're not being reasonable," Ophelia said. "She stole from me… from us."

"If I look like I give a fuck, I'm a better actor than I gave myself credit for," Ryske said. "Fuck off, Fi."

"I'll walk you out, Miss Hagan," Bale said, again, doing what needed to be done to protect his brother from acting in a way he might regret.

There was movement and then the sound of a curtain being pulled on a rail. A door closed and then there was silence.

"Are we alone?" she murmured, afraid she wouldn't be able to stay awake for much longer.

"Yeah, baby," Ryske said, gathering her hair away from her face. "Go to sleep."

"Promise you'll stay."

"I promise."

With a smile on her lips, she relaxed. There had been a time he wouldn't have made that promise. Offering any kind of promise had been against his rules when they met. Back then, neither of them had known that they would become so intrinsic in each other's lives. After all they'd been through, Harlow couldn't imagine life being any other way.

FOUR

THE HOSPITAL was horrible.

Harlow never wanted to spend another night in hospital if she could help it. The food was bad. The smells were bad. The noises were awful. The only time she enjoyed herself was while Ryske held her in her sleep.

After a bunch of chest x-rays, radiation probably glowed from within her. In spite of repeated signs that she was okay, Bale insisted on keeping her until Saturday. His resolve seemed stupid given that she was going back to his apartment. She'd literally be living with a doctor; it wasn't like she could die while under his care.

Ryske had been at the hospital throughout her stay. No one had confirmed it, but Harlow was pretty sure he hadn't left since she'd got there. Even though he'd showered, had a change of clothes, and brought her food from the outside, he didn't need to leave to get any of those things. The guys were on call to bring them whatever they needed.

When Saturday came and Bale discharged her, relief for her liberation almost matched what she'd felt getting her ankle monitor removed. Noon was there to take her and Ryske back to Bale's, where everyone was staying.

Going inside, she took a minute to observe their

refugee camp. The TV emitted a din. There were things everywhere, strewn across any empty space on the floor. The apartment seemed so much smaller. The couch had been pulled out into a full-size bed, and there were two air beds on the floor as well.

"Hey!" Maze said, leaping out of the armchair to dump his laptop on the pull out couch where Anwen was sitting.

Grabbing her away from Ryske, he hugged her tight, giving her a chance to see what was lying around. Mostly, it was clothes and boxes, which she guessed came from Floyd's. The structural assessment confirmed the building was sound. Although that was great news, they'd have to wait until the structure dried out to fully assess the damage.

"I'm glad you're okay, Harlow," Anwen said, but didn't bother to get up.

With an arm around her, Maze pulled her deeper into the room. "We're a riot without you, babe."

"I can see that," she said, stepping over a sports bag. "We better get home soon or Bale will euthanize all of us… Where is everyone sleeping?"

"We decided to let Bale keep his bedroom when he's here," Maze said, guiding her toward the second bedroom. "Anwen slept in there the first night; that was her room when she was here after the attack." Which wasn't that long ago. "So, we figure she can sleep there when Bale is on nightshift. I'm on the pull out couch. Noon and Dover are on the airbeds… Though Dover hasn't been sleeping much."

That wouldn't be good for his health but was no surprise. More stress meant more aggravation. Harlow didn't want him to burn out. Maze directed her into the second bedroom. It was small, and barely had enough room for a full-size bed and a dresser. Still, it was the tidiest room in the house, which was something.

Ryske kissed the top of her head. "This one's for you," he said, going past to dump her bag from the hospital on top of the dresser.

Maze pulled her closer. "You get to pick who you want to bunk in with… We're taking bets it won't be Anwen."

All the guys had popped into see her in the hospital the previous day, even Dover, who was more distant than she'd ever seen him.

"Yeah," Ryske said. "And I told you she doesn't have a choice."

Tipping her head up, she accepted Maze's kiss on her cheek. "Do you need anything?"

Harlow shook her head. "Ryske said there were some clothes around. I'll pick through what's left and find something suitable for tonight, then I'll have to get washed."

Maze frowned. "Are you allowed to do that?"

"Wash?"

"No, tonight," he said. "Are you going to the meet?"

"You're damn right I am," she said, slipping off her shoes. "I already fought with Bale today and Ryske. Please don't make me fight you too." She opened her arms. "Look at me, I'm capable."

"You look beautiful," Maze said, making her smile because she actually looked anything but. His head swung the other way. "We don't want you to get hurt again."

"Ryske will be there," she said, sitting on the bottom corner of the bed. "And it'll be quick. These things never take long."

"I already spoke to Noon about waiting outside," Ryske said. "You should come too, just in case."

Maze nodded. "I'll be there."

Watching Maze admire her was touching. She didn't often think of him as sentimental, but he couldn't take his eyes off her. He smiled and came over to kiss her cheek again.

"Okay, man, she gets it, you're happy to see her," Ryske said. "Now fuck off."

Holding up his hands, Maze backed out of the room and closed the door.

"Be nice to him," Harlow said. "You've been in a bad mood for days. I don't know what's wrong with you."

"You got hurt," Ryske said. "Do you expect me to be celebrating?"

"It wasn't a big hurt," she said, pulling the tie from her hair and trying to work her fingers through the knots. Her hair hadn't been washed since the blaze and still smelled like bonfire. "We better have conditioner."

"Maze hit the grocery store and Dover brought a bunch of stuff from the bathroom at home," he said. "I'll go see what's there."

Nodding, she didn't look up when he started for the door, but was grateful when he handed her a towel. At least she didn't have to go hunting for it.

As she got undressed, Harlow peeked in the dresser to find it was full of her and Ryske's things. From the smell of it, everything had been laundered… more than once. Good. Going through the clothes and accessories, she picked out what she'd need for that night, then wrapped herself in the towel.

Although physically fine, being in a hospital bed, bored, for almost two days, made her sluggish. She'd pep up once she washed and started moving around again.

Thinking about asking Ryske to make coffee, she slipped out of the bedroom and ducked into the bathroom that was between the two bedrooms. The last thing she expected was the place to be lit by a dozen candles.

"Fire insensitive?" Ryske asked, closing his lighter and slipping it back into his pocket.

Speechless, she wasn't prepared for romance. "No, it… it's beautiful."

While she'd been in the bedroom, he'd drawn her a bath and taken the time to stand up the candles like he'd watched her do for Anwen.

"I'm not leaving you alone," he said, backing up to the vanity to slide up onto it.

Getting herself together, they had a limited time window available. "You know what I love about Bale's apartment?"

"The bathtub?"

Harlow reached behind her and clicked the lock on the door. "The bathroom door locks," she said and he smiled. Pulling the comb out of her cleavage, she went to the vanity and tossed it down by the sink. "For the last two days I've been thinking about this."

"Thinking about what?"

Untucking her towel, it dropped to the floor. She slid her hands onto his thighs, giving him some of her weight when she rocked forward.

"Seducing you."

One side of his mouth curved as he scooped a hand onto each side of her face. "You just did."

Pulling her forward, he married their mouths, holding her in his firm grip, angling her to deepen his kiss.

There was no way they'd be able to have a typical relationship, not now. They couldn't waste time on dinner and movies and playing it coy. Time wasn't a commodity to be wasted. Each second they had was one closer to the moment they'd lose each other.

Thinking of being without him made Harlow grab for the hem of his shirt. Renewed urgency prompted her to pull it off over his head as fast as she could. His belt was next. In the same moment the buckle hit the floor with a thud, her frenzy took her fingers to the buttons of his fly.

"Baby," Ryske said, capturing her hands and pressing them flat on his bare chest. "Take your time."

While he might think it was okay to smirk or tease, Harlow wasn't in the mood to play. One of the best things about their sex life was the variety. They were just as at home being rough and dirty with each other as they were being tender and slow.

But this moment was unique... to her anyway.

Shaking her head, she pulled her hands out from under his and went back to unfastening his jeans. "I want to make a life with you, Crash," she said because that was one thing she had to say out loud. "I don't want to be me and you anymore." Cradling her head, he slid his thumbs across her cheeks, up and down, just listening. "I want to be us... I'll always be independent and I know you're strong-minded. We'll fight and follow our own paths. But I don't want a gray area between us anymore." To say the next part, she had to garner all her courage. When she thought she had it, she swallowed hard. "I want to belong to you, Ryske."

"That's all I ever wanted to hear, Trink," he said.

"Doesn't mean we can't take our time."

They were on a clock because they were due at the hotel in less than two hours. She could choose to make her point by being mushy with him, but that was less his style.

"Oh, okay then," she said, using her grip on his thighs to push herself away.

Turning her back on him, she sashayed to the tub and bent over, sweeping her hand through the water to test the temperature. It was warm enough. Hot, but not too hot. Her focus moved to the bunch of soaps and bottles at the end of the tub.

"Where'd you go, Trinket?"

"I'm right here," she said, putting the conditioner on the end of the tub near a candle.

"We were in the middle of something."

Twisting around, she spied him over her shoulder. "You said we had all the time in the world," she pouted and bobbed her head in an innocent nod. "I should take my time and look my best for you."

FIVE

"HA, THAT'S NOT what I meant," Ryske said and slid down off the vanity.

Harlow dipped a toe in the water to climb in and just got her footing as he captured her waist. Given that she was standing in the tub, he couldn't pull too hard. It would be a risky move to wrestle her out of the water.

"Hmm?" she asked, pretending to be oblivious to his frustrated disappointment.

"Come on, baby. Get out of there," he said. "Seduce me."

Harlow maintained her innocence. "Will you please pass my comb, honey?" she asked, pointing at the vanity and sinking down, catching the sides of the tub to tip back so she could soak her hair. "I like having my man in the bathroom with me."

The bathroom was somewhere they'd spent a lot of time. Sometimes the shower stall in Floyd's was the only place they got a semblance of privacy. Though that in itself was an illusion because there was usually at least one person on the other side of the glass going about their business.

"Come out and let me play with you," he said, grabbing the comb and slapping it off his thigh.

Sitting up, the water cascaded from her head. She slid

down to grab the conditioner bottle. "I'll let you skull fuck me if you condition my hair for me first."

Hunkering down at the side of the tub, Ryske folded his forearms on the edge. "I don't want to fuck your face, I want to fuck your pussy."

After tsking at him, Harlow opened her mouth in horror. "Wow," she said, faking offense. "You're being all kinds of insulting today."

"Baby, your language isn't—"

"It's not about language, Crash. You're just being rude."

"Rude?" he asked. When she sank back to wet her hair again, she noticed his smirk from the corner of her eye. As she sat up, he rose enough to lick a drip from her ear lobe. "Trink, you want me to be rude all over that gorgeous body of yours any damn time I want."

"I threw myself at you over there and you rejected me. Then, I offer you my mouth, which you've enjoyed before, and that wasn't good enough for you either."

"Baby, every part of you is good enough for me. The word rejection doesn't enter my vocabulary with you." Dipping his hand into the water, he moistened it and then ran it across each of her breasts, fondling his favorite part of her. "Come out and play."

Hitching her chin, she pulled her shoulders back like she was going to let him play with her. Except it was another tease.

Harlow put his hand back on the side of the tub. "Maybe we should come up with some sex ground rules," she asked, playing the priss that had once entertained him so much.

"Ground rules?"

"Yes," she said, pouring conditioner into her hands to begin working it through her hair with the comb. "We've never been a couple before. We've never discussed a relationship. Everything has always been fluid."

Doing a bad job of pretending to take her seriously, Ryske pushed out his lower lip and nodded. "Mmm, good point," he said, sitting on the floor to take off his boots and socks. "Spell it out, baby… Gimme rules."

"Okay," she said, wondering what he was doing when he stood up and pulled down his jeans and underwear in one swoop.

"Slide forward," he said.

Harlow didn't have much of a choice when he gave her shoulder a push and started to climb in. "Be careful," she said, steadying his leg when he launched it over the edge of the tub. "The conditioner makes everything slippery."

Lowering into the water, he put his legs around her waist and pulled her back to him, twining their legs in front of her. "Mmm."

"I thought you didn't like bathtubs."

"Never seen one with you in it," he said, taking the comb to run it through her hair.

The water was getting dirty fast; there was so much soot still in her hair. God, she couldn't wait to be clean.

With Ryske reclined against the head of the tub, and her sitting up in the middle, he combed her hair. Once he'd said she liked taking care of him. In truth, he was the one who took every opportunity to help with her grooming.

"Just didn't do it with the right girl," she whispered, drawing her nail down over his knee.

"I love this conditioner. It would make great lube."

"It doesn't go inside me," she said. "We can get actual lube for that."

His combing stopped. "You'd let me?"

"My body is your playground, Crash… It turns me on when you choke me, what do you think I wouldn't trust you to do?"

She laughed at the long vibrating groan reverberating behind her, and sloshed down in the tub, tipping her head back to wash the conditioner out.

Space in the tub was cramped. Her head was on his groin, her hair swam and tangled in the slick water, mingling around his cock. Ryske watched her and ran his fingers through her locks at her hairline until they were both satisfied the conditioner was gone.

Rising in a twisting corkscrew roll, she slithered up

the length of his torso and stretched her arms over his shoulders to grip the back of the tub.

"So…" she murmured, her lips grazed his. "You didn't agree to my rules."

His hands spread on her waist. She loved how big they were. Their span. The width of his fingers. His capability. But given she loved everything about his body that was no surprise.

"I can do anything I want with your body, any damn time I want. That's what I heard and I agree with that."

Sliding down, Harlow shook her head and dragged her teeth over the ink on his collarbone. "I have rules."

"Rules you've had with every guy?"

Feeling sly and sexy, she took her smile to his lips to kiss him, then sank in the water again until it met the surface. Tipping her head back and gazing up with all the adoration she felt for him, her cheek rested on his chest.

She'd never had rules for any man. That was probably because sex had never been as dynamic and exciting with any other man.

"I have special rules for you."

"I've got limits other guys didn't?" he asked, wearing a frown. "Thought I was the love of your life."

Pushing up, she sucked his lower lip between hers to loosen his tension. "And I want you to be the lover of my life too," she said. "But if you're not up to the challenge…"

Spiraling her body, she was about to flip over, when he caught her and pulled her back. "Anything you want, or don't want, it's my job to serve you. Gimme the rules."

She kissed him again. "I want sex. Every. Day." His brows rose, expressing his interest. "I don't care if we have to sneak downstairs to the alley or rent a motel room for an hour… If we're in the same place at the same time, I want you inside me at least once a day."

"Wow, you're tough."

"I'm not done," she said, prodding his tattoo.

Shifting, she caught her weight on her hands on each side of the tub to push up. With her nipples just resting on his torso, she moved up and down in a rhythm akin to what he wanted to be doing.

"What else you want, ball-breaker?"

"I want you to take every opportunity you can to touch me," she said and received a hum of approval. "Take advantage. Put your hands on me. Get close. Occupy my space like you occupy my body when we're alone."

His laugh was a groan. "I'm loving your kind of rules, baby... I've got my own for you."

Coiling both arms around his neck, Harlow relied on him to support her and keep control. "Anything."

"I don't want you wearing panties another day in your life."

He meant it, but it made her smile. VPL was a pet hate of hers, so it was something she'd been known to do anyway.

"What about my breasts?"

His eyes dipped. "Oh, those I want to see as often as possible."

"Okay," she said. "I have another. No more condoms. Ever. I'll stay on the pill. If you have to sleep with other women for work, you use protection and get tested before you put your cock in me again."

"What happened to sex every day?"

Her grin was instant. "I'll let you use your tongue."

Pushing her hair away from her brow with his middle finger, he let it slide down to her lips. "Baby, I'm not gonna fuck any woman for anything. I might have to flirt with them, let them think I'm going to screw them, you know, do... stuff. But my cock's just for you."

She kissed him. "Let's not make promises like that, okay? It sounds wonderful and romantic, but we know how quickly life can flip on us... It's enough for me that you want to make that promise. And I know you'll never want another woman the way you want me."

"Never have, never will... Do you want to get married?"

They hadn't talked about that since she'd mentioned it in her drug haze in the hospital. "I want to get your name tattooed on my pussy."

He laughed and squeezed her tight in his embrace. "That's the same thing; works for me."

Dipping her tongue into his mouth, Harlow pushed hard against him, rubbing their slick bodies together. "Time to get out the tub," she whispered.

Without explanation, she rose up to climb out of the water. Although she went to the vanity, she didn't touch the towel balled on the floor. Chances were they'd need to wash again, either in the tub or shower. So it was best to keep the towel clean. That and she had something else on her mind.

Sitting up next to the sink, Harlow propped her damp heels on the edge and let her hips push forward until her legs were wide apart.

"You haven't had sex today," he stated.

Biting her lip, she shook her head. "You're breaking a rule already."

Slapping his hands to the sides of the tub, he leaped out, sloshing water over one set of candles and swamping the floor, making some of the bottles tumble.

He wasn't practiced with bathtubs, but Harlow wasn't with him for his finesse. Striding over, Ryske swooped both arms around her and grabbed her ass.

Harlow already had control of his dick and didn't ask permission to line up their bodies. Without hesitation, he slammed deep into her.

"Oh, damn," she gasped, her loose head falling back. "Mm, it's magnificent… Can I keep it?"

He laughed and kissed her. "What? Like a pet?"

"Yes," she said, wrapping her arms around him. "I promise to feed him, and bathe him, and give him a warm place to sleep every night."

He nuzzled her mouth with his. "Fuck, baby. How do you still tease me even when I'm balls deep inside you?"

Groaning, his head dropped to her shoulder and his hips began to move. "Ah," she said, dragging her nails down his arm. "I didn't say you could do that."

His hips slowed and he leaned back to meet her eyes. Doing her best to seem unimpressed, Harlow struggled not to pant and squirm against how amazing he felt filling her up.

In a flash of movement, Ryske grabbed her throat and thrust her against the mirror.

Need forced her mouth open in a yelp. "That's better," she murmured. His feral gaze was sure, but his fingers weren't as confident. "Tighter, Crash."

She had just come out of the hospital. They hadn't even checked with the doctor if sex was allowed. As far as she'd been told, there was no evidence of damage to her lungs. She could tell that the nurses thought Bale was being cautious. She'd fainted, that was what she said and what she still believed. Except the doubt in Ryske's mind held him back.

"Hold me as tight as you love me, Crash."

Renewed vigor seized him. His fingers clenched so hard that they closed her throat. Her hands leaped to his shoulders. Her legs clamped tight around him too, which pulled his cock deep into her again.

His eyelids lowered until he was scowling at her. "Say pretty please, little bird. You want me to follow your rules, you better be a good girl."

His grip loosened. She gasped for breath, arching against the hand that had her neck, giving him the opportunity to squeeze her breast with the other.

"Crash," she moaned, more desperate for him than she could ever remember being.

"Pretty please, Trink… Let me hear it."

His fingers began to tighten and his dick began to withdraw. Harlow couldn't believe that he would really do it, that he would really walk away from her when he wanted her so much. If he was playing a game of chicken, she lost.

Just before he slipped out of her, she dug her nails into his upper arms. "Please! Pretty please!" she called out, louder than she should have.

There was an apartment full of people through the flimsy bathroom door, but she didn't care.

He thrust into her and she cried out again. Fucking her, he used her throat as an anchor with his other hand on her hip as a way to make her move exactly how he wanted her to.

She didn't care he was using her body like it was a toy

designed only to pleasure him. She teased sometimes and he let her. But when all was said and done, Harlow wanted him to want her with an overwhelming animal desire. One that would drive him to act on instinct not sense.

They'd always been electric together. Now they were embracing that connection, exploiting its full power. Harlow never felt stronger than she did when at Ryske's mercy.

SIX

"ARE YOU READY?"

Sitting in the back of Noon's car, Harlow heard Maze's question and looked to him peering over the shoulder of the front passenger seat. Except he wasn't talking to her, he was focused on the man at her side, preoccupied by the sight of her thighs.

Squeezing his hand locked in hers, Harlow drew his attention. "He's not talking to me, Crash," she said, wearing a smile.

"Yeah, I can trust Nightingale to keep her head," Maze said, scowling at his friend. "Where's yours at?"

Ryske was raw, vibrating with need. "That skirt is fucking short," he murmured.

The observation wasn't a judgment. It was more resigned than that. They'd been twined around each other on the drive, so her arm already overlapped his. Sliding her shoulder blade across his chest, getting even closer, she tipped her chin up to tease him.

"And you know what I have on under it," she purred.

The answer to that was nothing.

Harlow was preparing to go into a room where she'd been attacked by a man intent on raping her in a dress that just flirted with the top of her thighs. There wasn't a scrap beneath it to create a barrier to any would-be assailants.

His smirk betrayed how he enjoyed her sass.

He ducked to kiss her. "You don't want my head in the game, do you?"

Bouncing their joined hands on his thigh, she confessed. "The first time I went into a meeting with Ophelia, an official meeting, I swore… Fuck. Fuck. Tits. Ass. Cock. Fuck. And then I imagined you kissing me." That pleased him more. "I don't know why, but I've learned going into these meetings a little turned on actually helps."

Probably because of the chemicals released when her body was in that state. Arousal was easier to acknowledge and deal with than the adrenaline caused by anxiety or panic.

"Huh," Ryske said. "Interesting. I don't have time to give you everything on your list, but…"

Harlow was grateful they'd parked in shadow; it darkened the back of the car. Ryske slipped a hand between her legs, forcing them apart and driving his middle finger into her hard.

Sucking in a sharp, loud breath, one of her arms flew out to brace on the door while the other grabbed for his thigh.

"Shit, Crash," she gasped when he pulled the digit back to her threshold and then thrust it into her again. "Oh, God."

"Really?" Maze asked. "You gotta do that back there?"

"I'm getting her head in the game." His voice went from friendly to seductive in an instant. With her eyes closed and her teeth digging into her lip, Harlow didn't care about their audience. "That feel good, Trink?"

His breath heated her lips, betraying how close he was. Snatching the back of his head, she kissed him hard but got no response from his lips or his tongue.

Letting him go, she was determined to get a reaction, and shifted to give herself access to his pants. If she could get her hand inside…

His hand slipped away from her core. "Ah, no, baby," he said, smudging her taste on her lips.

Slipping a finger into her mouth, across her eager tongue, he teased her. Harlow sucked his digit hard, but he pulled his hand away. Bending the arm he'd had around her, he took a handful of her hair and pulled her head back to plant his mouth over hers, sampling her taste from her tongue.

Dragging his mouth away, he trailed it to her ear. "Turned on, not satisfied, Trinket," he breathed into her.

"I'm coming into the meeting with you," Maze said, interrupting their salacious moment.

Ryske turned to the front of the vehicle becoming aware of the others. Seemed he'd forgotten about them while agitating her insides to soup.

"Yeah?" Ryske asked. "Ready to shame your mama?"

"I think we both know I shamed my mama long ago," Maze said, not dissuaded by Ryske's taunting.

"I'd love to have you, man. Any backup for Nightingale's ass is welcome, but this is the kick off. If you're on the field when the whistle blows, there's no halftime subs."

"Nightingale's already done time for the team. I'd feel left out if I didn't throw my hat in the ring for the next round. Besides, who'll protect you from being raped in prison if we get picked up? And, you know, my parents can afford a better lawyer than any of us. So… co-defendants?"

"Co-defendants," Ryske confirmed. Both men looked at her. "Babe?"

"Do you think they'd let the three of us share a cell?"

"Yeah, if they added torture to my sentence," Maze said. "We'd have years ahead of us and no way to pass the time."

Sliding a hand down Ryske's thigh, Harlow wriggled. "I have a few ideas."

"Yeah, that's what I'm afraid of," Maze said and opened his door. "Come on."

Harlow skootched to the edge of her seat and Noon twisted expecting a goodbye, but Ryske pulled her back. "Don't kiss him, babe. You taste like… you."

"Hey, I don't mind," Noon said.

Harlow laughed, though she didn't know if he meant it or was just trying to rile Ryske. Whichever he was going for, he succeeded in the latter.

Ryske lunged over her to smack Noon's head. "You keep your eyes on the road, asshole."

They weren't going anywhere; the car was parked. Noon wouldn't be moving until everyone was back in the car… unless something unforeseen happened. Ryske gave her a shove toward the door, so she elected to blow Noon a kiss just as Maze opened the door to help her out.

"So what's the plan here?" she asked, walking like Dorothy with her arms looped through both Ryske's and Maze's. "Am I screwing you both?"

"As always the number one rule is…"

"Go with it," she replied to Maze, meaning everything would stay ambiguous.

They would let people think what they wanted to think without offering specifics or explanations. Though if one of the three of them made any sort of assertion, the others would accept and adapt to it without question.

"Maze's folks were our in with Parratt back in the day," Ryske said.

"Not a deliberate in," Maze explained. "I heard them talking about the guy, thought he'd make a good mark. So I invited Ryske along to a function to cultivate the guy. It went from there."

From there they'd met Ophelia. Their friend needed the switch done at the Hagan auction and Ryske met Anwen in the alley… It all started with Maze hearing something benign in his adoptive parents' conversation.

"They know who you are? Who your parents are?" she asked. "Are you Rowe?" Grinning, she squeezed herself closer to him. "Or should I call you Aston?"

"No," he grumbled. "You definitely shouldn't call me that."

Aston Mazer was his real name. His father was of Croatian descent, hence Maze's height and Slavic appearance. But his adoptive name was Aston Rowe. Given the money his adoptive parents had, a lot of people would assume he'd identify as descending from the affluent tribe.

Ryske helped her out. "We just call him Maze. Most

people assume it's a nickname… which it sort of is."

His passions were programming and hacking. Plenty of labyrinths to find his way out of in that digital plane.

"Okay, so if they assume we're sleeping together, I'll go with it… Good thing I've seen your pee-pee."

Ryske's step faltered. "Uh, what?"

"Relax, baby," she said to the suddenly tense Ryske. "I've seen every dick on the crew." They shared a bathroom. Though some were more discreet than others, they'd all been confronted by each other in the buff at one time or another. But Ryske wasn't calming down, his breathing got shallow and more huffy. "You should be flattered. Think about it. I've seen every cock on the crew, and I chose yours… It's a compliment."

Maze laughed as they rounded into the service alley behind the hotel. "Man, she's good," he said. "Just like you, she could sell condoms in a convent."

"Thank you," Harlow said, hoping that put a period at the end of the discussion… and Ryske's mood.

They went up a set of external stairs next to a loading bay. Maze opened the door and checked inside before allowing her to enter first.

"You got any concerns about coming back here?" Maze asked, staying at her side while Ryske took the lead.

"Because this is the place my boyfriend came back from the dead? No. I've been back since then."

"Well, yeah that, but… isn't this where Hagan attacked you?"

Taking his arm again, she rested her head against it without missing a step. "Maze, honey, I put him on his ass without any assistance. Now I have you and Ryske with me. If anyone tries to hurt any of us… we'll own them." With the men in suits, she was the only one with bare arms. She turned hers to show her stars. "'Til we're dirt in the ground."

Maze bowed to kiss her head, still keeping pace. "Good girl."

They reached the door of the meeting room and shared a look, each nodding to indicate they were prepared. Ryske dipped to kiss her, opened the door and went inside as his lips ebbed from hers.

It wasn't a typical 'get in the game' ritual, but it wasn't one she'd mind starting.

Following Ryske, Harlow had Maze behind her. He took her shoulders, giving her an encouraging squeeze.

"Now it's a party!" Ryske declared, opening his arms.

The door swung shut behind them, and they kept on going deeper into the room. Ryske stopped a few feet behind the couches that faced each other in the large drawing room. When she went to his side, Maze did the same, putting her in the middle of their crew.

Everyone was on their feet. Parratt and Yarker were in front of the furthest couch with a female between them; the same female who'd been with them before. Ophelia was standing by the couch closest to them.

"You're late," Parratt declared.

"Your daughter likes taking it in the ass," Ryske said, sauntering around the couch. "Is this a game of state the obvious?"

"She's his daughter," Harlow murmured to Maze, observing the woman next to Parratt.

Why would a man get his child involved in something like this?

Maze slid an arm around her shoulders. "That's his mistress. Lydia."

"My… my daughter? H… Hannah?" Parratt stuttered. Ryske dropped onto the middle of the couch closest to them. He laid his arms along the back, slouched and at ease like he owned the whole building. "You… My princess angel…"

"So that's where that pet name came from! If I'd known I was playing you, I wouldn't have been so generous with her," Ryske said and nodded at the woman next to Parratt. If Harlow knew him—and she did—he'd accompanied that nod with a wink. "Hey, Lydie." Harlow smiled at the way the woman blushed and dropped her attention to hide a smile. Trying to hide it anyway. Ryske noticed too. "Don't be shy, babydoll, let it all out… I'm right here if you want a real hello."

That tone, the way he spoke to women, made them feel so precious. Had she ever fallen for it? Every damn day since they met. Not that she'd admit it out loud in public.

"What's Rowe doing here?" Yarker asked.

The stunned Parratt sank down onto the edge of the couch. Rigid and mouthing silence, he wasn't doing a good job of getting to grips with the new information. Why had Ryske shared it, now of all times? Whatever, her job was to go with it.

"He's my buddy," Ryske said. "Figured we need a little more muscle on this… Are you gonna fight off the sex crazed if they OD? You know he's connected up the yazoo, right?" Ryske snapped his fingers and pointed. "That's right, you do, 'cause his father owns forty percent of your company!"

Yarker sat hard.

"You're just going around the room shocking the shit out of people," Maze said. "I'm here because I might want in… I have to get a feel for your setup first."

"Never hurts to have a little Rowe credibility, does it?" Ryske asked, lifting his hands at the wrist then strengthening the one closest to Ophelia to point at her. "You raiding Harlow's closet?"

Ophelia's outfit was a replica of the one Harlow wore the night Ryske came back from the dead. Wow, Ryske paid attention to what she wore, she wouldn't have called that. Of course there would be exceptions, like when he was figuring out how to get her out of it.

"No!" Ophelia objected a little too hard. "I've had this for years."

Ryske tipped his chin toward the back of the couch. "Trink, get where I can see you."

Maze nudged her along, guiding her between the end of the couch and the fireplace. Because Ryske was in the center of the couch with his arms stretched along the back, there was equal space on each side of him. Ophelia put herself in the furthest space, making it clear she wouldn't give up a place beside him.

SEVEN

HARLOW THOUGHT ABOUT waiting until Maze sat down and then sitting on both of them, but the aim was to give Ryske dominance. To underline his point—if he had one—about his power with women, and maybe to irk Ophelia too, Harlow stepped over Ryske's foot and sank down onto the floor between his legs.

"Now that we're all sitting comfortably…" Ryske said.

Picking up the ends of her hair with splayed fingers, he spread it on his thigh. Coiling her arms around his lower leg, Harlow rested her head against the inside of his thigh while he continued to stroke her.

"We have a lot to talk about," Ophelia said.

"Not so much," Ryske said. "Parratt, Yarker, you got the product en route?"

"Uh… yes," Yarker said.

Parratt was only just beginning to shake off his shock. "You… you slept with my daughter."

"I fucked your daughter," Ryske said. "She was actually the first of the set." His hand left her hair; Harlow twisted to watch him count off on his fingers. "Daughter, wife, mistress… I gotta ask, is your mom still living? 'Cause I feel like I should complete the collection." Outrage opened Parratt's mouth; he puffed out his bluster. Ryske's gaze dropped to her. "What you smiling at?" Was she smiling? Yep, oops. She shook her head and sucked her lips into her mouth. "Oh no, let me have 'em."

Pressing a finger to the underside of her chin, Ryske guided her up onto her knees, higher and higher until her body was angled on his, pressing into him. Kissing him in front of their audience felt different than doing it in private. It wasn't worse. It was naughty… and hot.

In spite of his bravado, Harlow knew she was his prize, his valuable beloved, more important to him than any other woman. His kiss infused her with the power they got from their bond. Pushing her tongue further into his mouth, she wasn't ready to lose the connection. Harlow reveled in their union. Everyone probably wondered what kind of woman could hear him talk of being intimate with other women and still share herself with him.

But she knew something they didn't. Harlow had been inside him in the deepest, darkest moments of the blackest night. She'd pushed at him, and every time his grip grew stronger. Losing herself in him would be her bliss.

"You've forgotten how short her dress is," Maze muttered.

Ryske pulled his mouth from hers. With his fingertips, he combed her hair from her cheekbones, his heated gaze adoring.

"This is a business meeting," Yarker objected. "Must you entertain your whore?"

Harlow's eyes flared as a fire of ire shot through her. Twisting around, she surged onto her feet, but didn't get one step before Ryske and Maze seized a wrist each, holding her back. Pinning her feral anger on Yarker, his dismissal boosted her adrenaline. Her goddamn money was in the pot; she had as much right as anyone else to be present.

"We'd hoped she wouldn't need this," Ryske said and slid something onto the forefinger of the hand Maze held.

She looked down at her pointed full-finger ring seated in its place.

"Now, do you want to apologize to the lady?" Maze asked. "Or should we let her go?"

"You remember..." Ryske said. "The only thing that stopped her ripping out Hagan's throat was me... No chance I'm doing that tonight."

"I... I'm sorry," Yarker said. "I am. I'm sorry..."

Ryske's hand slid up her inner thigh. "You're a goddess, Trink," he murmured, caressing the sensitive flesh at his fingertips. "We're at your command."

Maze's fingers loosened from her wrist to descend and twine with hers. Both men were telling her they were ready to fight at her side if Yarker's apology wasn't enough. Except they weren't there for a fight. Technically, Ryske had disrespected Parratt more than Yarker had insulted her.

Loosening, her anger ebbed and unlocked her knees to sink onto the floor between Ryske's feet again.

"Good," Ryske said. "You're a lucky man, Yarker."

"Who you kidding?" Maze asked. "You love it when she launches that fire on you."

Ryske's grin was audible in his voice. "Yeah, but I get a happy ending."

"I just didn't..." Yarker cleared his throat. "I didn't think there was any need to be so amorous in front of others."

"Welcome to my world," Maze muttered.

"I thought..." Lydia spoke, her voice so meek that it took a second to pinpoint the source. "I thought you were engaged to Ophelia."

"Nah," Ryske said. "I came to my senses on that one... I've been fucking with Harlow for months anyway. Seemed smart to make the change official."

"Official?" Yarker asked. "You're... together?"

"Doesn't mean your women are safe," Harlow said, rubbing her cheek against Ryske's knee.

"I don't want there to be... difficulties," Yarker said, his attention going to Ophelia, then around to Parratt.

"There's no animosity," Ophelia said. "We are the closest of friends."

The innuendo suggested more than friendship. The way Lydia's chin rose caught Harlow's eye. Was she shocked or interested in being part of that scenario? Ryske had been with Yarker's wife and Parratt's favorite mistress, Lydia, in a threesome. Did the quiet woman have a thing for group sex?

Ryske must have noted Lydia's reaction too. "What you doing after, Lydie?"

"Excuse me," Parratt said, putting an arm across Lydia's lap.

"Hey, man, I've got no problem with you excusing yourself right now," Ryske said. "Or taking Yarker with you. Maze and me will take care of the women."

"We have Pothos samples," Lydia said, more animated than she'd been all night.

"Lydia!" Parratt exclaimed in a way that reminded her of mom, Jean.

Harlow turned her face against Ryske's leg, hiding her restrained laughter.

"No, Lydie, babydoll," Ryske drawled. "You don't need chemical enhancements. This is me we're talking about, not your sugar daddy. Don't tell me you forgot what it's like au naturale with me."

Lydia was focused above her, the woman would be getting a glimpse of Ryske's intense, consuming stare. Shifting position, Harlow pressed her breast to his shin and let her fingers wander up the leg of his jeans to graze her nails on his skin.

Grabbing the length of her hair, Ryske twined it around his hand, once and twice until his fist was locked against the back of her head. Her neck ached when he pulled it back, but it was a nice ache.

"We've gotta give Lydie a refresher, wanna watch or join?"

"No one is giving anyone anything," Parratt snapped.

Ryske winked at her, then raised his chin to glare at the blustering man. "I've got a short attention span, Parratt. When there's entertainment on offer, I take it… You want to talk business, talk. Otherwise, I'm taking my wares and moving this pussy party upstairs."

"How will you react when we hold an event?" Yarker asked. "There will be half naked women everywhere. Women who may be sexually aroused. Women who will certainly be available."

Hookers. Yes, Yarker was right that there would be women available at Pothos events. Ryske was the one providing them. It was the only reason these men tolerated him.

"Yeah," Ryske said. "All trained or sampled by me… How many do you think? Twenty to start? Thirty?"

"You can…?" Parratt started. "You can get that many immediately?"

"I've got fifty on standby," he said. "But we've got to judge demand. We don't want to oversupply or my girls don't get the return they deserve… We don't want a price war."

This was the reality of Pothos and what kind of an event it required. She'd been the one to reach out to Svetlana in the first place. In addition to her investment, she had to bring something to the table. Back then, they'd all believed Ryske dead, so it had fallen to her to fulfill his commitment.

Ryske began to pitch his idea about crossing over the casino and Pothos nights to tempt interested parties into coming along without feeling any pressure. They didn't want to scare people off.

Harlow didn't hear everything he was saying. What would being in a room with fifty of Ryske's ex-lovers feel like? One or two was fine; it didn't register as intimidating. But fifty? Harlow hadn't been with even close to that number of guys. She'd had some experiences in college, but after getting with Rupert, she'd been faithful. Since the age of twenty-two, she'd only been with two men: Rupert and Ryske.

She wasn't sexually insecure and never had been. Ryske enjoyed having sex with her, no doubt about that. Yet being lost in the melee of dozens of his ex-lovers, would she be diluted in the crush?

"Friday," Ophelia said. "We will commence on Friday. Everything must be in place."

Whether deliberate or not, the choice of that night was a slap in the face. Usually, she, Ryske, and Maze would have to veto a Friday because it was Floyd's busiest night. But that didn't matter anymore, not now the place was charcoal.

Forlorn at the reminder, she breathed out and coiled her arm around Ryske's leg again. Taking comfort from her guy, she offered it to Maze too. Without looking, she raised her arm to seek his hand, which he gave her.

"Excellent. We'll meet early, get the women organized… What is your capacity?"

"The twenty rooms off the main game floor have been refitted," Ophelia said. "Each is an individual bedroom with storage and a restroom."

"Ten would be a good number for a soft opening," Parratt said. "We must have an agreement that investors are not allowed to sample product."

"Works for me," Ryske said. "I didn't give you a dime." Meaning he wasn't actually an investor. "Another thing to get clear, my girls should be respected at all times. They are not product. They are businesswomen who make their own choices about what can and can't be done with, and to, their bodies. No one forces them to do anything they don't want to do. If any of them are harmed or feel disrespected, hell will be rained down on the perp."

He'd have made that clear whether she was present or not. Ryske was good at treating women with respect. Even when he got rough with her or talked dirty, he never stopped respecting her. He'd never force her, or any woman, to do anything against their will.

"Yes," Parratt said. "Happy employees are productive employees."

"They're contractors. They work for themselves," Ryske said. "Allowed to leave at any time without notice… I want panic buttons in every room."

Breathing in, Harlow opened her mouth, trying her best not to show her appreciation for his concern. Digging her teeth into his knee, her nails dug deeper into his shin.

"I'll have them installed this week," Ophelia said.

"Good," Ryske said, dragging his fingers through her hair. "If we're done, we're getting out of here. My girl needs some attention. She's about to draw blood… Not that I have a problem with that, but we've learned our lesson about leaving blood at potential crime scenes."

Ryske and Maze slid forward, but Ophelia spoke. "Actually, I would like a minute alone with the women," she said and stood up. "I assume both of you can speak for your parties."

Parratt and Yarker were friends and Lydia had been present throughout negotiations. The mistress was as clued in as Harlow, maybe more given that she'd been involved since the beginning. But Harlow didn't envy Lydia being between her and Ophelia. Their relationship was fractious to say the least.

"A minute alone for what?" Parratt asked.

"Do you trust your woman or don't you?" Ophelia asked and swept an arm around to gesture toward the door in the far corner next to the bar.

"I… yes," Parratt gave Lydia the nod.

Harlow stood up and was about to follow when Ryske caught her hand. He trusted her to speak for him and their crew, without question. His hesitation was rooted in the knowledge Ophelia was a murderess; not everyone in the room was aware of that.

Crouching because she couldn't bend without flashing the other couch, she brushed her lips across his. "Go with it," she whispered and retreated, forcing him to let her hand drift out of his.

Ophelia was holding the door open for her. Harlow strode to her without looking back and crossed the threshold to join a waiting Lydia. The new room was smaller, used for storage with a table in the middle and boxes all around. It didn't have the same fine décor they'd enjoyed next door.

That didn't matter; they didn't sit.

Ophelia closed the door and turned to face them. "We have to trust each other," she said, surprising the hell out of Harlow. "I know we have reason to dislike each other. But, really, we don't want to give in to the stereotype. We shouldn't claw at each other. There doesn't need to be a queen bee. Yes, I have the most invested in this and it's possible my brother lost his life for it, but—"

"Hold on," Harlow said, raising a hand. "Did you just have the audacity to call me in here and tell me to respect you?"

"Harlow—"

"No, wait a second. You really want me to be your buddy? You know what's funny about that? I *was* your goddamn friend."

"I was your friend too," Ophelia said, folding her arms. "Yet you were fucking my man for months… Isn't that what he just said?"

With her lips parted, Harlow's tongue caught at the back of her teeth. Oh, Ophelia was some piece of work. Ryske had never been hers. Ophelia Hagan was the only woman he hadn't fucked. But she had the nerve to stand there and claim ownership over him just because there was a witness in the room.

Clucking her tongue, Harlow breathed out a laugh. "You know, I'm tempted to go out there and ride him raw right in front of you."

Lydia yelped. "Oh my goodness."

"Yes," Ophelia said with feigned sympathy. "You see now why Yarker called her a whore… She's quite uncouth."

"Sling another name at me, Ophe, and that pretty face won't be quite so flawless in the morning…" Leaning in, Harlow oozed malevolence. "I do my own dirty work."

"Really, Harlow, must you be so vulgar? Perhaps if you were more ladylike, he wouldn't stray on you."

This woman had gotten away with too much already. Everyone had a breaking point.

Harlow didn't remember coming to a conscious decision to move. But her fist did. It flew through the air, taking Ophelia by surprise, smacking her in the face, sending her tumbling against the wall.

Ophelia called out; Lydia's scream was louder. Harlow braced for Ophelia who leaped back to her feet. The rage burned until her reddened cheeks puffed out.

"You bitch," Ophelia shouted and jumped forward.

Harlow ducked out of the way. Ophelia sailed past, missing her target, though she quickly whirled around. Evading another of Ophelia's swings, Harlow used the clumsy move to catch her opponent's arm. Exploiting Ophelia's momentum, Harlow spun around to clamp an arm around the woman's neck.

Grabbing her own bent arm pulling on Ophelia's shoulder, Harlow got her in a chokehold. Using the strength Costello taught her to channel, she clenched hard, ignoring how Ophelia clawed at her forearm.

"Trinket…"

Her head rose.

Apparently, Lydia had retrieved the men from the other room.

EIGHT

"OH MY GOD!" Parratt said. "Oh my God!"

The smirk on Ryske's face was struggling not to become a laugh. Maze wasn't as restrained. Although he was shocked, he didn't hold back and let himself enjoy the view.

"Baby, let her go," Ryske said.

Harlow tugged her victim, giving her another shake. Ryske shook his head.

Puffing out her irritation, Harlow relented and threw Ophelia forward, out of her hold and into Yarker who caught the woman.

"She called me a name," Harlow said.

"Only I'm allowed to do that," Ryske said.

"She's an animal!" Ophelia tried to scream, except her voice was hoarse and she lost her words to a coughing fit.

Harlow growled again and tried to advance, but Ryske merged into her path, blocking out Ophelia.

"Trink," he said, taking hold of her arms. "We're business partners. We don't attack our business partners."

"I think… uh…" Yarker said. "Your girlfriend has impulse control issues."

Her impulse control was impeccable. She'd been out of jail for months and this was the closest she'd come to taking

Ophelia apart for what she'd done.

Harlow's volatile reactions didn't only have negative outcomes. Yarker had been calling her a whore ten minutes ago. Now he was calling her Ryske's girlfriend. Whether he had respect for her or not, he'd learned to show he did. That was an improvement.

"I encourage my girl to act on impulse as often as possible," Ryske said, sinking his fingers into her hair. "Wanna fuck? Will that make you feel better?"

Screwing would make him feel better and she'd forget about Ophelia. Though that reprieve would be short lived; the female Hagan wasn't finished yet. Her insanity could jeopardize their whole agenda. She had to hear whatever Ophelia wanted to say and gather whatever intel was available.

Though it went against instinct, Harlow clenched her jaw and locked her eyes on Ryske as she spoke. "I'm sorry, Ophelia," she said, grinding out the words. "Won't you please give me another chance to be reasonable?"

Though she huffed, Ophelia relented. "Control yourself and I will… Gentlemen, would you excuse us?"

Ryske bent down to kiss her. Still cupping one side of her head, he took his lips to her opposite ear. "You deserve a fucking Oscar for that one, Trink."

Knowing he understood how difficult it was for her to defer to Ophelia, Harlow felt better. Her love's wink gave her reason to smile. No matter what, she wasn't alone. No matter how she had to prostrate and humiliate herself, it was all for the greater good of her crew.

The men retreated the way they'd come. Once they were alone, the three women stood in silence.

Lydia looked terrified, genuinely afraid for her life, like Harlow might snap on her next. It wasn't the mistress' fault she'd had to witness that violence. Harlow had been in jail for murder, so she had every right to be concerned. It wasn't like they knew each other or had personal history.

Ophelia rubbed her neck, scowling.

Instead of responding to that judgment, Harlow chose to show her sweetest smile. "So, Ophelia," she said. "You were saying we should all get along."

"I think it's ridiculous that you harbor anger toward me given all you've done," Ophelia snapped.

Harlow hadn't done anything to her. But that wasn't how the world would see it. As far as the world knew, Harlow had stolen Ophelia's fiancé and murdered her brother.

Evidence from the crime scene had been lost; everyone knew that was why she'd been liberated. Although, at the time, being granted her freedom from jail had been a relief, the way it happened left lingering doubts. She never had, and likely never would, get her day in court. There was no way to refute anyone's belief she had committed the crime. Forever more, she would be a murderess, whether she'd been sentenced for the act or not.

Sure, if it had gone to court, Harlow probably would've been convicted. Though Ryske would remind her without going through it, no one could ever know for sure how it would turn out.

"You're right, Ophelia," she said, going over to the table and pulling out a chair to sit down. "I should be more reasonable. It's not like you murdered your own brother, is it? It's not like you took advantage of a man who made his lack of feelings clear to you… It's not like you paid someone to beat the shit out of an innocent woman."

"You… you did that?" Lydia asked.

Harlow opened her arms, resting one elbow on the table and the other on the back of her chair. "Who knows what anyone did anymore? So, Ophe, why is it so important for us to be friends?"

Dropping her hand from her neck, Ophelia gave up on the victim act fast now that she didn't have the right audience. "Because we can't trust these men."

Raising her brows, Harlow was surprised. "You don't trust Ryske? Are you telling me not to trust him? Oh, he'll love hearing about this."

"Of course I trust him. We all do," Ophelia said, coming over to take the perpendicular seat. "But with all of those women around, the drugs, the sex, we need to keep our heads. The women will want him. All of them. They'll do anything to have him. Don't doubt for a moment that Ryske's head will be turned. Mr. Rowe's too. We can't rely on him." Mr. Rowe? Oh, right, Maze. "Yarker and Parratt are sex-starved dogs, so this nonsense about investors not sampling the women won't last. You know it won't. Ryske is right, he didn't invest; he's free to do whatever he likes. Parratt might not like him, but he's smart enough to know we need a man with connections like his."

Almost lost in Ophelia's eyes, Harlow's voice became a breath. "Wow," she whispered. "I'd forgotten how good you are at this." Although she disliked the woman, there was no doubting that the heiress could weave a plot. "You're saying that as women, we need to keep control of the chaos their cocks will cause."

"Yes," Ophelia said and sat back. "I also believe this should be a fair venture… The second floor of the club has been converted too."

Harlow wasn't sure what that meant and she wasn't the only one. Lydia seemed confused too.

"Converted to what?" Lydia asked after Ophelia didn't expand on her statement.

Lydia came over to sit at the table with them, choosing the place opposite Harlow.

Ophelia enjoyed her position at the top of the table. "Men are not the only ones who like sex. It seemed only right that we incorporate a softer space."

"For women?" Harlow asked.

"Or couples," Ophelia said. "We have to consider the possibilities for diversification. Not everyone wants to be with a prostitute. They may wish to use the product in a safe environment… with a partner of their choice."

"Yeah, 'cause I don't know many straight male gigolos… Ryske will… We could accommodate same sex couples too."

"One step at a time," Ophelia said.

Ophelia wasn't homophobic, but she dismissed the suggestion so fast Harlow suspected this was about more than just welcoming women into the sphere.

"It could be worth thinking about."

"You are speaking on behalf of your factions,"

Ophelia said. "You both have several members to support you. In the interests of fairness, I would like to bring someone in myself."

"Someone?" Harlow asked. "Animal?"

"No, of course not," Ophelia said. "I'm bringing in another woman."

"Who?"

Ophelia wasn't ashamed to sit up straight. "Anwen."

It wasn't easy not to be horrified and rethink everything they'd gone through. In an instant, Harlow doubted every second Anwen spent under their roof and every word she'd said.

"You're working with her?" Harlow asked.

"Actually, I haven't spoken to her about it at all," Ophelia said. "I can't get in touch with her… I know you have her ear and thought you might be the best one to recruit her."

This could be a ploy to draw Anwen out. "Why would you want her involved?" Harlow asked, embracing suspicion.

"Anwen, who is… Wasn't your brother engaged to a woman with that name?" Lydia asked. "I thought she died."

Ophelia took Lydia's hand. "Didn't we all?" she said. "That is why I wanted you to be present for this. I'm asking Harlow to help us, to entrust our agenda to Anwen and to ask her to work with us…" Harlow was wary. "You'll be doing her a favor. What does she have? She needs to get back into civilization somehow."

An illegal enterprise was one way to do that.

Harlow couldn't figure this out. Anwen had been staying with them and hadn't shown any signs of wanting to hurt them. But with the fire, and her own personal dramas, Harlow had to admit she had neglected the woman of late.

If Anwen wanted to be their ally, it would be an asset to have her on the inside. But if Ophelia recruited her away, she'd be a liability. They were supposed to be protecting Anwen from Ophelia. Bringing her into the open might be exactly what Ophelia wanted.

Except, Harlow acknowledged Ophelia made at least one good point. As noble as her crew's motives had been, Anwen needed an exit strategy. She couldn't stay locked up under their protection forever. One way or another, Anwen would have to take steps either to neutralize the threat Ophelia posed or take care of it.

Assessing the situation, Harlow tried to draw conclusions. Would it benefit their side if the women reconciled? Ophelia didn't want to hurt them, she just wanted Ryske. Ryske didn't want her, but their plan was to give Ophelia what she wanted until they could find an official way out. Once they were free, Harlow and her crew would put as much distance between them and the nutcase as possible.

She was still trying to figure it out when a long sharp whistle sounded from the next room. Almost as if she'd been trained to respond to the noise, she stood up and went to the door without saying anything to the women at the table.

Opening the door, Ryske and Maze stood near the couch they'd been seated on.

"We're leaving, Trink."

She couldn't say she was sorry to hear that. The guys left the couch and started for the door, so she went to intercept them. As she blended into line between them, she threaded the fingers of her left hand through Ryske's right and reached back to take Maze's left hand.

Ryske opened the door.

"It's a lie that will catch up to you, Ryske," Parratt called out.

The man in front of her paused. Whatever the discussion had been, it led to their quick departure. Harlow stayed between Ryske and Maze, waiting to see if they'd fight or flee.

Ryske's grip on her hand tightened and he started walking again, tugging her out of the room. Stalking down the corridor, he didn't falter in his step, but she hurried to catch him up while pulling Maze along with her.

They got outside and back into the car where Noon was waiting, without speaking a word to each other.

"So...?" Noon asked, pulling out of the alley. "How did it go?"

Sitting in the back with Ryske, Harlow watched his profile. It was set in a scowl focused on the passing streets.

Sliding away from the middle of the car, she looked out her own window trying to decide what she should do about Anwen.

When Noon's question was greeted by silence from the back, Maze was the one to answer. "Just drive, man."

Maze knew what was on Ryske's mind. He didn't sound too happy about whatever had been brought up either, or maybe he was just annoyed Ryske was upset.

They would loop her in after they were finished with their own reflection. She had some decisions to make before joining the debrief at the apartment. Asking Anwen about her affiliation with Ophelia could backfire; she couldn't be sure the woman's word was trustworthy.

Bale's assertions about her power over Ryske kept playing in her mind. If Harlow told her love she wasn't happy or didn't trust having Anwen around, he'd kick her out. No doubt that would force Anwen back to Ophelia's allegiance… either that or Ophelia would kill her.

Bale was right about the power she had with Ryske, though he'd failed to note that her love had the same power over her. If Ryske alluded to wanting something that was within her capability, or he expressed a need that she could fulfill, she'd do it. Whether he asked her to or not.

This wasn't fun, she felt alone. She wanted to do the right thing for her crew and protect them at the same time. Harlow was still thinking about it when they turned onto a street she recognized.

Sitting up straight, she grabbed for the door. "Noon, will you stop here?"

He glanced to the side. "You want to go home? The place is a mess."

"I know," she said. "I just need a minute." Noon adjusted to get Ryske's approval. Only after he nodded once did Noon pull the car to the curb. "Thank you."

Ryske spoke to the front of the car. "We'll get you back at—"

"No," she said, putting a hand over Ryske's. "You go to Bale's with the guys… I won't be long. I can walk back myself."

"Trink, I don't—"

Lunging over the car, she kissed him. "I love you. Trust me."

Though he glared, he didn't argue. Smiling, she slid toward the door and climbed out of the car to stand on the sidewalk until they'd driven away.

Only when they were gone did she turn around to face Floyd's… or what was left of it.

NINE

THE DARKNESS BROKE her heart. Many people would probably dub Floyd's depressing. Not her.

At this time of night, the sign outside, above the corner door, should be illuminated. Light should be emanating from the upstairs windows and seeping through the cracks around the shutters on the lower floor.

Floyd's had never been well lit. In fact, even she'd have called it dark. But it was different now. The life had gone from the place. The illumination of the bar, the jukebox, and the dull glow from the ceiling fans was gone too.

The corner door was nailed shut and she wasn't packing a crowbar this time. The side-alley door could still work, not that it mattered, she didn't have her keys. There was some kind of irony that when she went around to the back alley and pushed the window they'd escaped from, it gave.

Opening it as far as she could, Harlow grabbed the sill and hauled herself up. It had been easier with Maze's help, but a little exertion wouldn't discourage her. She got herself up and inside.

Jumping down onto the spongy den floor, the truth really hit home. Water from the fire hoses had drained or been pumped out, but the damage remained.

Witnessing the darkness from outside was nothing to the devastation of walking through the bar. Dover had already ripped out the burned panels from the walls. The reinforced-concrete structure was the same beneath the devastation, yet the energy was gone from the almost unrecognizable place.

She stopped, on the spot where Ryske was shot, and crouched to sweep her hand across the warped floor. Once the site moved her to tears, and here it was about to do the same thing again.

"Surreal, isn't it?"

She didn't expect anyone to be there. She should've. Where else would he be? Dover stood at the curve of the bar. She rushed over to wrap both arms around him.

"I'm so sorry, Dover," she said, overcome by the strength of her anguish. "So sorry."

"It's okay, Nightingale. It wasn't your fault," he said, holding her, running a hand down her hair. "It just happened. No one was seriously hurt, that's what matters."

"You were seriously hurt," she said, tipping her head back to look up at him.

He brushed her tears from her cheeks. "Don't cry, babe. We'll fix it."

Behind the forced smile, there for her benefit, was the pain he wanted to hide.

Frustrated, she tightened her embrace again. "This didn't just happen. Someone did this to you, to all of us. Dover, I know I wasn't here long. What I feel is nothing to what you're going through. I just need you to know, I… I've never felt so safe or happy anywhere else on Earth… If I feel this way about it, I can't imagine how you feel… I love this place. I miss it."

"Taking in special strays is in Floyd's DNA," he said. "And you were lost, Night, whether you know it or not… Why are you here tonight?"

His arms stayed around her. He wasn't angry she came around. If anything, it seemed he was grateful to see her. As much as she hadn't expected him, he'd have expected her less.

"I needed to feel grounded," she said. "We just came

from that Pothos meeting and I… I don't know… I feel like my head's screwed up with it all… Bale's is great, but I won't get space to clear my mind there… I need to figure some stuff out."

"Do you need a drink?"

She smiled and peeked up at him again. "You still have booze?"

"Stock? No," he said, linking their hands to lead her from the bar toward the spiral stairs. From what she'd heard, they'd need new stairs in the stairwell because they weren't exactly stable anymore. "But we have alcohol."

Up the spiral stairs, in the apartment kitchen, the place, even up there, looked so different. The curtains were gone, the couch too. Maze and Ryske's bed frames were without mattresses. Noon's box-spring was nowhere in sight.

Dover guided her to the counter that separated the kitchen from the long dining table. "I tossed all the soft furniture stuff," he said. "There isn't a lot of water damage up here. The fire was limited to the basement and first floor. The apartment was just stinking with the smoke."

Clothes they could wash. The curtains could probably have been washed too, but if it made him feel better to start over, she wouldn't argue.

One new box-spring and mattress stood in the furthest corner: Dover's spot.

"Are you moving back in?"

"Yeah," he said. "I'll get more done if I'm here."

Retrieving a bottle of bourbon from a lower cabinet, he poured some into a glass and then brought the bottle over to join her.

She took the bottle, leaving him with the glass. "Can I stay?"

Instead of drinking, he frowned. "Problems with our boy?"

He tossed the measure into his throat.

Harlow shook her head as she drank. "He's not the problem," she said, pouring more liquor into Dover's glass. "I just want to be home… That might be presumptuous to say, but… I don't know, I just feel like I've been so all over the place this year. This building has been the only thing that's made sense to me the whole time, you know? Does that sound stupid?"

Even when Ryske had been dead and she'd believed she was alone, Floyd's had been there, strong and reliable.

"It's not presumptuous, babe, but you'll have to bunk with me. I don't have anything else that's even an excuse for a bed."

"That's okay," she said and offered the bottle to him for a toast.

After another drink, he took the bottle from her to refill his glass. "Tell me what happened tonight."

Harlow took a breath and told him everything, from the car with Noon through to Parratt's parting words.

"You really choked her?" Dover asked. The smile on his face was far more genuine than the one he'd worn downstairs. "Wow, you're good, Nightingale."

She sighed. "Yeah, it felt good… I don't know what to make of it all, Dover. She wants Anwen in. Do you think she's been playing us this whole time? She couldn't have taken that beating for show, could she? It was bad, really bad."

"Yeah," Dover said, considering it. "Has she had time to be in touch with Ophelia since?"

"Maybe," Harlow said, trying to figure it out.

The truth was, as much as they tried to watch Anwen, the crew didn't often compare notes. No individual one of them knew where she was at all times. Bale's apartment had a phone. Floyd's used to have one in the bar. Anwen could've made a phone call at any time. Doubt anyone was checking the bills.

"You could ask Maze to find out, trace any electronic trail she's left," Dover said. "Maybe they made up."

In years gone by, she'd call him crazy for thinking anyone could reconcile with an attacker like Ophelia. But, in the past year, Harlow had been party to stranger things. In her work with family services, she'd seen plenty of domestic abuse situations where people were taken to the brink of death and still argued against pressing charges. Anything was possible.

After another sip, she sighed. "The problem is, if

Ryske thinks I'm uncomfortable around her or I suspect her of something, he won't waste any time."

Dover didn't disagree. "He'll toss her out on her ass."

"Exactly," Harlow said. "Despite her new ID, she's still alone without us. It could drive her straight into Ophelia's waiting arms."

"Then we'd have two of them coming at us."

"What do they know?" she asked and shrugged. "Maybe I'm overthinking this. They can't hurt us, right? I mean, why would Anwen want to hurt us?"

The bottle he'd been about to drink from left his lips. For the longest time, he just looked at her. Was she missing something?

"You're kidding," he said.

"Kidding about what? We haven't hurt them. You guys helped Anwen when you saved her from Hagan. Ophelia is the one who killed her brother, I didn't. And as for Ryske—"

"As for Ryske?" Dover said and snatched the glass from her. Somewhere along the way their drinks had become interchangeable. "I don't think you need that. You've gotta be drunk already."

"I'm not drunk," she said, stealing the bottle from him. "What are you talking about?"

"You think this is about Ryske, it's not. The catalyst was Ryske, but this whole damn mess is your fault."

"My…"

With a slow shake of his head, he trailed his thumb along her jawline. "You are so beautiful, Nightingale, so beautiful… Shame you're dumb as a box of rocks."

An offended 'ah' came from the back of her throat when she opened her mouth. "Dover!"

Smacking his arm, she was met only with his laughter.

"Babe, this whole damn mess is your fault. You made him fall in love with you. Not the fake kind he uses with every other woman. Real fucking love. He did more than face plant on the sidewalk the day you met. He fell head over heels… and he's never recovered."

What should she say to that? "I—"

"You don't get it, I know," he said, drinking from the glass. "That's because you didn't know him before you... Before you, Ryske belonged to everyone. Sure, he was on our crew and more loyal to us than anyone. We were his family. But when it came to women, Ryske knew how to give them just enough of himself. Just a little tiny piece to each one, sharing himself out among them all. Ophelia had a piece of him, Anwen too. Lydia. Hannah. All of them had that little shred of him they could carry around, knowing it belonged to them.

"Ophelia always had hope, Anwen too. Almost every woman he was ever with wanted to keep him, probably because he made it clear they never would. Everyone loves what they can't have, right? He'd give them some speech about not being good enough for them."

"Why would you want to tie yourself to a guy like me?" she recited, recalling something Ryske said to her once.

"Guess you got it too."

Shrugging a shoulder as she lifted the bottle, she watched it rise. "Some version of it. He told me he wasn't my white picket guy."

"Did you want him to be?"

She swirled the liquor left in the bottle. "I don't know what I wanted him to be back then... I was a different person."

"So was he. You changed him... and he fought against it. You might not know it, but he tried not to love you... For your sake, not his."

"Believe me, I know it, Dover. Not many women can say a guy's faked his own death to avoid a break up."

"That wasn't what he did," he said, but she dipped her chin and arched a brow at him. "Okay, so yeah, that was sorta what he did."

His brief laugh made her exhale one too. That was old news. Yeah, still a big deal, but not something she was going to rake Ryske over the coals for again.

They drank in silence for another minute or two.

"So what are you going to do?" Dover asked.

"Me?" She swayed forward to push on him. "You

mean we. You're supposed to be the one I can rely on to be level-headed. You're supposed to help me out."

Though he laughed at her meager form attempting to stand up to his, the sound drifted off. "I don't know, Night. With this place the way it is, I can't see me being much use to anyone for a while."

"You are the team, Dover. I know Ryske is the one with the big head, but you're the real anchor. This place grounds all of you."

"Not much use to us now, is it?"

Forcing him to hold her, she moved into his arms, coiling both tight around her as she turned her back to his chest.

"We are going to get this place back up and running in no time, you'll see. I know you think doing the big, brooding thing is what you're supposed to do. That's just because you've spent too much time with men."

On one forearm were his stars, the same as hers and everyone else's on the crew. She turned the other and was surprised to find new ink. Tracing it with a fingertip, she learned the shape. All black, it was only a couple of inches high. Two curved horns rose from a rounded base into pointed tips.

"Did it myself," he said, withdrawing the embrace and stepping back.

"It's a flame," she said. From the look on his face, she'd guess he hadn't expected her to figure that out. Picking up the glass from the kitchen counter, she tossed the remaining liquid into her throat. "Got a clean needle?"

Any lingering doubt or disappointment left his gaze and he smiled at her again. "Step into my studio."

He'd given her the stars on her arm; she had full faith in his work. The flame was a symbol of what happened. Of a night that bound them all.

Dover needed to feel he hadn't lost his bond with this place. Tying them all to it with such a permanent act was a good way of reminding him of their solidarity.

TEN

HARLOW WAS STILL asleep, so when a tongue slid against hers, she was sure it was a dream. Recognizing the taste and technique of her man, she didn't hesitate to respond. Rolling onto her back, she slid her hands up his shoulders and around the sides of his neck to pull him closer.

"Hey!" Dover hollered from somewhere. "Quit that shit in my bed!"

Jerking away from the kiss, Harlow blinked, attempting to clear the sleep and focus. Someone swept the hair from her forehead. She shifted her head back in the direction of the kiss to see Ryske lying there beside her.

"You've got some splainin' to do, Little Missy."

Still foggy and tired, she rolled her head back and forth on the pillow and tried to pull his mouth back to hers. "I want kisses," she mumbled in her morning voice.

He resisted her kiss, but did keep running his fingers through her hair, soothing and relaxing her. "You could've had all the kisses you wanted last night if you'd come home."

Smiling, she tucked her head under his chin, trying her best to use her weight to con him into lying on his back as opposed to his side. "This is home, Crash," she murmured, running her hand up and down his torso, only to be disappointed by the sensation of fabric under her palm. "Take your shirt off, baby."

"Not in my bed!" Dover called out.

From the angle of his voice, she guessed he was in the kitchen.

Respecting she shouldn't violate the man's space, any more than she had last night, Harlow sighed and sat up. Yawning, she ran her fingers through her hair, in a failed attempt to make some semblance of order out of it.

"Dover's bed is more comfortable than yours," she said to Ryske, who, of course, chose that moment to sink onto his back.

Peeking over her shoulder at him in his dark blue jeans and gray tee-shirt, she was too weak to resist the temptation. Screw it. Flipping over, she climbed onto his body to wriggle against him.

"It's a new mattress, that's why it's so comfortable," Ryske said, scooping his hands under her shirt to find her wearing his boxer-briefs. "What happened to no underwear?"

"It's not my underwear, it's your underwear. Besides, I was sleeping with another man last night. I figured you'd want me to make the exception."

"You shouldn't sleep with my friends," he said, accepting her kiss, gathering her hair in the crooks of each thumb to hold it in a ponytail at the base of her skull. "It's kinda slutty."

"I love Dover," she said and kissed him again.

His brows went up; amusement written all over his face. "Oh yeah?"

Nodding with her mouth resting on his, she rubbed them together. "See what he gave me?"

Kissing him quick, she didn't rise, but picked up her hand to present the black flame tattooed on the inside of her wrist.

"Shit, baby, what is it with you and ink?" he asked, catching her wrist to examine it. Once he'd looked for a good minute, he kissed it. "It's a symbol, right? Of the fire?"

She nodded and pressed her hands to his chest to sit up, straddling his hips. "It means something to him," she said, studying it herself. "Will you get it too?"

"If you want," he said, linking his fingers at the back of his head. "But I already have my wristband and my stars, so we'll have to figure out somewhere else for it."

"Okay."

Still sitting on him in Dover's distant corner, she unbuttoned the top few buttons of her shirt and opened it to show him her breasts.

"I don't know where this is going, but I like where it's starting," he said, sliding his hands out from behind his head to scoop a breast into each palm.

Leaving one to its fun, she checked his wristband tattoo which was made up of what looked like arrowheads and zigzags. He was right, there was no space. It would look out of place on his other wrist, crowding his stars.

The scar on his palm was fresh. She drew her finger across it then pressed her own palm to his.

"I love how much you love me, Ryske," she said, recalling the day he'd made them bleed into each other. "Don't ever think I take you for granted."

His hand skimmed down from her breast to rest inside her shirt on her hip. "What's wrong?"

They didn't usually do sappy, not at this time in the morning, and not unless something provoked it.

"We'll talk about it later," she said and tried to cast off her melancholy by poking a finger into his forearm, above the wristband. "Get it here, on the same arm as Dover and I."

"Whatever you want, baby."

She buttoned her shirt again. "Dover could do it while I'm in the shower maybe," she said. "I want to spend the day here. We have to strip the floor out downstairs. There's a lot of work to do. It's wrong we should leave it all to Dover."

"Okay. I'll call in reinforcements."

"Good," she said and started to climb off, but paused. "And will you order a new mattress, please? One like this. I want to move back here. Dover said it was okay."

He nodded. "Your sister called," he said as she got off the bed, tugging down her shirt. "She wants you to go to dinner at your parents tonight."

Harlow groaned. "Oh God, you know what that will be, don't you?"

He grinned and sank his fingers into his hair again. "The shit's gonna hit the fan."

"What did you say? You could've told them I was sick or something."

"You think they'd buy that?" he teased.

Harlow wasn't in the mood to play and raised her fists to her hips. "I think if you couldn't sell it, you need a new profession."

He laughed. "Sorry to disappoint, baby, I wasn't the one to take the call. Noon did. He said you'd be there."

Oh, that smug smile of his was just so proud of itself. It gave Harlow great pleasure to be able to wipe it off.

"I don't know why you look so pleased with yourself," she said. "If I'm going, you're going." The look of satisfaction slid off his face and onto hers. "That's right. They know about us now. It's all out in the open. I gave Rupert a whole speech about whether he liked it or not, you two are family, so I'm saying the same thing to you." Sliding a knee onto the bed, she balanced her weight with a hand on his chest and bowed to kiss him. "You've got an appointment with the in-laws."

Ryske didn't find it funny; his kiss was weak. Somewhere in the background, Dover laughed.

Ha! Yes. One of the great things about being in a relationship was having someone help counteract her mother's disapproval. But knowing what tonight was going to be about, Harlow was certain Ryske would have to utilize more than one of his many charming personalities to get them both through it.

***

"YOU NERVOUS?" Ryske asked.

In the car on the way to her parents, they were just a couple of turns away from what could be a head fuck of a night.

"No," she said, bending down to untwist the strap of her purse in the foot well. "Are you nervous?"

With his eyes on the road ahead, he frowned. "Why would I be nervous? I've met your parents."

"Never as a potential son-in-law."

"Potential?" he asked, flashing her a smirk and reaching over to give her thigh a squeeze. "Want to swing by the courthouse? We'll make tonight a double whammy for them… I can get you pregnant right here too, if you don't want to be left behind on that score."

"You're driving and it's Sunday… The courthouse isn't open."

Her love wasn't discouraged. "We'll give Maze a call, he'll slip us in there. Say we did it on Friday."

"I was in the hospital on Friday."

Laughing, he slid his hand higher. "Shit, babe, where's your sense of humor? Sure you're not nervous?"

Breathing out her frustration in a half-sigh, half-groan, she slid his hand higher and sank back in her seat. "I'm sorry."

"Don't apologize," he said, pulling her leg closer to him, away from the other one. "Talk to me."

"I think Lena and Rupert assume my parents will take this news better if I say I'm okay with it."

"Yeah," he said, stealing his hand back to lick his fingertips. "I'd say so… Are you not okay with it?"

His damp fingers bypassed their previous spot and went up her skirt to zone in on her clit, rubbing in slow circles.

"Mm," she whimpered and slid down in the seat, parting her legs further. "I'm okay with it. I'm weirded out, but I'm okay with it… That feels so good, Crash."

"Always feels good… Want me to pull over? My mouth is at your disposal."

Though she could barely see past her heavy eyelids, she smiled when he cast a look her way. "We're in a residential neighborhood."

"Yeah," he said. "It'll take the cops at least twenty minutes to get to a public indecency call… plenty of time to finish you off."

She swatted his arm in the same minute his finger plunged into her. On a gasp, her hips rose, pushing hard against his invading digit. Dropping and rising, she wasn't ashamed to ride his hand while his attention flashed between her and the road.

The frequency of her pants grew until yelping and squealing was all she could do. "Crash," she begged, snatching a handful of his shirt, yanking him to her.

He leaned over and drove his tongue deep into her mouth, kissing her with the same urgency his finger showed slipping out of her to speed over her clit. With a strong hold, he angled her back, arching her body and tearing his mouth from hers to trail it down her throat to her cleavage. Sucking on the swell of her breast, he tipped her into the screaming abyss of an orgasm that squeezed around her heart so hard she stopped breathing for half a minute.

Ryske kissed each of her breasts again, then sat up and ran his hands through his hair.

As she lay there, boneless and panting for breath in the front seat of Noon's car, she figured out they weren't driving anymore. Embarrassing, but, yeah, it took her a minute. Given the indulgence he'd bestowed, he'd used both hands and his mouth, she should've worked it out.

And that wasn't all.

She absorbed their surroundings. "Crash," she said, her attention sliding left and right.

"Yeah?"

"We're in my parents' driveway."

"Yeah. I parked five minutes ago," he said and licked his fingertips. "Do I get mine now?"

She smacked his chest. "What if someone saw us?"

Scooping a hand under her jaw, he drew her mouth to his.

After their kiss, he brushed his nose over hers. "Let's go meet the in-laws, Trink."

"You better wash up before you shake anyone's hand," she said, reaching for her door handle.

"Hold on, stay there, don't move," he said and leaped out of the car to run around the hood.

The smirk on his face when he opened her door was suspicious. He offered her a hand like some sort of professional doorman and helped her out of the car.

"Are we roleplaying?"

"I don't know," he said. "Want me to bend you over the hood and fuck you? You're prepped."

"I have never met a parking valet who did that to me," she said, turning around to bow into the car, reaching for her purse, sort of deliberately presenting her butt.

She'd just gotten hold of her purse in the foot-well when he smacked her ass.

Swinging her arm behind her to swat him away, she stood in a twist to face him. "You've done enough," she hissed. "Already I'm thinking about your cock. Not really the right headspace for what we're about to deal with, don't you think?"

Dipping, he kissed her, guiding her away from the door so he could slam it. Harlow was next to be slammed, right up against the side of the car.

"Don't think. Act," he said and kissed her again. "Right here outside your parents' house... You can do whatever you goddamn like to me, any time you want."

Licking her lips, she was maybe just insane enough to take advantage of Ryske's suggestion. Except, over his shoulder, the front door of her parents' house opened, putting paid to those ideas.

Her father stepped out onto the doorstep.

"Daddy," she said.

Ryske smirked. "Daddy? That's a new one."

She smacked his shoulder and nodded behind him. "Daddy," she said in a tone meant to explain she'd been talking to her actual father, not her boyfriend. She pushed away from Ryske, linking their hands to pull him with her. Her mom and Lena came outside too. "What's going on?"

"There was an issue in the kitchen," Brysen said, descending to join them.

"There was not an issue," Jean exclaimed. "I just decided I'd like to go out tonight... There's a new restaurant in town. Everyone's raving about it."

"Oh," Harlow said. "We're going out to eat…" She peeked over her shoulder at Ryske to murmur, "Did you bring your credit card?"

"No," he said, smiling at Jean and Lena as they came down the stairs. "Don't worry, I'll pick one up there." Harlow jabbed an elbow into his ribs. He laughed. "I'm kidding." As her family went past them, her eyes cut to his. "What? I was kidding."

Harlow wasn't all the way sure; he'd told her about his and Noon's pickpocketing days. When it came to sleight of hand, Ryske was a pro.

Her father opened the driver's door and the women got in the back. "Would you like to ride with us? Rupert is meeting us there."

"Sure," she said, pulling Ryske toward the car to shove him in the direction of the front passenger seat. "We'd be thrilled."

ELEVEN

HARLOW GOT IN the back of her father's vehicle with her sister and mother. The drive to the restaurant was mostly talk about the car, in the front anyway. She didn't really pay attention, but her father seemed to like talking horsepower and mod-cons with Ryske. The man didn't even realize he was being seduced.

It was sort of funny to watch Ryske work from a distance. The subtlety was impressive. He didn't make a big deal about flattering her dad. By complimenting the car, he was actually complimenting Brysen's taste and means. Oh, how the frog loved to luxuriate in the hot tub.

They got to the restaurant and parked out back. Inside, the maître d showed them to a reserved table. Ryske pulled out her mother's chair and Lena's while her father talked to a passing client.

Harlow waited at the bottom of the table. When Ryske was done charming her mother and sister with his manners, she pointed at her chair.

"Help you with something, Trink?"

"I don't know," she said, wearing a smile. "How do you want this night to end for you?"

A smile contorted his lips, hiding a laugh. He came

over to do his gracious duty, pulling out her chair and guiding her down into it before pushing her in at the table.

He took his seat between her and Lena.

Harlow leaned in, running a hand up his thigh under the table. "You're doing good, cowboy."

"It's all in the wrist," he said without looking at her.

Her father was just taking his seat when Rupert rushed in. "I'm sorry, it's been a day."

Rupert went around the table, kissing each of the women. Her ex wasn't subtle about ignoring Ryske in his greeting.

"Such a friendly bunch," Ryske muttered while Rupert settled himself.

"Come on," Harlow leaned sideways to whisper. "He's not the first man to be intimidated by you."

Turning to meet her eye, his smile was wide and mocking. "Oh, I see what you did there, Trink. Very clever," Ryske said, pretending to have figured something out. "You complimented me so I'd forget he insulted me. That's good. Very good. You have talent."

"If you let it go, I'll suck your dick later."

He straightened his fork and mumbled, "You already owe me one. You're racking up a helluva debt."

"Mr. Ryske," Jean said, drawing his attention.

With three places on each side of the long table, Ryske had Harlow on one side, her sister on the other. Rupert sat opposite Lena, next to Jean, leaving her dad in the last spot.

Leaning back and stretching an arm along the back of her chair, her love was at his happiest spreading himself around. "Just Ryske is fine, Jean."

"Ryske," Jean said. The way her mom averted her eyes swung Harlow's jaw loose. Her mother was blushing. Blushing! What the hell was it about Ryske that he could just turn it on like that? Mom hadn't been quite so coy when she believed him to be just another businessman. "I'm a little confused. What is it you actually do?"

"Oh," Ryske said, bending his wrist to trail the back of his thumb up and down the outside of her arm. "I guess you could call me a jack-of-all-trades."

The shivers his thumb left in its wake were unnerving in their ability to touch more sensitive corners of her body. The man wasn't even looking at her. His arm wasn't exactly around her either; it was just draped along the back of her chair with his forearm loose.

"Like a carpenter?" Lena asked.

"Sure," Ryske said. Harlow kept her mouth closed, but that didn't dam the surge of snorted laughter that caught in her throat. He glanced her way. "What? I work with wood."

In the broadest possible definition. While she wasn't buying it, and Rupert had a rather severe look on his face, the rest of the table nodded along.

"What else do you work with?" Lena asked.

Ryske's arm left her chair when he twisted toward her sister. "Well," he said, taking Lena's wrist from the table. Turning it over, he trailed the tip of his finger up the inside of her forearm at an excruciating pace. "I know how to manipulate electricity." His voice dropped an octave and slowed to a purr. Resting Lena's arm on the table, he kept stroking her forearm from elbow to wrist with that barely there touch, and raised his other hand to her face to caress her cheek. "I can subdue waterworks… inspire moisture and humidity…" Rolling his hand over, the back of his fingers slid down Lena's slack jaw to her neck. "Turn up the heat…"

Harlow could only imagine the smolder he'd be pinning on her sister. Given the girl's daze, there was no doubt his spell mesmerized her.

Harlow grabbed a passing server, catching him off-guard. "We need some alcohol at this table," she said and let the guy go. Stretching across Ryske, she eased his hand away from Lena's décolletage. "Let's stop seducing the youngsters, honey."

Lena and Jean gaped at him. They couldn't even get it together to order drinks, so Brysen ordered for them. Once the server scurried off to fill the orders, they were left to peruse their menus.

"There's been something on my mind," Brysen said.

Uh-oh, this felt like a red flag moment. Her father was peering over his menu at Ryske. Everyone was doing it;

he was like a zoo exhibit at their table. They'd really believed he was what he'd told them he was, except now he was there in front of them, a completely different person. He sat differently, talked differently, had a whole different air about him. Everyone at the table was fascinated. Except Rupert, he was still glaring.

"What's that, Brysen?" Ryske said, not moving his eyes off the menu.

He was taking all of this in stride; she was proud of him for that. It was his way to go with it, but this was her family.

"What made you target Harlow?"

Oh. Wow. That got Ryske's attention in a different way and he lowered his menu. "You want to know if she's a weak spot." Her father nodded. "She's not naïve if that's what you're asking. She knows the world better than any of you do."

Though that statement startled her father, he gathered himself and seemed to look at Ryske with new respect. "But you targeted her…"

Ryske's laughter surprised everyone. "For sex," he said. "She was never a professional mark."

"Honey," Harlow said in an attempt to temper him.

The moment she realized she'd just done exactly what her mother would do was the same one she vowed never to moderate him again.

Folding his menu, Ryske put it on the table and laid his hands on top. "Harlow's no fool," he said, meeting Brysen's eye. "You'd be surprised what she's capable of… I wasn't, but I saw something none of the rest of you did."

Pushing his chair back, Ryske removed the suit jacket he wore and hung it over the back of her chair. One at a time, he offered her his cuffs. Sensing what he wanted, Harlow removed each of his cufflinks and put them on the table.

"What did you see?" Lena asked.

"Her true self," he said, watching her fold up his sleeve. The second it was out of the way, he picked at the corner of the dressing over his new tattoo. "The glue's catching, Trink. It's pissing me off."

Grabbing the corner he'd unstuck, she ripped it off fast and hard.

Her grin followed his growl. "Oh, baby, did that hurt?"

"You'll pay for it later," Ryske said, pulling himself back in at the table.

Bending down to get her purse from the floor, Harlow put his cufflinks away and folded up the dressing, sticking it to itself. They knew not to leave evidence behind, so she tucked it into her purse to be trashed later.

"I think you took advantage of her when she was vulnerable," Rupert said. "You played us once. There's no reason to believe you wouldn't do it again."

"And I think you didn't hear her. You wanted her to be something she wasn't," Ryske said, linking his fingers on the table. "You're right to be suspicious of me. I'd think you were an idiot if you weren't. You don't know what I'm capable of." He pressed his weight to an elbow to lean a fraction closer. "I'll give you a hint, there's not much on the incapable side."

Lena gasped. "Oh my God, you're some kind of outlaw!" And damn if that didn't sound sexy. "That's what this is about."

Her sister never had been the quickest wit. She was too easily distracted. At least they knew she was caught up, for now, at least.

"I think it's a little suspicious that immediately after meeting you," Rupert said, "Harlow goes to jail for murder."

Harlow grabbed for Ryske's thigh under the table, telling him in her own way to keep his cool. "If Harlow would've let me do that time for her, I would have."

"Oh, so you take your orders from her?"

"You don't know what you're talking about, Rupe," Harlow snapped.

"Seems to me your boyfriend should take care of business."

"Like you did," Ryske said, picking up the drink the server put down in front of him. "You don't have a damn clue what she's been through."

Her heart pumped harder. No one had mentioned the half million yet. Maybe that was why Rupert was being so salty. Could be that he thought he'd been the mark and she'd facilitated Ryske taking him for that money. The sooner they could get it back to him, the better.

"She said she tells you everything," Rupert said.

Rupert laid eyes on her. Was he thinking about the money? Was this him trying to decide if he'd been conned?

If she'd been honest with him about her need and lack of options, Rupert may think Ryske didn't know about the money. Going to an ex to bail her out might be emasculating for some men, so she might have kept it a secret... if she'd been with a lesser man.

"Yeah," Ryske said. "We don't spend a lot of time discussing your sex life if you're having a crisis of confidence."

Harlow slid her hand to the inside of his knee. "He's not thinking about that, Crash," she murmured and looked at Rupert. "It's complicated."

"Does he know?"

"Yes," she said. "He does now."

"He didn't at the time?" Rupert said. She shook her head. "Was it him?"

"No and he wasn't happy when he did find out about it," she said. "I told you. It's complicated."

Shaking his head, Rupert wasn't stingy with his disappointment. "I never thought you'd lie to me, Harlow."

Oh, she wasn't going to sit there meek and sorry when he didn't even understand the full situation. On top of that, Rupert was supposed to make an announcement of his own that night. If anyone should be judged, it should be him.

"Yeah?" she asked, heated by anger. "Well, I never thought you'd fu—"

"These linens are beautiful, aren't they?" Ryske said, smoothing a hand over the tablecloth next to his plate.

The quick subject change was unexpected. Décor was more Jean's wheelhouse. So, after recovering from conversation whiplash, Jean went into a speech about the restaurant, the history of the building, and how it had been refitted. There had been a lot of gossip about the owners, and she was happy to regale them with it all.

Jean was still talking when their food came. They got through the rest of the meal without any more animosity.

"Who's for dessert?" Harlow asked when the server brought back the menus. "We always get a sweet when we're out."

Ryske leaned in to murmur against her ear. "My Sweeting isn't on the menu… Think I can order it on special?"

"It?" she asked, peeking at him, wearing a smile. "I think if you're talking about me, you can order any damn thing you want, but it's your job to make it special."

He grazed his lips on hers. As he was about to withdraw, she put a hand to the back of his neck to pull him back for a deeper kiss. They were still nuzzling their mouths together when a shadow cast over them.

"Harlow," Lena whispered, crouching behind their chairs. "Come to the restroom with me. Mom is busy talking to Gayle… Sorry, Ryske."

"No, restroom emergency, I understand," he said, curling his fingers around a strand of her hair and letting it drift away. "You ladies want another drink?"

"Please," Harlow said, smacking a quick kiss on his lips.

Lena was nervous. "I, uh…"

"Virgin, I know," Ryske said and winked at her. "Get lost. Let me weave my magic."

"I love you, Crash," Harlow said and snagged Lena's arm to guide her away from the table.

"What does that mean?" Lena asked. "His magic?"

"He'll keep the table busy," she said. "No one will notice we're gone."

Pushing her sister into the restroom, Harlow dragged Lena into the large stall at the end and locked the door.

"Oh, Harlow," Lena said and fell into her arms. "This is all going wrong…"

Going wrong? Harlow held her sister, stroking her hair and soothing her. Things had probably started to go wrong for Lena when she slept with Rupert.

"You have to tell them," Harlow said, taking her arms

to set Lena straight on her feet. "Just do it like I did Ryske's dressing. Rip it off hard and fast."

"I… I don't know how. Where do I even begin?"

That seemed like the wrong question. The situation had begun with sex, but Harlow wouldn't recommend telling their folks about that.

"You have to say it," Harlow said. "Both things at once. Don't delay the reveal."

"But I—"

"No," Harlow said, aware they may not be alone in the restroom. "You have to because one of the first things they'll ask is, you know, who's half-responsible."

Breathing in, Lena blew out the breath. "You're right… I know you're right…"

"Or you could have Rupert do it. He's close to dad."

Lena regained some hopeful spirit. "Will Ryske help?"

Harlow opened her mouth to respond, then closed it again as she tried to figure out what he could do. "I… You want him to tell Mom and Dad?"

She didn't get it.

By the way Lena groaned and rolled her head, it was clear she was off base. "No, but he has a way of talking to people, of calming them down."

"Yeah, he can piss them off too and he's not Rupert's biggest fan."

"I don't know why they can't get along," Lena muttered. Squeezing her lips together, Harlow didn't offer any explanation. She'd let Lena reach her own conclusions on that one. "We were supposed to eat at home. I'd feel better doing it in private. What if there's a scene?"

It wasn't easy to imagine her mother creating drama in public. Yet, if there was anything capable of causing Jean to lose awareness of their environment, learning her youngest daughter got knocked up by her eldest daughter's ex-fiancé would be it.

"We'll go back to Mom's for drinks after," she said, rubbing Lena's arms.

"They'll know something's going on if we make a big

deal of—"

"Ryske will do it."

"How will he know to—"

"Trust me, honey. He'll make it happen," Harlow said and kissed her cheek. "We're all frogs in warm water when he's around."

TWELVE

TAKING LENA'S HAND, Harlow guided her out of the restroom. They only got a few steps before someone appeared from the shadow at the end of the hallway nearest the dining room.

And that was no stranger.

Harlow pulled Lena close. "Go back to the table. I'll meet you there."

Despite also knowing the approaching woman's identity, Lena didn't ask questions and released her hand to continue to the dining room.

The woman came to a stop in front of Harlow. "You recognize me?"

"Yes," Harlow said. "The Rowe family are famous. Most people around here know the Rowe Estate. It's less than twenty miles from town… and you go to my father's country club."

The woman's head tilted. "Is that why you recognize me?"

Harlow didn't want to give any indication of her feelings, but sensed she wasn't a bullshitter. "No," she said. "That's not why I recognize you, Mrs. Rowe."

Her chin rose. "You know Aston."

"I live with Aston," Harlow said. The woman's surprise put a smile on her face. "I'm not sleeping with your son."

"Well, I… No, I… I didn't think you would be."

"Why not? He's hot," she said. The woman didn't have a response. If she didn't do something, they'd be there all night. "What can I do for you, Mrs. Rowe?"

"I… I'm not sure if I should say anything now."

"Aston is safe… he's happy. It might not be the life you would've chosen for him, but he's one of the best men I know."

Amelie Rowe blinked at her. Maybe she hadn't expected Harlow to be so forward. It must be strange to hear someone talk about your child, adoptive or not, with such authority.

"I saw you with Ryske."

Inhaling, Harlow's mouth opened in understanding. "Ah, and you're here to warn me he's a bad 'un… Yeah, I know. The asshole can't make a bed." More surprise. "I'm sorry, Mrs. Rowe. I appreciate that you wanted to warn me, to make sure I wasn't being taken advantage of. But I'm not being taken advantage of… Ryske and I are in love." She raised a hand. "I know, he's in love with a lot of women. A lot of women think they're different or special to him. You've done your duty. If I get crapped on, it's my own fault… I'll give Aston your love when I get home."

Leaving Amelie in the hallway, she went back to the dining room to find a dessert at her place.

Ryske stood up to help her into her chair. Having such a gentleman as a date when she'd been living with Crash for so long was a bit of a strange experience.

"What is this?" Harlow asked, looking at the dessert.

"Dessert," Rupert said from the opposite corner of the table.

"How do I know I like it?" she asked.

Ryske put his forearm on the back of her chair. "There's booze, coffee, and chocolate in it," he said. "Eat it."

"Hmm," she said, scooping some onto her fork. "Missing just one of my favorite ingredients."

"What?" Ryske asked.

She offered the fork to his lips. His brow twitched in confusion, but he opened his mouth to accept the creamy dessert. Harlow fed it to him then put the fork on her plate, eyes locked to his.

"You," she murmured, cupping his face to draw him down for a full tongue kiss.

He hadn't swallowed all the dessert; the kiss was full and sweet and intoxicating. If Amelie Rowe had seen them together, others had too. Most wouldn't know what Ryske did. The Rowe's didn't advertise what their son and his friends were into. To the majority of the room, her love was just a curiosity.

Anyone could look, but Harlow was going to make sure they knew he was all hers.

"Mmm," Ryske made a sound of approval when their mouths parted. Picking up a napkin, he wiped a smudge of dessert from the corner of her mouth. "We should get some of these to go."

"Maybe we should," she said, nuzzling closer, kissing him again, dragging her teeth along his jaw to take her lips to his ear. "You need to get us invited back to my parents."

Ryske didn't respond to her words, but he'd heard her. Her guy understood discreet... in certain arenas. He kissed the soft spot under the curve of her jaw open to him at this angle. He kissed beneath her ear, the side of her neck, sliding his hand up her skirt under the table.

"This is an upscale restaurant," Rupert said. "Your behavior is inappropriate, Ryske."

It was tough to put a man in his place when everyone used his last name.

"I started it," Harlow said, twisting toward her dessert.

"Yeah," Ryske said. "You should see what she's doing to me under the table. Harlow the Harlot, that's what they call her back home."

Breathing out a laugh, she enjoyed another forkful of dessert. She ate one, then fed another to Ryske. His accusation was rich given he couldn't keep his hands out of her skirt.

"Crash, I don't need to play with you under the table. If I wanted you, I'd take you by the hand, lead you out that side door and have you."

"Harlow!" Jean said. "Really? Must you speak like that?"

If her mom was worried people would overhear, she'd probably been worried about the kissing too, which may have been why Rupert spoke up. Turning her fork, Harlow flattened her tongue on it to lick it clean. The dessert was good; it had been a good choice.

"Mom, I'm the Sweeting girl who went to jail for murder," she said, scooping up more dessert to feed it to Ryske. "Just be glad the room doesn't think I'm a lesbian."

"I could be your beard," Ryske said, stroking her inner thigh and accepting more dessert.

Her lips curled. "Could be. With all the sex we're having, you're convincing even me."

"That you're straight?" Ryske asked, catching some of the dessert with the end of his tongue. "Don't worry, baby, I wouldn't let that happen." He leaned in to whisper in her ear. "Pussy's way too much fun."

Nudging him away with her body, she ran her little finger around the rim of her dessert dish to gather the smudges. Ryske caught her wrist on its way to her mouth and tugged it up to his instead. Opening wide, he took the full digit into his mouth. Squeezing it between his tongue and palate, he sucked it clean, dragging his teeth down her finger as he did.

Her teeth caught her own lip. The sensation on her skin and the force of suction awakened every part of her. She couldn't tear her attention away from his mouth. That mouth. The side door loomed large. God, she wanted him.

Snaking a hand onto his thigh, she was still watching him nibbling on her finger when she pressed her palm to his groin. Harlow had only been half kidding about taking his hand and leading him outside. She'd known she could do it but hadn't thought temptation would be so hard to resist.

Stimulating him through his slacks, it didn't take long to get his full attention. When he gritted his teeth, she leaned in and licked his lower lip.

"We should go out for dinner more often," she said. "I didn't realize it turned you on so much."

He only held his control because her parents were opposite them. Even in spite of that, it was fun to take him right to the edge of his restraint.

"Oh my goodness," Jean said. Harlow expected they were about to be chastised again. Except it turned out her mother wasn't talking to them. "Mrs. Rowe, it's an honor."

The name raised Ryske's head. Harlow twisted around to see the woman standing at the end of the table.

"Charmed," Amelie said, flashing Jean a smile that faded when she shifted her focus. "Harlow, I feel I should apologize."

"I won't tell him you offended me," Harlow said, picking up her drink. "Though now I've said that in front of Ryske, he probably will."

"Tell Maze you were offended?" Ryske asked and took her glass from her when she lowered it from her lips. "Yeah. I probably will."

Amelie's attention rose to Ryske. "Ryske," she said in acknowledgement.

"Ame," he said.

There was enough tension in that exchange to tell her all she needed to know. These two people had known each other a long time. That went without saying given Ryske had known Maze longer than Amelie. They were both suspicious of each other. Leaning back, Harlow rested in the crook of his shoulder between his body and his arm resting on the back of her chair.

Sliding a hand down his knee, Harlow tipped her chin toward her shoulder. "She thought I was sleeping with him."

"Yeah, this is me stealing her away," Ryske said, sipping from her glass. "How do you think I'm doing?"

"I… I apologize for my presumption in approaching you, Harlow," Amelie said, contrite and polite. Harlow didn't know the woman well enough to decipher if it was genuine or an act. "I wouldn't like for there to be bad feeling between us. I would like to be friends… Maybe we could meet for lunch one day I'm in the city."

Harlow didn't see Ryske smile, but she guessed he did because the burst of his laugh vibrated through his throat. "Oh, Ame, that's an incredible idea," he said and rubbed her arm. "Baby, you should go to lunch with Mrs. Rowe. You guys could be BFFs." He took a long loud breath. "You know Harlow was in jail, right? She's not his redemption."

"Yeah," Harlow said, nodding, playing the dumb bimbo. "They think I killed a guy, can you believe that?"

Ryske kissed her hair. "Hey, baby, if blowjobs could kill, you'd need a license."

Tipping her head back, she whimpered and kissed the underside of his jaw. "Oh, you're so romantic, my love."

"Ryske," Amelie said. "We never wanted this."

"I know what you wanted," Ryske said, becoming sinister. Harlow remained slouched against him. A tickle of awareness prickled the hairs on the back of her arm. "What I want is for you to turn around and walk away. Go back to your ivory tower, Ame, because until my boy tells me otherwise, you and me are not okay."

Unsettled, Amelie cast a feeble smile at the others before retreating. When she was gone, Harlow turned expecting she'd have to soothe Ryske. She didn't.

Her man was all ease again as he straightened and laid a hand on the table to push back.

"Brysen, want to bring the car around and I'll take care of this?" Ryske said, gesturing at the table, showing no signs of upset or aggravation. "I say a drink is in order, don't you? Everyone back to yours?"

Ryske stood up and helped her to her feet too. When they were up, he draped his jacket over her shoulders. Everyone else rose in a hurry to catch up.

"You are going to pay?" Harlow asked over her shoulder, keeping their conversation quiet and private.

"Yeah," Ryske said.

Spinning all the way around, she laid her hands on his chest. "No, I mean, you are *actually* going to pay… aren't you? Did we even bring any money?"

"Have faith, Trink." He winked and bowed to kiss

her. "You know me."

His hands drifted from her shoulders as he retreated toward the front desk.

"Yeah," she muttered and called after him. "That's what worries me, Crash!"

THIRTEEN

RYSKE HAD JUST disappeared around the screen that separated the front desk from the dining room when Rupert came up behind her. Seeing him so close so suddenly was a surprise. He must have rushed all the way around the table. The poor guy was stressed, that much was obvious. Harlow could understand why and didn't envy his position.

Without a word, Rupert grabbed her hand to drag her through the restaurant and out the back exit to the parking lot.

"Uh, I'd like to keep my arm, if possible," she said when they stopped in the shadows of the perimeter.

Spinning around, Rupert's momentum almost caused them to collide. "I don't like him."

"Don't sleep with him," she said and opened her hands to exaggerate brushing them together. "There. Problem solved."

"Harlow," he said, pulling her back when she reversed a step.

But she wasn't going to be dictated to or patronized. "No," she said, raising her voice a fraction. When a nearby couple returning to their car stopped to look at them, she lowered her volume again and got closer to her ex. "No, Rupert, you don't get to comment on my relationship. You don't get to say a damn word. Are you insane? You fucked my baby sister. You got her pregnant. You're going to marry her… Do you hear me busting your balls about that?"

Bobbing his head, he relaxed as understanding settled over him. "That's what this is about. You're trying to get back at me. I'm sorry, Harlow. I don't know what else I can say."

"I didn't ask you to say a damn thing," she said. "You and your dick are your problem. Am I pissed? Yeah, probably, but only because I'd like my sister to have the best."

"You don't think I'm good enough for her?"

Closing her eyes, she tried to imagine she was talking to Felipe. Someone she had to keep her cool with even when he was pushing her buttons.

Rubbing her forehead, she took a moment to lick her lips. "Rupert, I think you're an incredible man. I think you have a kind heart and a generous nature—"

"Yeah, and that worked out for your special new friend, didn't it?"

"I didn't give him your money," she said, losing her cool to exasperation. "He didn't ask me to take money from you! I took your money and I gave it to someone he has no love for. I told you that you'd get it back and you will. Ryske was fucking livid when he heard what I'd done."

"He knows what you did with it?" Rupert said, pointing at the restaurant. "So if I go in there and demand to know why he let you get mixed up in something that required a half million dollars…"

"Oh. My. God!" she said, spacing out the words, grabbing for her hair. "Ryske doesn't *let* me do a damn thing! He'd suspect he'd slipped into some sort of parallel universe if he thought for a second that I deferred to him or any man. It might be difficult for you to understand this, but I am not the same woman you shared your bed with. I've grown. I've changed."

He wasn't deterred. "For the better? Is that what you think? When you were with me, you would never have been making out in restaurants, using the language you do… accused of murder! How can you be so relaxed? Your life is spiraling!"

That made her laugh. "My life? Are you shitting me? Rupert, look at the state of your fucking life! Everything I've done, it's been my choice. I stand by my decisions. Right or wrong, I take ownership of them. You're standing here giving me the righteous speech when we both know your future has been dictated to you. Don't get me wrong, I hope you'll both be very happy, but God, Rupert… How could you be so stupid?"

For a minute, he just looked at her. She witnessed the moment he surrendered his high horse. "Harlow," he murmured, paling suddenly. "I feel like I'm losing my grip."

"Hey." She rushed forward to scoop her hands around his jaw when it looked like he might fall on his face. Loosening his tie to give his throat more space, she also unfastened his top button. "Look at me, Rupe… Look at me." His eyes met hers. There was such resignation in them that her heart broke. "You are an amazing man and you're going to be an amazing father," she said, stroking his face and widening his smile. "I'm honored that your blood will mix with the Sweeting line."

The softness in his gaze gave her confidence in his ability to stay upright. "Harlow," he said like he got comfort from the word.

Holding his face, she brushed her thumbs back and forth on his cheeks. Dread trickled in when he licked his lips and dropped his attention to her mouth.

She leaned back. "Not that honored…"

The familiar whistle startled both of them. In the shadows, they weren't easy to spot. She spun around, expecting to alert Ryske to where they were. Turned out that wasn't necessary. Ryske was at the edge of the parking lot with her already in his sights.

"Was that him?" Rupert asked. "Whistling at you?"

Didn't take long for his judgment to return. "Come on," she said, grabbing Rupert's hand to lead him toward the group.

"Are we ready to leave?" Jean asked when they got there. "Harlow, will you and Ryske ride with us?"

She was tempted to say they weren't riding with

anyone and asking Ryske to call Noon. But her sister was there, shaking and sweating, so she gave up notions of abandonment.

"No," she said. "We'll ride with Rupert." The declaration surprised her parents. Harlow let go of Rupert to take Ryske's hand and caught Lena's hand too. "You come with us."

It was only a short trip, so she doubted her parents thought twice about the kids riding in a separate vehicle. Ryske got in the front passenger seat while Rupert drove. Her father pulled out of the restaurant parking lot. Rupert put his car in drive; Harlow bounced forward to pat his shoulder.

"Hang back," she said, watching her parents' taillights disappear. "Go to the quarry."

"What?" Rupert asked. "It's dangerous out there."

"It's dangerous in here," Ryske muttered, his focus sliding to his side window.

"It's in the wrong direction."

"It's five minutes," she said. "We're not going to swim or climb. We just need somewhere quiet. Out of the way."

Muttering something inaudible, Rupert drove in the direction she'd requested. Sliding back in the seat, Harlow put a comforting arm around Lena.

"Quarries are good places to get rid of bodies," Ryske said. "In my experience."

Something must've happened in the restaurant to upset him. She'd get the details later. They drove over the no entry sign ripped down by kids years ago and up around the sweeping road that wound through the trees.

At the highest ridge of the quarry, Rupert stopped the car. It was dark and the moonlight bright, but they weren't there for romance.

"Everyone out," Harlow said and they all did as told.

"What are we doing here, Harlow?" Rupert asked, checking his shoes like he was worried they might be ruined on the damp grass. "This is insane."

"Ryske," Harlow said, catching him up and snagging his ribs to back him up against the hood of the car.

"Harlow," he said, mirroring her scholarly tone and hooking her hair back behind her ear.

Wrapping her arms around one of his, she propped her hip against the hood and leaned on him. "What's the most important thing you need before any op?"

"Blowjob?" he asked, earning himself a smack in the stomach. He laughed. "A plan. You need a plan."

"Right," she said and gestured at Rupert and Lena standing about ten feet apart, both displaying differing expressions of unhappy. Slipping off Ryske's jacket, she took it to Lena and put her in it before going back to Ryske. This time, she leaned back against him instead of the hood and laid her arms over his when he wrapped them around her waist. Slanting to the side, she peeked up at him. "Tell me, baby, do they look like two people with a plan?"

His smirk was quick. "No," he said and kissed her forehead. "They don't."

Rupert stretched an arm toward them. "You expect us to trust him?"

"Trust him with what?" Harlow asked. "He knows you got Lena pregnant."

"Yeah," Ryske said. "I'm the only guy here who *hasn't* slept with every woman present…" He paused. "Huh… that's the first time I've ever been able to say that truthfully."

Nudging her elbow into his ribs, Harlow silenced him. "Ryske is excellent with a plan. He's also excellent at thinking on his feet; something neither of you do well. You're about to reveal something to two people who could alter the course of your lives… Rupert, what are you going to do if my dad explodes and fires you?"

Stunned, Rupert blustered. "He can't fire me for personal reasons."

"Can't he?" Harlow asked. "And, Lena, you live at home… What if mom and dad flip out and you need to get out of there fast?"

Lena's jaw sagged, that was her only response.

"She can stay with me," Rupert said. "But it won't come to that."

"Yeah, God forbid you let the woman you knocked

up into your apartment," Ryske muttered.

"Wait a second," Harlow said and looked at Rupert. "Am I still on the deed at the apartment?"

He shrugged. "Possibly… Yes, you must be."

"Oh my God," she said and shifted her weight to her feet. "Did you have sex in my bed? Wait. Don't answer that." With a shudder, she settled back against Ryske. "I'm so glad we're getting a new bed."

Ryske's lips rested on her hair. "We did it in Bale's bed."

"That's different. It wasn't his actual bed, it was a guest bed," she said. "Anyway, he's not my ex… and you didn't get me pregnant."

"Something I'm sure the doc will check on again soon."

Bale tested his brother's girlfriend more than any regular brother would. At least she understood why it was so important to him. If Ryske got her pregnant, he'd have to live a safer life. Bale was just looking out for his brother's well-being.

Getting back to the point, they didn't have a lot of time. "Look, this isn't complicated. Just get your stories straight. Decide what you will and won't tell them. What do you want to share?" Neither of them looked any more certain. "Okay, try this… let's role play."

"Oh," Ryske said like she'd just piqued his interest for the first time.

She ignored him. "Pretend we're mom and dad, tell us," Harlow said. Lena looked to Rupert. "Come on, just do it."

"That's what got them into this mess."

"Crash," she whined at him.

"Sorry, yeah, okay," Ryske said and cleared his throat. "So, young man, little lady, what is it you want to tell us?"

Harlow laughed. "That sounded nothing like my dad."

"I'll play daddy for you later," he said and kissed the top of her head. "This is for the kids."

Harlow dragged her nails up and down his arms still

tight around her torso. "Who's going to break the news?" she asked. Neither of them said anything. "One of you has to do the talking."

"I'll do it," Ryske said, urging her forward to stand them a couple of feet apart facing each other. He cleared his throat. "Mr. and Mrs. Sweeting…" He leaned back to side whisper at Rupert. "Never hurts to show a little respect." He turned his focus back to Harlow and spoke in a calm, slow, even tone. "I have something to say that's going to surprise you. I expect you to be surprised, shocked, maybe even disappointed, but I must be honest with you. This is something you have to hear."

"What would you like to say?" Harlow asked, doing her best to play her mom straight.

"I fucked your baby girl, shot my load in her snatch, and knocked her up."

Harlow slapped his shoulder. "Crash!"

He laughed. "Okay, I'm sorry…" Ryske took a moment to compose himself and then straight as an arrow, he spoke. "In a moment of weakness that has proved to be the most crucial of my life, I gave in to something I shouldn't have. I let my baser desire overtake my good sense and my great respect for you and your family," he said the words with such sincerity that even she was enthralled. "In a dark moment when we were both in need of comfort, Lena and I sought refuge in each other… We made love…"

He paused like he was letting that sink in. "You… you slept with Lena?" Harlow asked, trying to remember her role in this play.

"I did," Ryske said, showing nothing but contrition. "I know I shouldn't have done it. I disrespected you and what I once had with Harlow. We both agreed it was something we shouldn't entertain again. We hoped karma would bring our penance… Instead, it chose to give us a gift." Ryske took a couple of steps backward and grabbed Lena against his side, bringing her with him to his previous spot. With his arm around Lena's waist, Ryske smiled and rested a hand on her stomach. "We're expecting a child… Your first grandchild."

"You… you slept with Lena?" Harlow said again,

sure that would stick in her mother's throat for a while.

"I fully understand this is a surprise," Ryske said, still stroking Lena. "It was a surprise to both of us… But we've talked about it, we've absorbed it, and… we're going to do the right thing."

"The right thing?" Harlow said on impulse; that was her reaction, not the one her mother would have.

She didn't think it was necessary to marry a man for the sake of a baby, so she took exception to the characterization. Except this wasn't about her ideology, it was about her mother's.

"Yes, Mrs. Sweeting," Ryske said, sliding over her error and incorporating it as part of the scene. "I asked Lena to marry me… and she's made me the happiest man alive by accepting my proposal."

Harlow was sure Rupert had said something along those lines when they'd told her parents about his engagement to her.

"Oh God," Rupert said, drawing everyone's attention. "Harlow."

FOURTEEN

RUSHING PAST RYSKE and Lena, Harlow took hold of Rupert's arms. "Don't freak out. I know this is a lot."

"It's more than a lot," Rupert said, driving a hand through his hair. "Your father is going to kill me."

"He won't," Harlow said. "He will be disappointed and I'm sorry, Rupe, but you have to take that on the chin."

His eyes fixed on hers. "What were we thinking?"

"You were thinking you were lonely. That you were in shock and weren't in your right mind. It's just one of those things."

"Hey," Ryske snapped and she turned to his scowl. "Don't make excuses for him."

Letting go of Rupert, she faced Ryske, folding her arms. "Oh, are we going to fight about this now?"

"Yeah," Ryske said. "Yeah, we are." Easing Lena aside to a safe distance, he marched over to her and Rupert. "He fucked your little sister. No, forget that, he fucked both the man's daughters. Brysen might be an easier mark than he'd like to admit, but he gave this jerkoff a legacy, a career, a fortune. He's given him security, invited him into his home and shared his family with him. I don't think he expected to be taken advantage of like this!"

"Oh, come on," she said, throwing up her arms. "Lena was there too! They're both as responsible as each other."

"For the sex? Yes," Ryske said. "But the betrayal is his." Thrusting an arm out, he pointed at Rupert. "He has the bond with your father. Where's the loyalty?"

"Loyalty? Did you get confused? We are not talking about the guys here," she said. "I think I've slept with every single one of your friends."

"Yeah, but you haven't fucked any of them. They wouldn't come near you. You think if I doubted any of them that damn bathroom door wouldn't have been fixed the day you moved in? Damnit, when I got back last night and found out Dover was at ours, I knew you'd spend the night there. I knew you'd get in bed with him. It didn't occur to me to doubt either of you."

Ryske would never assume to tell her how she felt about her ex or her sister with regards to betrayal or loyalty. But he could see the situation from the male point of view. Still, that didn't mean she understood why he was reacting so vehemently.

"I don't understand how—"

"That's what Brysen felt," Ryske said. "He trusted this guy, trusted him with his family, his business, his money… Fucking up his relationship with you would've been a kick in the teeth."

Her arms folded again. "That was my fault and you know it."

"Yeah," Ryske said, exaggerating his nod. "Right, 'cause you wanted to be an independent entity instead of a walking womb, I get it, how dare you."

His disgust was palpable through his sarcasm. "Ryske," she warned. "None of this is about Rupert and me."

"Sure it is, because he's going to say what I said just now and the first thing Brysen is going to think is that this man is not who he thought he was… And if he wants someone to smack the fucker in the face, I'll be right there on hand."

"You are not muscle for hire," she said, prodding his

arm.

Ryske captured her wrist and whipped it aside so fast her body smacked into his. Seizing her throat, he wrenched her to the very tips of her toes. That intensity in his animalistic glare blocked out Lena's screaming and Rupert's blustering.

"You think there's anything I wouldn't do to keep your family happy?" Ryske growled, his mouth almost on hers. "I've gotta please your father 'til the day he gives you to me."

"I belong to no one," she hissed, ignoring her instinct to grab for his arm. "If you don't take your hands off me in the next three seconds, you better be ready to snap my neck or fuck my throat... Don't start something you're not willing to finish."

"Never do," he said, spinning them around to which Lena screamed again.

"Let her go!" Rupert called when Ryske rushed her back against the side of the car.

"Don't you fucking dare," Harlow hissed.

Pushing against her, he blocked the others view with his hip and pulled up her skirt to rub her clit. "Hmm, my baby's wet," he growled, pleased with himself.

He ducked down to push his tongue into her mouth. If they were just in front of the guys, they'd be fucking already. Harlow could feel the insistence of his erection trying to get to her through his slacks.

Grabbing his shoulders, she pushed him back. "We gotta stop."

"Oh no, you don't, Nightingale."

"Don't call me that," she said, pulling him down to coil both arms tight around his neck.

A cellphone rang, and Rupert answered. "Yes, Brysen, I'm sorry, we…"

Forcing herself from Ryske's kiss, Harlow darted away and grabbed the phone from Rupert. "Daddy?" she said, straightening her dress.

"Harlow, where are you? I thought you were right behind us."

"We were," she said. "We're just showing Ryske the sights."

An arm slithered around her. Someone coiled around her to lick her cleavage, she didn't need too many guesses as to who it was.

"We'll be home soon," Harlow said, hanging up the phone and tossing it back to Rupert. Trying not to broaden her smile, she ran her hands into Ryske's hair. "Those are sights you've seen before."

"He's always on you," Rupert said, not disguising his disgust.

Inhaling, Ryske lifted his attention. "Not true. Sometimes she's on top."

"Baby, I don't think that's what he meant," she said in an attempt to calm tensions.

Rupert was about as interested in keeping the peace as Ryske. "Well, it is her favorite position," her ex said, surprising her.

Ryske stood straight, his brows rising as he did. "On top?" he said and then smirked. "No, it's not."

"Okay," she said, holding out a palm to each man. "Let's stop talking about Harlow's sexual preferences."

Neither man listened.

Rupert challenged Ryske. "It is."

"It's not."

"What's her favorite?" Rupert asked, widening his stance.

This was an odd kind of pissing contest; she wasn't sure she wanted either of them to win. "Actually, we like to mix it up. Variety is important. But if she could pick just one way to take my cock for the rest of time, it would be flat on her back with my hand around her throat... or against the wall in the shower."

Rupert laughed. "She hates shower sex."

"Not anymore..." Ryske's swagger grew. "Who do you think schooled her?"

"Okay," she said, pointing at him. "You didn't school nothing, buster." She turned to Rupert. "You have more important things to deal with tonight than this bullshit." Grabbing Rupert, she shoved him toward Lena. "Go talk it out." Though Rupert glared until the very last second, he did eventually stomp away to speak with Lena. Once they were occupied, she moved in closer to Ryske. "What the hell do you think you're doing?"

"He started it."

"Not the sex stuff, the other stuff. Why are you picking on him?"

"He fucked your little sister."

"If I needed a man to look after me, I'd have married Rupert and I'd be the one carrying his child," she said. "Cut it out, Ryske. I don't need you fighting my battles."

Grabbing her arm, he twisted it to present her stars between them. "This says different."

"No, it doesn't," she said and pointed to the first star. The one meant to honor the memory of him after his death. "Do you want to know what that says? It says I got along just fine without you."

"So in one breath I'm part of your family and in the next it isn't my business?"

Stepping closer, she whispered. "You didn't see him in the restaurant parking lot."

His gaze darkened. "Oh, I did... You bet your fucking ass I did, babydoll," he said and grabbed her arm to squeeze her tight. "Tell me he wasn't thinking about kissing you." Harlow did her absolute best to blank her expression. Just her lack of a response was enough to vibrate his anger. "Oh... I'll fucking kill him... This is an excellent spot for it."

Slamming both hands to his chest, she used all her strength to push him away from Rupert and Lena until she could shove him behind one of the rocky outcrops away from the edge of the cliff.

Pushing away, she put him against the rock and took a step back. "I love you, Ryske. You know I do. This jealousy—"

"No one will take you away from me," he hissed, lunging down to get in her face. "You hear me? No fucking asshole will put his hands on—"

"Hey," she said, clamping a hand over his mouth. "No more anger, okay?" Softening, she twisted her hand away from his mouth to caress his jaw. "I love you, Ryske. I'm not going anywhere."

"Yeah? That's what I thought when the cops came and slapped you in cuffs," he said. "Probably what my dad thought before my mom fucked around on him too."

Her hand slid down to her side. "You… you think I'm going to cheat on you? Really cheat on you? Not the bullshit screwing around for a con stuff, you… You think I'd actually leave you for another man?"

"No," he said, blowing out a breath and curling a hand around the back of his neck. "No, baby, I don't think you'd do that. It's just stupid, dumb, irrational—"

"Oh my God," she exhaled.

Ryske was the most confident man she'd ever met. In bed and out. He could command a room, be anyone, do anything. She'd never considered it could be a smokescreen. An overcompensation for a masked fear he'd never admitted aloud.

It made sense. So much made sense.

For years, he'd screwed around without any concerns. He'd never settled down, never let himself love or commit. Even when she came along and their feelings consumed them both, he'd fought giving into it.

"If I didn't trust you a hundred percent, I wouldn't be with you," Ryske said. "Shit, weren't we just talking about you sleeping with the guys?"

"Yeah, but is it them you trust or me?" she asked. "What if I slept in a bed with Clyde or with Rupert?" His jaw ticked. "Oh my God, Crash."

"It's not you I don't trust, it's them. The sap I just don't fucking like," he said. "I'm your guy. It's my responsibility to keep you safe and if some bastard corners you—"

"Like Hagan did?" she asked, losing some of her incredulity. "I can take care of myself, Ryske. You know I can. You did see how fast I subdued Ophelia, didn't you?"

"You shouldn't have to," he said, grabbing for her arm, but she tugged it from his reach. "Trinket—"

"No, I have watched you kiss other women. I've heard you proposition them. I hear you flirt all the time, and you know what? I like it," she said. He blinked in surprise. "Yeah, I do. Do you know why? Because the whole time I'm thinking that's *my* guy. I am so confident and sure of your love that I could probably walk in on you balls deep in another woman and I wouldn't even think for a second that it meant a thing, or even that you'd chosen to be there. You'd be doing it for a purpose. I like seeing you charm other women. I like watching you touch them and seduce them, because I know that no matter what, you're coming home to me. They can't touch that part of you that belongs to me."

"I don't want to see any guy take advantage of you."

She scoffed. "If you think I'd let a man take advantage of me, you don't know who I am at all."

"Harlow!" Lena called.

The fear in her sister's tone hurried her around the end of the rock to stride back over to the car where Lena was waiting.

"Are you ready to go?" Harlow asked, rubbing Lena's arms to heat her up. "Are you okay?"

"I think we're ready," Lena said.

Rupert was already standing inside his open car door, his hands on the roof. "What's wrong?" he called to her.

"Nothing," she said, and kept smiling even after Ryske touched her hip. She knew better than to let their relationship issues show to anyone. "Let's get back."

FIFTEEN

EVERYONE GOT INTO the car again. The return journey to her parents' house was silent. Noon's car in the driveway was so tempting that if she'd been wearing Ryske's jacket, Harlow might have jumped in and sped off.

But she was in this, and had no choice but to face the drama with her sister.

Rupert went inside first with her and Lena behind him. Ryske was at the rear of the party.

"We thought you got lost," Jean's voice carried from the foyer beyond the entryway. "Where have you been?"

"I was showing Ryske the best make-out spots," Harlow said as they all fanned out in the foyer. She helped Lena take off Ryske's jacket, which she handed back to him.

"Oh, Harlow," her mother chastised her. "Come into the living room. There are drinks for everyone."

Her parents sat in their usual seats in front of the window. Harlow reached behind her for Ryske's hand and took him with her to the loveseat. That left the larger couch for Lena and Rupert, which, incidentally, was closer to her parents.

There were glasses of alcohol on the table for each of them. She went to retrieve hers and Ryske's. When she sat back down, he took her hand onto his lap and left it there to touch the underside of her chin with a single finger.

Bringing her focus around to him, Ryske admired her. "Thank you, baby," he murmured and guided her mouth up to his for a light kiss.

"Ryske," Jean said. "Are your parents living?"

Typical that she should ask a question like that when his parents had just created contention between them.

"As far as I know, yeah," Ryske said. "We're not what you'd call close."

"I thought perhaps your parents were your connection to the Rowes."

"Harlow and I are close to their kid."

Just the idea of Maze as a child was amusing. Opening her hand on his thigh, where he'd put it, she appreciated being close to him. When they got in each other's faces, they both reacted with emotion either positive or negative.

Ryske was her man and his confidence got her every time, even when she tried to push back against it.

Her fear of losing him wasn't about other women, it was about death. She'd been through that and didn't want to repeat the experience. If he was worried about losing her to another man, she would have to address that.

She'd never had to think about anything like this before. Ryske had full confidence in her around the guys he trusted. What should she do with the guys he didn't? She couldn't cut them out. Men like Costello and Clyde were her friends. No matter what, she had to respect Ryske's boundaries and his vulnerabilities. Just like she'd expect him to respect hers.

Pressing his hand on top of hers, Ryske was trying to mend their rift with a physical connection. Opening her fingers, she accepted his between hers and hoped he got the depth of her love for him.

"I haven't met the Rowes' boy," Jean said.

"You don't want to," Harlow said. "He's an asshole." Ryske laughed and kissed her hair. "No, not really, Mom. He's wonderful. Nicer than Ryske most of the time."

She didn't want the conversation to get too off course

and didn't want it to get too late either. Jean Sweeting wasn't often up late. If Lena or Rupert didn't speak soon, their news would be delayed again because her mother would go to bed without hearing it.

Making deliberate eye contact with her sister and Rupert, Harlow tried to encourage one of them to say something and missed that her parents were looking at her.

"Harlow, is something wrong?" her mother asked, glancing back and forth between her and Lena.

"Not with me," Harlow said, patting Ryske's knee. "Me and my man are just fine. No news over here." She tipped her chin up. "Right, honey? We're fine?"

"We're in bliss, sweetheart," Ryske said. "No news here. Not yet."

He took her cue, as always, and was probably eager for Rupert or Lena to get on with it.

"I feel like we're missing something," Jean said. "Brysen?"

"Yes," he said. "I feel the same way."

Jean gasped. "Oh my, Harlow! You're pregnant!"

Despite all her time spent working, maybe she should be paranoid about her weight.

"Oh my God," she said. "I'm getting goddamn buttons made. No, I'm not pregnant! Yes, we have a lot of sex. Yes, we live reckless lives. But we are responsible fornicators." Holding up a hand to God, she followed it by crossing her heart. "We're not pregnant!"

"You don't think," Ryske said. "We've had sex today. The doc hasn't gone in to check, has he?"

She prodded his leg. "You're not helping... and we are not the ones with news."

Being less subtle this time, Harlow presented her hands toward the other couch. Her parents' focus went to Lena and Rupert sitting at opposite ends.

"Yes, uh..." Rupert started when Lena made no move to speak. "I have something to say... Uh... In a moment of weakness, I gave in to something I shouldn't have. I let desire overtake my good sense and my great respect for this family. In a low moment when we were both in need of comfort, Lena and I sought refuge in each other… and… uh… We made love…”

Harlow couldn't believe it! Rupert was using Ryske's words, almost exactly. He'd missed out a few details, but the speech was the same. For all his complaining, Rupert didn't mind using Ryske's skills when they suited his needs.

Lena looked at Rupert and wouldn't face her parents. Harlow could understand why. There wasn't horror or outrage there, they were just dumbfounded. Blank and still, barely reacting at all.

Ryske turned over his hand, so they were palm to palm.

When there was no response, the awkwardness of the silence prompted Rupert on. "I know I shouldn't have done it. I disrespected you and what I have with Harlow. Lena and I agreed it wouldn't ever happen again. But the universe had other plans and we've found ourselves in a forced position." Well, that wasn't a very nice way to say it, but Harlow didn't want to jump in. Probably as another tribute to Ryske's mock run, Rupert moved along the couch to touch Lena's stomach. "We're expecting a child."

"You… you slept with Lena?" Jean asked, her pallor quite bleak.

"I understand you're surprised," Rupert said. "We didn't expect it, but we're going to do the right thing. We've agreed to get married."

Agreed to get married didn't sound romantic.

"You're with Lena?" Jean said and turned to the loveseat. "Harlow?"

Making sense of this wasn't really her job, though she'd do whatever she could to help her family. "I know it's unexpected, Mom. I was shocked when they told me too." She smiled. "But it's okay. Rupert is a good man. He'll take care of her and we know he fits with the family."

"But… he was with you," Jean said. "How can he… how can he be with Lena? When did this happen?"

Harlow shouldn't be surprised that she was the one answering questions. Lena was focused on her knees, ignoring everyone and their father was completely still.

"While I was in jail," Harlow said. Jean gasped in a squawk. "Mom, you have to sit with this. Let it sink in. Don't react too quickly."

Her father got to his feet so suddenly that Ryske moved her aside like he was preparing to jump if he had to. Harlow slid away to give him space.

Except her father didn't say a word. He strode across the room and out, with the direction of his footsteps taking him upstairs.

Jean leaped up and rushed to the door. Spinning around when she got there, she was flustered and didn't quite know what to say.

"Everyone stay the night," Jean said in a hurry. "There are towels in the closet upstairs and linens for the guest rooms and…"

Harlow got up and went to take her mom's hand. "We'll take care of it, Mom."

Breathing in, Jean seemed to hold the oxygen in. "We'll talk about this at breakfast."

Offering a comforting smile, Harlow nodded once and then Jean spun to scurry off after her husband. From the living room doorway, Harlow watched her mother disappear up the stairs. After hearing her parents' bedroom door close, she whirled back around to face the room.

"Okay, well done everyone," she said. "That wasn't so bad."

"Daddy didn't say a word," Lena wailed.

"Neither did you," Harlow said and extended a hand to Ryske. "Naked time?"

"I was just thinking you've been wearing those clothes too long," Ryske said, leaving the couch, swiping the bourbon off the table as he passed.

"You can't go to bed," Rupert said. "Don't you want to talk?"

Ryske tossed his arm around her neck, giving her some of his weight.

"The last thing I want to do is talk, Rupert," Harlow said. "Stay in Lena's room or the guest room, I don't care. You guys know where everything is. We're going to bed. We'll see you in the morning."

SIXTEEN

RYSKE SWEPT HER around in an arc to guide her upstairs and into her bedroom. The moment the door was closed, she unzipped her dress and stepped out of it. Ryske toed off his shoes and put the booze on the floor. Grabbing for his belt as soon as he straightened, she unbuckled it and backed him toward the bed, stepping out of her shoes on the way.

Ryske didn't argue or object when she pushed him down on the bed and climbed on top of him. She'd only undone a few buttons on his shirt, but she gave up on that and rose onto her knees to grab his cock. Guiding him inside of her, she breathed out and sank down, feeling better the moment their bodies were fully engaged.

Rocking back and forth, she just let herself feel him long and thick inside her. Having him occupying her body made her whole.

She moved her hips in circles. With her eyes closed, her head went back, her hair was so long that it probably tickled his thighs.

Ryske crunched up and grabbed his shirt at the back of his neck to pull it off. While he was still half sitting, he snatched her hands and pulled them to his chest. When they were flat on his pecs and he was lost in her hair, Ryske encircled her with his arms and swung her onto her back to take control.

Harlow needed this; she needed them to be them. With him, when they were together, everything beyond them became oblivion.

His kisses were brief and his caresses more like demands. Somehow, he knew that she didn't need a seduction or a paint by numbers experience. She needed it hard and fast and in its most basic form. Penis, pussy, bliss.

Pulling back, the drag of his dick through her juices arched her body. Her whimper of need became a call when he slammed forward and thrust her into orgasm.

The clench of her inner muscles around his member gave him the push he needed to go off inside her. Once the explosion of their furious union was over, his arms buckled and he toppled onto the bed beside her.

Harlow scooched over and propped her head on his diaphragm.

"Mad?" he asked, combing his fingers through her hair, spreading it on his chest.

"Hurt," she said, drawing her fingernails around his abdominal tattoo right in front of her face.

"Baby, I'm not a words guy… I'm not worried I'm hooking up with a girl like my mom…"

It wasn't like him to undersell himself; he was better with words than he claimed. But she understood what he was trying to convey.

"I've never felt like you didn't trust me," she said. "I kiss the guys, hug them, sit with them. You have never looked at me with suspicion. Even with Clyde and Costello, it felt primal, not insecure. I don't mind you making it clear to outsiders that I'm yours. It's hot when you and the guys are possessive of me. I always thought you wanted to protect me."

"I do, baby."

"That doesn't mean it's okay to hurt my friends," she said, digging her nails in a little deeper.

"You've made that clear," he said, scratching his fingers on her scalp. "You really like seeing me with other women?"

"Not sleeping with them, I don't want a threesome…

I guess its ego. I've always just known I was more to you than they were… Dover thought I was. Maze too… I had no idea, no notion of how little you thought of me."

"Hey," he said, taking her shoulder to roll her onto her back, her head still resting on his torso. "You're my Juliet. I'd slit my own throat for you. I worship you, Trinket."

She rolled her head on him in a shake. "You can't think that and say you expect to lose me to another man."

He rested a heavy hand on her forehead, and stroked her hair back, then returned his hand. "My dad didn't lose my mom because she was a ho…" Though she turned her head further to try getting a better look at him, Ryske chose that moment to raise his chin so his focus was on the ceiling. "He lost her because he was an asshole and a drunk. Getting out of there was the right thing to do. She should've got out of there sooner. No woman should put up with a guy like that."

Something about his tone flipped a switch on her thinking. Slowly, Harlow sat up, almost in a trance. After taking a few seconds to gather herself, she curled her legs beneath her.

Grabbing his chin, she forced his head around, compelling him to look at her. "Have I ever been shy with you?" she asked. "When we met and you wanted to sleep with me, was I coy about saying no?"

"You didn't mean it."

"Ryske," she yelped. "If I was unhappy with you, or thought you were an asshole, I'd tell you. And if you beat me or mistreated me, I'd sure as shit be out of there in a flash… Though that would be after the guys put you on your ass. You are not your father."

"Fuck my parents," he said, flying up out of the bed. "The guy who decked out the sap in Floyd's, that's who you hooked up with, babydoll. That's who I am and you're just gonna have to live with that. I am not letting you go anywhere and I promised I would never leave you again."

"Okay," she said and had to admit he was right. "Good, this is the Ryske I know. I expect you to confront guys in bars. You fly off the handle, but you bring yourself back. You're reasonable with Clyde, most of the time. You apologized to Costello. This is never a huge problem. You have your moment and it ends just as fast. But it feels different with Rupert. Whenever he's around—"

"Because he had you," he growled, leaping to the side of the bed. "He fucking had you!"

"Shh," she said, clambering over the bed to rise on her knees and touch his lips with her fingertips. It was unlikely the others in the house were asleep; they didn't need to be sharing their grievances with the whole family. Everyone had their own issues to process tonight and there were various other mumbles echoing through the house. Theirs were all she cared about. "What do you mean, Crash? I meet your exes all the time. Rupert's the only one of mine you've met, but we broke up long before you and I ever met."

"Not in my head," he said, stabbing his finger to his temple.

Her hand slipped away. She sank down to sit on her feet, trying to figure him out. Ryske turned his back on her and went to the window.

He was quite a sight there in front of her window seat, bathed in the moonlight and completely nude. Thinking about the nights she'd lay in bed arguing with him in her head, this was how she'd pictured him. Ethereal in the darkness, bathed in an almost blue moonlight, cocooned in night. When she'd thought he was dead.

"When you were with Anwen," she murmured, catching up. "You thought I'd gone to him after you died."

"You know all those weeks lying in that bed, every time the door opened, I wanted it to be you coming in with soup and cookies. Like you did at Bale's when we met, remember?" He didn't wait for a response or turn to look for one. "I'd imagine you coming in and kicking off your shoes like you always did. Climbing into bed with me, running those damn fingernails all over me. Just the memory would get me hard. I knew I loved you. Goddamnit, the pain of loving you was worse than the bullet."

Lying down on her side, Harlow curled an arm under her head and drew up her knees toward her chest.

He kept talking. "What we have is perfect. Yeah,

you're a pain in the ass with an answer for everything and you're too independent for your own good. But, damnit, baby, I can't imagine how any other woman could ever be more right for me. You don't bust my balls over shit that you know means nothing. You can see what I feel for you, how real it is. You don't demand I prove it all the time. I'm not great at the romantic gestures shit, you know? I mean, I could be. But I think it would always feel fake and I don't want that with you."

He'd spent so long protecting himself from feeling anything. Pushing away women who got too close to him. When it came to addressing his true emotions, he was a little more resistant.

The man could sell any line, so long as it was a lie. The truth wasn't so easy to part with.

"And the shit when you're with other guys, there's theater to it. I like playing the macho boyfriend. Scaring the sap is fun. I love you; every minute of every day I'm grateful for that. I'm grateful for the faith we have in us. Whatever the fuck this is between us and wherever the fuck it came from, we're not ever going to find it again. I'm not sure it exists anywhere else. This isn't love like I ever understood the word." The almost childlike sentiment of the last sentence made her smile. "We don't have to be together twenty-four seven. It's always there whether we're together or not... I can know you're with him, that you're here or he's around, and it doesn't affect me. But..." His fists clenched and a growl slipped into his voice. "When he's talking to you like you're his, or acting like you are and you... It feels like I'm back there, lying in that fucking bed at Anwen's, miles away from you. When I lay in the dark thinking of you, baby, when I thought of you with him, building a life with him... It's not even the fucking, you know? I mean, that's bad, but..."

Turning around, he scrutinized her lying naked in the bed where they'd just been joined. Relaxed, sleepy, adoring him, Harlow was warm and content to be existing with him.

Tilting her head, she smiled. "What? Finish what you were saying."

"This is what I envied him," he said, coming over to sink down in a crouch by the bed, sweeping one of her hands into both of his. "Being with you when no one else is. Seeing you in the dark." Leaning in, he pressed his kiss to her knuckles. "Whispering with you… These are the moments I want, when we can be us and nobody else exists."

Slipping her hand from his, she ran it through his hair, stroking and admiring him. Witnessing Rupert talk to her with tenderness or need, it reminded Ryske of the possibilities he'd tortured himself with when they were apart. That's why he was so hard on Rupert, even in his vulnerable moments.

"But you spent time with him," she murmured. "When you were at SweSec, wheedling your way into my father's good graces so he'd bring you home. You were kind to Rupert then."

"My claim to you wasn't so strong back then. I wanted us to be this, but I didn't know we would be, you know? And when I'm running a con, there's a part of me that switches off. I guess it's a defense. I can't have a weakness in the field. I can't react. I've had to watch men scream at their wives and then listen to them quip about what a bitch she is. If that part of me was on, I'd put my fist through their teeth. I've made love to women I'm not attracted to, women I don't even like… Anwen used to instruct me to be tender with her; I was basically her puppet at that point. I fucking hated every second. Resented the shit out of her for blackmailing me into her bed. Those first few weeks, if I'd let that part of myself lead, I'd have throttled her."

"Damn," she whispered, enjoying the intimacy of the dark. "Lucky her."

Exhaling a laugh, he picked up a loose section of hair from her brow to tuck it back in her locks. "There's no woman like you, Harlow Sweeting. I know I'm an arrogant ass. Every time you've called me off one of your boys, I've taken your orders, but with him…"

"I understand."

"I always fucking managed to push it down deep. It was there, but I controlled it. Except with this Lena shit… I fucking sent you to him, Trink. A guy who's capable of doing this to you. What if I hadn't come back and you'd married him? How long do you think before he fucked your little sister and your family in the process?"

"He was always faithful to me," she said. "He's a good man. We weren't together when he slept with her. He just got a little lost. I don't know why he fell into bed with Lena when he could've had any of a dozen other women…"

"She's a substitute for you," he said. "He doesn't love Lena; he still loves you."

"He doesn't, that's your bias talking," she said and tried to roll away, but he caught her shoulder and pulled her back.

"You remember how I dismissed you when you said Ophelia was into me?"

Rolling her eyes, she tsked at him. "That's not the same. Ophelia never got a chance with you."

"Yeah, but he did and he blew it. He knew what he had with you and how incredible you are. He's probably hated himself every day since he lost you."

"Ryske…"

Tracing the back of his finger down her cheek from her temple to her chin, he soothed her. "He doesn't love you like I love you. Maybe he's not in love with you. Maybe you're just familiar and he doesn't want to let go. I took you seriously when you told me to watch my ass. Just tell me you'll take me seriously too."

Easing herself up, she kissed his mouth. "I promise to take you seriously if you get your fine ass into this bed and hold me." Wearing a smile, he stood up to leap over the top of her. Scooping her into a spoon position, they twined their arms. "Ryske?"

"Yeah, baby," he said, kissing her head.

"Ophelia asked me to make a move."

He didn't tense, but she did feel the air in the room alter. "Tell me."

"Not yet," she said, turning her head to rub her lips on his arm. "I have to talk to someone first. Dover knows all about it, so I do have backup. But… if I make an odd suggestion this week, I… I need you to support it."

SEVENTEEN

FOR A SCORE OF seconds, the room was quiet. "Parratt wants control and he's not against using our past to get it."

Ryske and Parratt's past wasn't a happy one. "Is that the lie he was talking about?"

"He lied about what happened to the money he gave me," Ryske said. "If he tells the truth…"

To authorities, it would get their crew into a lot of trouble. Even if Parratt couldn't prove Ryske's deception, they could be opened up to all sorts of scrutiny. The last thing they needed at Floyd's was people snooping around.

Having that threat hanging over their heads put more pressure on all of them. Relying on each other was more important than ever. Sharing her own suspicions, even though she had no proof, could lead to them having ammunition of their own against Parratt.

"I think they had an affair," Harlow said. "Him and Ophelia. I think that's how she found out about Pothos and got the idea to pull you and Hagan into it."

"Think they're still fucking?"

"Maybe," she said. "She told me I should… Back when you were dead, we talked about it."

He cleared his throat. "I know."

Sensing he was holding something back, she twisted herself toward him.

Still in his embrace, she looked up at him. "Ryske?"

"I was at Ophelia's," he said. "That day you went to see her after I got back… The day you found me in bed at home, when we talked and you got that call and left Floyd's… I went over there. I was there when you arrived. I stayed in the hallway outside the kitchen. I heard every word."

"Oh my God."

"That was how I knew you'd come back to your parents. From there, I made the plan to infiltrate through SweSec… which was how I got to your parents' dinner table."

It hadn't occurred to her to question how he knew where she was. Thinking about it, there had been no delay between her coming back to her parents and him conning his way into SweSec. There were only a few days between her leaving the city and him showing up. He'd used every one of those to endear himself with her father.

"I… guess honesty is good." Even if it was late. Sagging against him, Harlow tried to remember what else she might have disclosed in that meeting. "I was so hurt then," she murmured and then smiled. "I can't really have been thinking straight, I still considered Ophelia a friend."

"I knew I had to have you back," he said, squeezing her tight. "No matter what it took. Soon as I heard you were back at Floyd's… I don't know. I knew you were mine. Karma was telling me that it was okay. That I was allowed to have you… The guys told me to wait, to come up with a plan, but… you before them, that's what I told them."

"I'm surprised they didn't resent me after that."

Running a hand down her body, she felt his appreciation for her, inside and out.

"You don't understand how mad they were that we left you," he said. "They knew what you were before I was willing to admit it."

"And what am I?"

He bowed to kiss her. "One of us."

Smiling under his mouth, she hadn't thought it was possible to be closer to him. Yet, somehow, they'd strengthened their bond with their honesty.

"Any more revelations?"

For a moment, he considered it then shook his head. "Don't think so."

Before he could kiss her again, she pulled her head back. "I have one." He crooked a brow. "The night of the fire…" He nodded, a frown forming on his features. "I heard you and Anwen… in bed."

The frown faded and he brushed his lips on her. "I figured."

Harlow subdued a laugh. "And you can keep your balls," she murmured. "You win the bet." Seemed from his expression of confusion that he didn't remember. "I do love you… I did then, I do now."

"Never doubted it."

Recalling that conversation gave her an appreciation for Ryske's possessiveness. Something she had to remember in context of their conversation that night.

Anwen's assumption she could speak about their relationship at all was really aggravating.

"Kind of made me mad," she said.

Ryske made an assumption of his own. "Nothing happened."

That wasn't her implication. Harlow had no doubt he hadn't been intimate with Anwen on the night of the fire.

Squeezing her eyes closed, she touched his mouth. "Don't ever say those words to me," she said, and opened her eyes to look at him. "I told you I didn't want promises."

His frown came back, more fierce than before. "That was before."

"If you have to say those words to me then I've failed you. I've failed to express how secure I am with you, how much I trust you… How much I love you, Huntley Ryske. I don't want promises because we don't need them. With the kind of life we live, anything could happen. Either of us could be conned or cornered into doing things. We could be blackmailed or coerced because we both have secrets. Our love for each other and for our crew, it makes us vulnerable. We want to protect those things; we'll do whatever it takes to keep them safe…" He inhaled behind her fingers, but she carried on before he could talk. "But it doesn't matter, Ryske. What matters to me, is this." Her hand trailed down to his chest. "It doesn't matter if we're together or not. It doesn't matter if we're fucking other people or not… You said it. You got it perfect when you said every breath you are is me. You are my soul, Crash. All I need is your heart. So long as you promise that belongs only to me… I don't need any other promise."

Brushing his fingers across her face, he let them sink into her hair beneath her ear to cradle her head. "You're amazing. You've no idea how completely I belong to you, baby. God, just breathing with you teases me… I want you every fucking second."

Skimming a hand up his arm, she curved it around his shoulder. "Except when you're with your crew," she said, recalling something he'd said to her a long time ago. "You don't think about sex around them."

"Oh, yeah, that was a lie," he said. Her mouth opened in mock outrage. "I was always thinking about sex when you were around whether they were in the room or not… Still am… And you are my crew, so… yeah… total lie."

He lowered to try kissing her, but she shoved hard at his shoulder. Using more force, he started to shift their positions, telling her with his actions that he wanted more sex.

Before they got distracted, she had to ask one more question. "Baby," she said, letting him kiss her for just a moment.

"Hmm?"

"Will you move back home with me? Our support means so much to Dover. I don't want him to be alone, and I want to be there too. It makes me feel better to be there, and we should help—"

He cut her off with a kiss. "The guys moved our stuff back tonight. They were picking up the mattress for our bed too. Everything will be there ready for us when we go back."

"*Our* bed," she said, trying to figure out why it felt so significant that he'd used that word.

"Yeah," he said, lifting his body to slide his hand

down her torso, between her legs. He bypassed her pussy to grab the inside of her thigh. "Everything is ours, baby… And as soon as you're ready to make it legal…"

Dropping to suck on her neck, he left his mark on her. Raising her arms to the frame of her bed, she gripped it tight and parted her legs further.

"My crook," she said. "Who'd have thought you'd ever be trying to coerce me into doing something legal?"

"I know, it feels kinda dirty," he said, trailing his tongue down to her cleavage.

Melting into the bed, his mouth stirred her insides to soup.

Purring out her pleasure, Harlow dragged her knees up his sides to his ribs. "We should get cuffs."

Picking up his mouth, he made eye contact. "Says the woman who's been in jail to the guy who's been under threat of prison his whole life."

Her lips curled. She opened her arms wide only to bring them back together as she draped them over his shoulders. "Leather cuffs or silks then," she said. "I want to tie you up."

He licked her lip. "Baby, you don't need ropes to restrain me. I'm yours to command. You tell me not to move, I won't move."

"It's not the same," she said. "I want to be under your power too. You know how I love it when you dominate me."

"Want to do that wax thing as well?" Nodding, she was excited by all the possibilities. "We'll stop somewhere tomorrow, get whatever you want."

"Anything?"

He must have noticed the way her eyes lit because he became dubious. "Why do I think I'm the one who's going to need a safe word?"

"I just want to try things, baby," she said, sliding her hands through his hair. "Any limits you want to tell me about in advance?"

Tilting his head, he almost nodded. "There's one major one I can think of."

Widening her smile, she tightened her body around

his. "I don't want to do that… I'd never cause you pain. I'm not a sadist."

"No, but you are a masochist," he said and grabbed her throat tight. Gritting her teeth, she let out a hiss of pleasure. "I won't draw blood."

Playing with the twist of her lips, she did her best to be sly. "No needles then."

His suspicious eyes narrowed. "Do you get turned on when Dover's putting ink on you?"

Pointing her tongue, it touched her upper lip and he took a turn to growl, forcing her head further back with his grip on her neck.

"Think it's…" With the constriction of her throat, she struggled over each word. "The vibration."

"I'm gonna have a word with him about that."

After what triggered the tension between them that night, she was so pleased to hear him teasing her about other guys. His trust was real; he just had to remember to trust himself too.

"I don't…" He must have heard the strain in her voice because he loosened his grip enough to let her speak easier. "You can always say no to me."

One side of his mouth lifted. "But I never will, Trink… Fuck, I love you."

"Prove it," she said, trying to reach for his dick, but he had her pinned. "Fuck your cock in me."

Pushing his lips to one side, he surprised her by being more quizzical than lustful. "Hmm."

Leaping up off the bed, he strode across to her closet and put the light on.

Rising to her elbows, she wondered where her sex had gone. "Baby… what are you doing?"

A shout from somewhere else in the house made her look to the door. Ryske stuck his head out of the closet to look too. After a moment of eye contact, he went back inside.

"We don't need special products from a store," he called out. "We can improvise… You've got plenty in here, belts, scarves… garters we keep, panties can go." A smile rose to her lips. She let her weight fall from her elbows. "I don't know what this is, but I'll spank you with it."

She laughed and rolled onto her side. "There's a riding crop in there somewhere."

His moan of approval thrilled her. "You got a vibrator?"

"No," she said and he poked his head out to land suspicion on her. "I don't. Rupert didn't like that stuff. He said using sex toys and props made him feel like he was lacking."

Ryske disappeared back into the closet. "It's okay," he called out. "We've got a backup."

That was curious, so she rose onto an elbow. "What backup?"

One of his palms appeared and he wiggled his fingers.

She laughed. "What about your tongue?"

"That will be busy somewhere else," he said.

Harlow had no idea what he was planning. Her man valued having a plan going into an op, so she didn't doubt she was in for a good night. Relaxing, she was ready to surrender herself to his mercy.

The rumble of raised voices quaked through the wall from the guest room. Rupert must've chosen to sleep in there… or at least that's where the argument had traveled to.

Harlow felt safe in her room with Ryske and took a moment to appreciate just how lucky she was. Out there, in the rest of the house, people were hurt, and angry, confused, sad… There were so many emotions beyond her sanctuary, so many negative ones. Only one ruled in this room: love.

Ryske appeared from the closet. The bundle of things in his arms flared her eyes.

He let out a short whistle and dumped everything on the end of the bed. "Flip over onto your front."

Harlow started to do as he asked. "What are you going to do to me?" she asked, tilting back to look over her shoulder to watch him sort through his wares. Except when she noticed that his cock was already hard, she was distracted by his appeal.

"Eyes front," he said. "Grab the top of the headboard."

"Ryske," she said, rising onto her hands and knees. "Maybe I could play with you first."

Something cracked across her ass, sending a shot of pain up through her. A yelp escaped her throat. Assuming he'd found the crop, she tightened the circle of her hands around the top of her headboard.

"You're my slave, Trinket," he said in a deep drawl. "When I want you to do something to me, I'll tell you to fucking do it."

Biting on her lower lip, she let the sting on her butt and the heat of his words course through her. Ryske knew she was independent and headstrong. He also knew that in their intimacy, she'd always been aroused by him in the dominant role.

Adopting a lifestyle on a permanent basis wouldn't really work for them. But they had such an innate way of reading each other that each could trust the other to know when to exert power and when to surrender it.

She started to turn her head. The end of the riding crop brushed her cheekbone; Ryske used it to push her back around.

"Breaking the rules means punishment, slave," he said.

Something warm and soft covered her eyes. He tied a scarf around her head plunging her into darkness. She couldn't look even if she wanted to.

Silence followed. She was about to ask what he was doing when the bed shifted beneath her. Except, she didn't move *on* the bed. It felt like the whole bed moved.

Confirmation came when he cupped her face and drew her head up so he could kiss her. From the angle, he had to be standing behind the headboard, meaning he must have pulled the whole bed away from the wall.

He kissed her cheek and then her ear. "You owe me two and the night hasn't even started," he murmured on her ear. "My cock's gonna spend a lot of time in your throat tonight… Say thank you."

"Thank you," she said, her lips curling while her body fizzed with anticipation. This was more daring than anything she'd ever done and they hadn't even done anything yet. "Cr—"

"You call me sir if you've gotta call me anything," he said. "But you're only gonna speak when I tell you to… which I won't."

Something soft touched her chin, more fabric… a gag.

Harlow ducked back before he could do what he was going to do with it. "Sir, before I surrender myself to you…"

"What is it?" he asked, part him, part playing.

"I love you so fucking much."

Bowing down, he rubbed his cheek on hers. "You're about to love me a whole lot more," he whispered.

The fabric went over her mouth and he tied a tight knot at the back of her head. At his mercy while he tied each of her hands to the top of the headboard, she couldn't begin to imagine what he was planning, but she didn't question for a second whether or not she'd enjoy it.

Gagging her was a gift. He was ensuring they wouldn't rouse the rest of the house with their antics. Though, Harlow suspected her family wouldn't miss there was something going on in her bedroom that had never happened before.

Ryske was a sexual force unlike any she'd ever known. Whether they were playing and teasing, or kissing and making love, she loved every second, and every inch of his body.

Tomorrow they'd go back to life and dealing with the problems that swirled around them. For tonight, they belonged to each other and if this was a test of their trust, she didn't doubt they'd both pass with flying colors.

EIGHTEEN

BREAKFAST WAS NEVER going to be fun.

Sneaking into the shower with Ryske had been fun. Having sex in there before he washed her body and her hair had been fun. But the inevitable had to come eventually. Harlow's grin vanished the minute she stepped into the dining room with Ryske.

Lena was there in her usual seat beside Jean. Neither were speaking and there was a sadness hanging in the air that hurt her heart. Going around the table, Harlow could tell Ryske sensed it too, but he knew better than to comment.

Through the French doors, she spotted her father and Rupert at the far end of the backyard engaged in conversation. She couldn't tell how heated it was or what was being said. They were at the other end of the lawn, facing each other, maybe eight feet apart, and Rupert was making hand gestures.

"Uh oh, that's his you're being unreasonable gesture," Harlow said, tucking her hair behind her ear and sitting down in the chair Ryske held for her.

He'd never pull her chair out at home. Sometimes the con required him to be of high breeding, so he did know how to act with impeccable manners. She guessed he'd gotten into the habit here or still wanted to impress her family.

Jean inhaled a long, tired breath. It didn't seem like anyone had slept well. Lena's posture was terrible, but that could be because of her mood too.

When her mother breathed out again, she laid a hand on the table. "Ryske, I don't mean to be forward. This isn't a question I would usually ask…"

Alarm bells rang.

Ryske didn't flinch. "Ask me anything."

"You may not be the man we thought you were, yet you stated that everything you've done for this family has been because you have an affection for my daughter."

"I love your daughter, Mrs. Sweeting."

Vehement in his respect, he always sounded a little defensive when anyone equivocated on his feelings for her.

"That's what leads to my question," Jean said. "My husband, he… He wants to know what your role will be in this family."

There was no chink in the proverbial armor he'd donned after Jean's slight. "I won't lay hands on Lena, if that's what he wants to know."

Lena's horror was obvious when she straightened like someone had prodded her. Jean just looked downcast.

Her sister's alarm swung from Ryske around to her. "Harlow, I wouldn't—I would never—"

"It's okay, honey," Harlow said and took Ryske's hand. "I'm not planning to be done with him any time soon anyway."

"That's not what my…" Jean shifted in her seat. "He wants to know if you will be a part of this family… If you plan to be a permanent member of this family…"

Harlow was dumbfounded. Was her mother asking Ryske to marry her or telling him to get out if he wouldn't?

"Mom, if you ask him to leave, neither of us will ever come back," Harlow said, infected by Ryske's defensiveness.

Frustrated, Jean frowned at herself. "No, I… Brysen wants to know if Ryske plans to be a stable fixture in the family because this is a difficult time for us all and we need support."

Seeing her mother's exhaustion, Harlow's heart broke some more. "Mom, Ryske isn't going anywhere. He's here for whatever any of us need. You can rely on him. Both of you can. Dad too." Rupert maybe less so, but she didn't think now was the time to highlight that. She smiled. "He's even better than most guys because he has far fewer morals." The attempt at a joke only garnered anxiety from the other side of the table. "Except for the sex with Lena thing. He definitely won't do that."

"Thanks, babe," Ryske said, picking up her hand to kiss her knuckles. "Am I blushing?"

"Ryske," Jean said. "Your relationship with Harlow. Is it frivolous? Please, be honest."

This time he was more solemn. "No. Harlow and I won't part for anything. I'm her guy. Period."

Jean sighed. "I don't know why I believe you, but I do. Maybe I'm tired or you're very good, but I believe you."

Ryske glossed over that doubt. "What do you need, Jean?"

"Harlow's father has traditional views. He feels Harlow should have a representative… someone to speak on her behalf. An advocate…" Closing her eyes, she gave up on explanations. "Brysen would like for you to join them."

"Harlow doesn't need me to speak for her," Ryske said. "She's capable of speaking for herself… She'd kick my ass for presuming to—"

"It's okay," Harlow said, probably surprising the shit out of him. "I trust you to speak for our corner of the family."

Ryske trusted her to speak for their crew at the consortium meeting. She trusted him to keep his cool. Her father would only clam up if she was to march on out there. There were things he'd voice in front of men that he would never even whisper with his daughters in earshot.

It worked both ways anyway. Harlow needed a chance to talk to her mother and sister in private. They'd be more open without Ryske listening in.

He smirked and put a hand to her forehead. "You feeling okay, Trink?"

"Yes," she said, smiling and shaking her head at him.

"I love you."

"I love you too."

"Go be a man with the men." Ryske pushed out his chair. As he turned, Harlow caught his face. "Just... control yourself, representative," she murmured and kissed him.

Leaving via the French doors, Ryske strode across the lawn. When her father spotted him, Harlow turned back to face the table. She really didn't want to see how Rupert would react when Ryske showed up.

Picking up the coffeepot, Harlow poured. "I should've given him coffee," she said. "Though he functions fine without it, unlike me."

Harlow selected a pastry and figured her mom had the deli deliver because she hadn't cooked this morning. She certainly hadn't made what was on the table.

"Will they be okay?" Lena asked. "Will Ryske calm daddy down?"

"If anyone can, he can," Harlow said, pulling a piece off her pastry. She could see that Lena was on alert. Jean seemed too tired to even focus. "Mom, if you need to go back to bed, just go. We'll take care of everything down here."

"I have to be here for your father," she said. "As you've seen, he didn't go to the office today."

Neither him nor Rupert were at SweSec, which may be a first. Harlow couldn't think of another time when either of them hadn't been there when it wasn't a holiday or event.

"He's so mad, Harlow," Lena said. "He came down this morning and just looked at me, he didn't even speak."

"He's disappointed," Jean said. "Can you blame him, Lena? Neither of us were expecting this and we don't... We don't know how to process it."

Harlow drank some more coffee. "Yeah. The ladies at the lunch club will be horrified," she said, startling both her mother and sister. "I'm sorry. Mom, I didn't take the news well either... Where do you think dad's Dalmore went? But it is what it is. We're here now and we just have to face the facts. Lena is pregnant. She's going to have a baby. The baby is healthy, a good size, perfect... She had an ultrasound. There are pictures."

Jean seemed surprised but perked up to look at her younger daughter. "You have pictures?"

Lena nodded.

"Go get them," Harlow said to her sister who leaped from the chair and dashed out, probably just happy to be doing something. Jean was blinking, in a sort of daze. "Mom, Rupert and I weren't together. I know it's not conventional, and maybe they're not crazy in love. But he's a good man and he's been a part of this family for a long time. He's not going to beat her or mistreat her. Dad always wanted him to take over the reins at SweSec. I remember that's why he was so disappointed when Rupert and I split up… Now he has another chance. Rupert will be marrying into the family, just like you both always wanted… And he's mortified, Mom. Rupert didn't want to hurt anyone in this family."

Jean leaned over the table. "Have you forgiven him?"

"There's nothing to forgive, Mom. When Rupert and I broke up with each other, we lost the right to dictate to the other what they did with their body. The only concern I have is for Lena."

"Lena?"

Harlow nodded. "She'll need our support. She didn't expect to be a wife and a mother so young. Her life isn't going to be what she expected it to be… And… this might sound ridiculous, I don't know if you understand, but… in a relationship things are shared, habits learned. You get to know your partner better than anyone because you see them the most often and in the most situations… There can be a language, a behavioral understanding between a couple. Something that no one else understands…"

"Rupert had that with you," Jean said, proving that she did comprehend.

"Their relationship will be different than mine was with him. And I stand behind my statement that he's a good man. She's an incredible person. They will be happy. But Lena's lost that chance to introduce a man to us who she knows better than any of us will. Ryske is mine. He'll always be a part of this family. You'll make memories with him; we'll all make memories together. But he'll still be mine. Ryske can touch me or look at me in a certain way and we'll understand each other… I've seen you do it with Daddy."

Nodding, Jean became forlorn. "You'll understand Rupert too."

Harlow shrugged. "I won't get in anyone's way. I'm sure in time all that, I guess you could call it institutional knowledge, will fade, but… I know more about Ryske than any of you ever will. I know his past. His family. His friends. I know everything there is to know about his life now, where he spends his time, who he talks to… Those are the kind of things a woman knows about her man and vice versa… I'm just sad Lena will miss her chance to discover a man like that. She won't have the excitement of a new relationship and integrating herself into his life. They'll miss out on that."

"I do understand," Jean said. "I understand what you mean. You regret what her impulse has cost her. Are you sure you harbor no animosity?"

Harlow shook her head and ate some more. "None. I was shocked. But Ryske and I have the ultrasound on our fridge." Or it had been there before the fire. "We're looking forward to this little guy or girl getting here." They hadn't really talked about Lena's baby, but Ryske was great with kids. She liked the idea of him being an uncle to her niece or nephew. "Focus on the positives, Mom. This is where we are. We have to move forward. We can't change what's happened. Just think, there will be a wedding for you to plan."

Jean's whole demeanor changed. She grew in confidence as her spine straightened. Lena came running back in carrying the ultrasound pictures.

"A wedding," Jean said when Lena sat back down.

Startled by her mother's change in attitude, Lena's attention darted back and forth between them. "You… you seem happy."

Jean took the ultrasound pictures to coo over them. "Oh, he's adorable… he? Or she?"

Lena was still stunned. "I… we don't know yet."

"If you ever want to know my friend will give you another scan," Harlow said, tucking into her food. "Though you can probably go to a clinic closer to home now."

"When were you thinking of having the wedding?" Jean asked. "Soon? We'll have to budget. How many guests will there be?"

Harlow raised her hand. "I'll need a plus six."

Jean laughed. "Will they all be eating?"

"They're all guys, so… yeah, they'll all be eating… Probably their portions and whoever else is around them too."

The French doors opened.

"You're bringing six dates to my wedding?" Lena asked. "Six… men?"

The men filtered in from outside.

Ryske looked at her. "Six?" He did a mental head count wearing a frown and then groaned as he deflated. "You're bringing the sap?"

"We should have dinner with him this week," she said as Ryske came to sit beside her again. She offered him her mug. "We haven't seen enough of him recently."

Ryske gulped her coffee down. "How many will you owe me after putting me through that charade?" he asked and flashed her a wink.

"Brysen?" Jean said, drawing everyone's attention to her father who'd just sat down.

"Rupert and I will be going to the office this afternoon," he said, watching Jean pour his coffee.

"I—"

"That's it, Jean," her father said in his *'I'm finished talking about it'* tone.

Rupert sat down beside her. Harlow took the coffee pot her mother had just placed down to pour some caffeine for him.

"You okay?" Harlow murmured.

Once she'd put down the coffee pot, she took Ryske's hand under the table. Although she was focused on Rupert, she wanted to remind her man that she belonged to him.

Rupert, despite appearing completely drained, nodded. "We worked it out."

Jean took a big breath that seemed more optimistic. "We were just talking about the wedding," she said, turning to her husband. "We'll need a budget."

"You'll already be halfway there," Harlow said and smiled at Lena. "You can use the money Rupert and I saved... His mom will match it and our mom and dad said they would too."

"You... you'd let us use that money?" Lena said. "Isn't it half yours? Don't you want it back?"

Shaking her head, Harlow put a pastry on Ryske's plate. "These are really good, baby, try them." Picking it up, he took a big bite. Harlow leaned toward her sister. "Ryske pays for everything I need... or someone does..." That made her straighten and turn to him. "That's a point. Who does pay our bills? I haven't paid a dime to anyone since I moved in... Noon pays for my Chinese food, I know that. Dover pays for the liquor."

Curling a hand through her hair to the side of her neck, Ryske pulled her to him and kissed the side of her head. "Don't worry about it, baby."

His confidence was enough for her. "Consider it a wedding gift from Ryske and me."

Harlow didn't know how much money was there, but she hadn't missed it so far. Rupert probably paid in more than she ever had simply because he earned more.

"I've never lived on my own," Lena said.

So much about her life was changing fast. It had to feel like these changes were happening to her rather than through choice.

"You won't have to live alone," Harlow said. "You'll be living with Rupert and the little one..." Harlow swung a finger between Ryske and Rupert. "You two should switch seats from now on so Rupert's opposite Lena. Then when the little one comes, he can sit at the top of the table and have his parents on either side."

Jean was actually smiling when she next spoke. "What if you and Ryske have a child? Where will he or she sit?"

Harlow pointed at the bottom of the table. "He or she can sit there. Ryske's great with kids. Babies and teenagers anyway, I don't know about in between."

Ryske put an arm around her. "Everyone loves me," he said and kissed her.

Lena laughed. "You know, I always thought you had this like crazy, dangerous life full of drama and action in the city… But you're talking about babies and Chinese food and bills. You just have a normal life, don't you?"

Harlow took the coffee from Ryske's hand. "Who? Us?" she asked, raising the cup to her lips. "Our life is completely normal. Normal and boring." Taking a sip, she put the cup down and laid a hand over Ryske's. "Isn't it, honey?"

Bobbing his head in agreement, Ryske picked up his pastry with his free hand. "Yep. Totally boring."

NINETEEN

THE HULLABALOO OUTSIDE Floyd's was obvious from down the block. Harlow waved to those who noticed them as Ryske drove by to park Noon's car around the back of the building. It felt like an age since she'd been with her friends, so she was eager to get out of the car and leave the alley to find out what was going on.

Ash and char-encrusted furniture was piled near the wrapped new planks that were stacked outside. The block wasn't only busy with people. A couple of trucks pulled up just as Harlow spotted Noon and Maze loitering on the corner in the midst of a bunch of other folks.

Letting go of Ryske's hand, Harlow squeezed through the groups and ran to Maze and Noon, grabbing them both into a hug at the same time.

"Oh, I missed you," she said and smacked a kiss to each of their mouths.

"Geez, lady, do we know you?" Maze said.

Noon blinked and then looked the way she'd come. "Don't you have a boyfriend?"

Harlow waved a hand over her shoulder but didn't turn. "Yeah, he's around somewhere. What's going on?"

Maze opened his arms. "Everyone turned out to help.

We've got the place stripped out inside. They're taking up the floors and we've got most of the paneling out. A couple of the guys are doing sanding and we've got folks scrubbing the windows, checking out the frames… The place will look brand new when we're done."

"Hey, you got a new thing," Noon said, pointing to her necklace.

Ryske stopped at her back and slung an arm around her to loop his thumb into it. It didn't look at all like what it was, which was one of the things she loved about it. The accessory was another inside secret for her and Ryske to share.

Just like he'd promised, they'd stopped at a specialty store on the way back into the city. They'd bought so much stuff they'd got a new sports bag to put it in. It was currently in Ryske's other hand, in the fist he had propped on his shoulder.

In the same store, Ryske picked out the necklace for her. Noon didn't know it, but he was admiring a BDSM O ring. It rested just on the groove of her throat, suspended on a silver chain. Ryske stood behind her with his arm hooked around her neck, holding the ring in the crook of his thumb.

It was a simple piece that could be mistaken for normal jewelry. From the front anyway. At the back, it fastened with an engraved padlock, which Ryske had the key for. Harlow never considered wearing a slave day collar before. Now, knowing what it signaled to her love, she couldn't imagine ever taking it off.

"What's going on?" Ryske asked just as Harlow spied Anwen coming out the corner door.

Maze was repeating to Ryske what he'd said to her. Harlow wasn't really listening and spun around to face her man.

Putting a hand to Ryske's throat, she got his attention. "I'm going over there," she whispered and touched his jaw, asking for a kiss without words.

While still listening to Maze and Noon, Ryske glanced in the direction she pointed. He probably wondered why she was so eager to see Anwen, but he didn't question her and dipped to touch his lips to hers.

After what she'd told him the previous night, he probably had his suspicions about what she and Anwen would talk about... Though, given what had happened after their twilight conversation, he could be forgiven for forgetting.

Heading over to Anwen, Harlow was pleased to be greeted by a smile, figuring that was a good start.

"Hey," Anwen said. "Where have you been? I feel like I haven't seen you in forever."

"Not since Saturday," Harlow said. "You want to go inside? Talk with me?"

Dubious confusion made Anwen frown, but she didn't let it linger and quickly changed it to a smile. "Uh, okay, sure."

Going inside, Harlow weaved through the workers. Neighborhood folks grafting to get Floyd's back to its former glory. She didn't see Dover but knew he'd be around. No doubt he was outside loading or unloading the trucks, or down in the basement.

Tiptoeing her way through the den, Harlow went up the spiral stairs to the apartment and was happy to find it empty. Discovering the coffee machine on and hot liquid in the pot was even more welcome.

"Coffee?" Harlow asked, picking up the pot. "There is booze somewhere, but... it might be a little early."

Though liquoring the woman up would be an easier way to get straight answers. "Is this about me and Ryske?"

"No," Harlow said, pouring the coffee.

Apparently, they had new stools because Anwen took a seat at the breakfast bar, with her back to the dining table. "Oh, well, I kind of wanted to talk to you about that."

"Okay," Harlow said, taking the drinks over and sitting down with her.

Anwen left her drink on the breakfast bar. "He's really in love with you."

"Yeah," Harlow said, holding the rim of her cup and resting it on her lower lip.

"And you..." Anwen pointed at her. "You said you weren't that into him, and I... I just want to know if that's still true."

"I stand by what I said, if you can steal him, you can have him," Harlow said. Any man who could be stolen wasn't worth having. Though, as far as she was concerned, that didn't really apply. She didn't doubt for a second that Ryske wouldn't be stolen from her. "But… we are together."

Anwen released the cup she'd been about to pick up. "Oh."

"I… I don't know. The fire put things in perspective, I guess… The fear of him not coming out after us reminded me of what it felt like to lose him the first time. And in the hospital…" It was hard to believe how much had happened in less than a week. "I love him, Anwen… and you're right, he does love me."

The silence that followed quickly got awkward. Harlow didn't know how to fill it and just had to wait for Anwen to react. She didn't have to wait too long.

"So that's it, you're just… together?" Harlow nodded. "And screw the rest of us?"

"Well, I didn't—"

"You know, I don't get it," Anwen said, jumping off her stool. "Last week you didn't want him, now you do, and he's just like yours, just like that?"

Anwen's heritage slipped out when she was emotional. Usually, she was the picture of poise.

"Look, if you want the truth…" Harlow said because she didn't know how this was going to play out. She'd never get answers if Anwen hated her. "We are together. Yes, we are. But… I don't know that means he's mine."

Anwen faltered, losing some of her anger. A moment later, she slid back onto her stool, then was laughing. "God, I'm an idiot."

Harlow was confused. "I don't—"

"I was all 'Oh my God.' I actually panicked for a second." Laughing, Anwen picked up her coffee and took a gulp. "How could I forget this is Ryske we're talking about? No woman ever has him all to herself." The smile Anwen wore was more than happy; it was optimistic. "We'll always have to be willing to share him, won't we?"

Still a little unnerved, Harlow tried not to let it show.

"Yeah, I guess we will."

"So, I guess what you meant to say is that you're fucking again," Anwen said, loose as she enjoyed her coffee. "You know, it's a weird setup here…" Twisting around, she hung her elbow on the counter to scan the apartment. "But it works…" When her perusal was finished, Anwen set her focus on Harlow and lowered her volume to a whisper. "Have you ever…?" Harlow's brows rose in question. Her chin dipped in expectation of what Anwen might say next. "You know… with any of the other guys?"

"Maze, Noon, or Dover?" Harlow asked. "You want to know if I've had sex with them?"

Anwen's excitement shimmered when she nodded. Harlow's finger curled into the O-ring around her neck to take comfort and support from it. Ryske was wearing the bullet. He had been since she'd given it to him in the hospital. Every time he put it on, after a shower or sex or whatever, he always glared at it first. It meant something to him. For now at least, she felt like she shouldn't get in the way of him working through that.

"They all look capable," Anwen said.

"Well, they all have dicks, I can confirm that," Harlow said, having seen each of them at different times during the course of living with them. "But I've never sucked or fucked any of them."

A whistle brought their attentions around to the stairs where Ryske ascended. He wasn't all the way up, only his head and shoulders were in view, but he had to have heard at least her last sentence.

"Need me?" he asked.

Harlow just smiled and shook her head.

Anwen got up and rushed over to him.

Taking his arm, she pulled him up the stairs into the kitchen. "Harlow and I were just talking about girl stuff."

"Right," he said, plodding forward, being guided by Anwen who had both hands around his forearm. "I just came upstairs to dump this."

He raised the new sports bag in his other hand.

"Oh, I can take that," Anwen said.

"Mm," Harlow said, shoving her coffee aside to leap off her stool. "No, I will."

Ryske lifted the bag over Anwen to hand it to Harlow. She kept it on her lap when she slid onto the stool Anwen occupied before Ryske showed up. Switching seats gave her a better angle to address the couple standing in front of the fridge. Not that she was really paying attention to them. She unzipped the bag and peeked into its darkness to explore their secret toys.

"I was thinking," Anwen said, guiding Ryske toward the stools.

Not wanting their things to be seen, Harlow zipped the bag again and put it on the counter behind the coffee.

"Thinking what?" Ryske asked.

Anwen stopped him in front of Harlow, which made her as suspicious as Ryske sounded. "Harlow said you two made up."

"Yeah," Ryske said. "So?"

Anwen touched the top of Harlow's head to stroke her hair, opening her fingers to comb them into its volume. "Harlow and I get along, you know… We're close."

"Okay, Annie," Ryske said, extricating his trapped arm. "I know where this is going."

Harlow pushed her shoulders back. "I don't."

He set an unenthusiastic gaze on her. "You don't want to."

"Maybe she does," Anwen said, sliding an arm around Harlow's shoulders.

The half-embrace was odd in itself. The moment only got weirder when Anwen took Harlow's loose hand from her leg. Harlow was about to ask what was going on when Anwen guided her hand onto Ryske's groin.

The implication was more obvious with actions. "Oh," she said, glancing at the scowling Ryske just standing there while Anwen rubbed Harlow's palm against his cock through his jeans. "Okay, can I just clarify? Do you want me to get him hard so you can use it, or do you want us all to be involved in this?"

"No one's involved in it," Ryske said and leaned over

her to grab the bag from the counter. "Because it's not happening."

Turning around, he strode off to unlock the closet and go inside.

"Wait here," Harlow whispered to Anwen and slid off her stool to go after Ryske.

Closing the closet door behind her, she found Ryske in their corner, putting the bag on one of the higher shelves. Going over, she wrapped both arms around him to unbuckle his belt.

"Now I don't know why you're doing that," he said, letting his arms fall to his sides. "Is it because you want to use it or are you getting it hard for someone else?"

"I've changed my mind."

He turned so fast that she almost lost a finger in his buckle. "You want a threesome?" he asked like he couldn't believe it. "With Annie? Fuck, Trink. When you said odd suggestion, I didn't think you meant—"

"No! What? No. Not about that." She inhaled. "I wasn't going to tell you what Ophelia said to me because I was worried you'd do something." Threading their fingers together, she used the contact to lead him to the couch to sit them down. "But now I think you should."

"Think I should what?"

"Ophelia wants Anwen in on Pothos."

His reaction was both angry and surprised. "What? Why wouldn't you tell me that? You think they're working together?"

Stroking his thigh, she twisted her whole body toward him. "I don't know. Ophelia says she hasn't seen Anwen since the beating. I can't believe Anwen would volunteer to get beat up. We're supposed to be protecting Anwen, so I don't want to give her up to Ophelia like it's nothing. But—"

"Anwen can't stay here forever," he muttered like he was reading her mind. "She could be a benefit to us… and she gets life beyond here… But if they're working together, or make up and decide to screw us…"

"Right," Harlow said, sinking back for a moment, then rising up to kiss him. "You're amazing."

"Thank you," he said and winked at her. "I already knew that. So what's your plan?"

"My plan was to talk to Anwen, to try to get a feel for whether or not she has loyalty to our side or sympathy for the other. But now I think you should do it. You bring it up, get a feel for her, and if you think it's okay, invite her on… She's more likely to be loyal to you than the rest of us. She wants to please you. She trusts you more than she trusts the rest of us too. I think she'll buy it. Whether you invite her, or warn her to keep her distance, she wants to believe you. That desire is stronger than anything any of the rest of us can cultivate in this short space of time."

"I don't know that it's our choice to make," he said. "If she finds out Ophelia invited her in and we hid that, it could turn her against us. This is a choice she has to make for herself."

Nodding, she agreed with the sentiment. "Just like we have the right to make our own choice about how much we trust her."

His smile was proud. He leaned down to kiss her. "You're amazing too."

It seemed she'd read his mind and finished his thought for him. Anwen could pick whether or not to be involved in Pothos. But, as a crew, they had to decide how far they would go, or even what they would do for Anwen, if she did come onboard.

"If we let her stay, we'd have to be careful about what we told her," Harlow said. "Make sure she only overhears what we want her to overhear."

She let him consider that for a second and expected a response. She didn't expect that response to include him curling his finger into the ring on her necklace to haul her lips up to his. Yanking his mouth from hers as quickly as he'd given it, he picked up her hips and pulled her over to straddle his lap.

"Fuck it," he said, in a weird kind of booming voice.

Confused, she was still trying to catch up when he drove his hands up her thighs, under her dress. Pushing it up over her torso, he kept on going until the fabric was free of her head and tossed it away.

"Fuck what?" she asked when her hair was cascading down her back.

With her still sitting on his thighs, he slouched and opened the fly on his slacks to pull out his dick. Already full and hard, he was prepped for her.

"You started it, baby," Ryske said in that same voice, swooping an arm around her pelvis to tug her up closer to him. "Fuck yourself on my cock." Linking his fingers at the back of his head, he was cock of the walk. He winked and whispered the next three words. "And be loud."

His eyes flashed to the door and she got it. He wanted Anwen to hear them having sex. She wasn't really sure why, but Ryske had a plan. He always had a plan.

Rising higher on her knees, Harlow brushed her nipple on his lips, coaxing a drowsy feral look to his eyes. "Maybe I don't want to—"

His arm locked around her. In the same second that he sucked her nipple into his mouth, he fired his hips up while pulling her down, slamming himself into her so hard she screamed.

"Fuck! Holy—fuck! Shit," Harlow called out and punched his shoulder. "Crash!"

His thin smile stretched, but he kept her nipple between his teeth when he spoke. "Yeah, baby," he growled. "Just like that."

Ryske did have a way of getting what he wanted no matter what. He wanted sex from her and he was getting it. He used his arm on her hips to start her moving. Once she had her rhythm, he stretched his arms along the back of the couch and tipped his head back to look at her.

"Look at my gorgeous girl go," he said. "You enjoying yourself?" Holding her lip in her teeth, she nodded, trying to quiet her panting. "Prove it."

Her mouth opened, but nothing came out until he seized her throat. The possession of his grip bled a desperate yelp of need from within.

"Ryske," she called. "Oh, fuck! Yes!" Gritting her teeth, Harlow hissed the word out again. "Yes!"

Releasing her throat, he grabbed her ass in both hands, squeezing her, making her work harder and faster. He leaned forward and tongued the ring of her collar into his mouth, catching it in his teeth and pulling her upper body forward when he leaned back. Turning his head, he restricted her breathing with the twist of the chain. His control forced her breasts to rub on his shirt as she rose and fell at the awkward angle.

Being at his mercy, being controlled by him, took her over the edge. It had made her forget herself the previous night and was doing the same there in their closet. Riding him hard, Harlow hit climax so suddenly that she wouldn't have been able to stay silent no matter how she tried.

Slumping against him, he released the tension of her chain. It slithered from his mouth and skittered back to its place against the nook of her collarbone.

"I don't want to move," she muttered, feeling the thump of his heart on her chest begin to slow. "I'm going to stay right here."

"Okay," he said, trailing his fingers up and down her back. "The guys could come walking in any second, but you've got a hot body, so…"

"They've seen my body before," she said, sighing and forcing herself to rest her hands on his shoulders to push her body away from his.

Smoothing her hands down his chest, she caught the front tails of his shirt and began to unfasten the buttons. "You going to send me out there naked?"

Smiling, she opened his shirt wide and dragged her nails down his torso. "How did you stay fully clothed while I'm completely naked?"

"This is not my first rodeo," he said, skimming a hand up her back while snagging the ring of her necklace in his forefinger to pull her down for a kiss. "Go downstairs and help the guys… Don't come back up."

"You're going to talk to her?" she asked, her mouth on his.

"Keep the guys downstairs until you see me, okay?"

"Can I tell them why?"

"They're our crew, right?"

Climbing off him, she went to get a shirt dress from the rack by their dresser. After doing a couple of buttons, she grabbed a pair of skinny jeans from the drawer. Jumping up and down, she pulled them on and turned back to Ryske still on the couch with his shirt and slacks open.

Their relationship was moving at a meteoric pace. They hadn't even been together last week and yet, in this moment, their feelings were the most stable, sure thing in her life.

Something about their bliss unnerved her. In the past whenever they managed to find happiness, something would change, and it wasn't usually something for the better. Harlow loved that man; there was no way to deny it anymore. But keeping him had always been harder than falling under his spell.

TWENTY

"THIS IS EXCITING and terrifying at the same time," Anwen said.

Sitting in the back of Noon's car with Ryske in the front, Harlow and Anwen were due to meet Ophelia in the Pothos venue.

All Ryske had told her about his conversation with Anwen was that he hadn't needed to persuade her. Harlow didn't know exactly what he'd said. Though it had to have been more than just a question and answer.

The pair had spent a lot of time upstairs in the apartment alone after Harlow went down to help with the cleanup operation. Long enough that Dover called time and sent everyone from the neighborhood home with the promise of free drinks on the night Floyd's re-opened. At a loose end, because they couldn't go upstairs to the apartment, Maze treated her and the other guys to Chinese food and cocktails. Somehow the conversation came around to the Anwen and Ophelia predicament, Harlow and Dover filled the other two in.

They'd been rowdy when they got back. Despite the late hour, Ryske had been working out, while Anwen was already asleep on his bed. He'd been kind of grumpy about being ditched. The rule that Anwen couldn't be left alone in the apartment was still in effect meaning he'd had to stay and babysit.

With everyone up to speed, they began to speculate and plan what was next on their Pothos agenda. She was sort of done talking about it. So, without permission, she'd kicked off her shoes, slipped out of her jeans, and gone to sleep on the closet couch.

The next morning, that morning, after sharing the shower with Ryske, Harlow called Ophelia to tell her that Anwen was in. That was when the female Hagan asked the two to meet her at the club.

Anwen was edgy and anxious. In contrast, Harlow was curious enough about what Ophelia wanted that she was sort of excited.

The energy in the car was such a mixture of different feelings that Harlow couldn't really blame rookie Anwen for being unsure about what to expect.

"Swear," Harlow said, bending to fix the back of her pump.

"Ah, excuse me?" Anwen asked, on a whisper of a snicker.

Sitting back in a twist so she could see Anwen's face, Harlow nodded. "Swear. It helps. I don't know why, but it does. Come on try it. Fuck. Fuck. Tits. Ass. Cock. Fuck."

She said the words in quick succession, so they almost blended into one. Anwen was stunned.

Ryske addressed Noon. "That turned me on. You?" Noon flashed him an amused smirk. "I thought she reserved her potty mouth for me. I'm hurting, baby."

"Everything turns you on, smarty-pants… And you know I do this," she said, tossing him the stink eye in the far edge of the mirror.

"Yeah, and I know what else you like to do before."

He blew a quick puff of air onto his fingertips and wiggled them in front of his face, eyeing her with salacious purpose.

Noon pulled the car to a stop in a wedge of shadow behind the club.

"Wave at yourself all you like, Crash," Harlow said. "Those aren't coming near me today."

"For the whole day?" he asked, snaking his arm into the back to reach for her knee.

Squealing, she slapped at his hand and flipped her knees the other way. "You're a sexual predator, you know that?"

"The one in your dreams, babydoll," he said, taking his hand back and slouching down in his chair.

"Come on," Harlow said, sliding on her pointed ring and opening her door to slip out.

Anwen took her time getting out and coming around the car. In that time, Ryske rolled down his window, which she only discovered after he stroked her ass under her skirt. Smacking his hand away, Harlow spun to glare at him.

Her love was the picture of innocence. "Just checking you're sticking to the rules." That wasn't what he was doing; she could read the swagger bleeding into his expression. "Come down here."

Anwen was next to her and ready to go inside. Assuming he had some last minute advice, Harlow didn't object when he reached out of the window to snag the ring on her necklace. He gave it a tug, so she bent over to rest a forearm on the door sill to look inside.

"What?"

"Nothing," Ryske said.

When he didn't follow the word with anything else, she sought his eyes only to find them staring down her dress.

"Geez, Crash," she said, shoving his face to point it the other way.

He laughed and caught the ring again so she couldn't stand up. "Seriously, babe…"

Harlow didn't know why he was in such a playful mood. If they were in a different place, doing a different thing, she might embrace it. But, there, she had to be in the right frame of mind to react to anything unexpected that may happen.

"We're right out here," Noon said, leaning forward to look past Ryske. "If you need us, holler or scream and we'll get in there, whatever it takes."

"Thank you, Noon," she said, opening her hand to present it his way. "See, that's what a real man does in this scenario. He reassures, he comforts."

"Yeah, yeah," Ryske said. "'Cept I have full faith you can handle anything that's thrown at you. And if you didn't already know that I'd raise hell to get to you if you needed me, then you haven't been paying attention."

Damn him for reaching into her and giving her heart a squeeze just a moment before kickoff. "Come here."

Sliding her hand onto his cheek, she brought him closer and parted her lips to enjoy his. Leaning further into the car, her tongue slipped into his mouth, and was ready to push further until his fingers slid down the front of her dress.

Pulling back, she shoved his hand away.

Ryske laughed and leaned back to talk to Noon. "Always get my hands on them one way or another."

"Just wait 'til I get my hands on your balls again," she hissed.

Ryske just grinned and winked. "Look forward to it, Trink."

Standing up, Harlow fixated on the building they were about to enter and tried to get herself into the zone. "Let's go," she said to Anwen and strode away from the car.

Ophelia had told them to use the employee door in the alley. She went inside and found herself in a well-lit wooden stairwell with ornate carvings in the coving. Her interest in the décor lessened when she noticed the man descending the stairs to meet them.

"Brash," she said, aware of Anwen just behind her shoulder.

"Harlow," he said, and his attention shifted. "Miss Windsor."

"Brash," Anwen said. "Didn't imagine you'd ever be running errands for Ophelia."

The way his jaw shifted was curious. Was he irritated she'd impugned Ophelia or... something else?

"My loyalty to Mr. Hagan extends even beyond his death."

Harlow smiled. It was such an inappropriate affect that it startled Brash. "I just… I think that's great," she said, putting a hand over her mouth to disguise her laugh as a cough.

Loyalty to Jarvis Hagan? Yeah, okay, she could buy that. It was impressive Ophelia had recruited a man so vehement to stand by his ex-boss. Given, you know, that she, in fact, was the one who'd erased said boss from the land of the living.

With gritted teeth, he leaned in. "You're lucky she told me not to tear your head off with my bare hands."

Pushing out her lips, Harlow bobbed her head. "Yeah, lucky me." Her finger left her mouth to drift around. "Are we going to shoot the shit here all day, or…?"

Hissing out, Brash didn't like her attitude. Shame he was under orders to take it. Spinning around, he marched up the stairs. Looping her arm through Anwen's, Harlow followed on.

At the top of the stairs, Brash opened a door and held it for them. Ophelia had spared no expense. With a thick carpet, recessed lighting and expensive furniture, the club was fully kitted out for a high-caliber crowd.

A walled-off area toward the back of the space meant she couldn't see the full room. Could be another stairwell or enclosed elevator bank. With plenty of space surrounding the booths and tables, this club had been custom designed for drinking and gambling.

Low music came from the speakers hidden in the coving; there wasn't a space for a stage or a DJ booth. The fully-stocked bar to the left was backed by pristine mirrors and glass bricks above. No painted wood or neon signs in sight, but she still preferred Floyd's.

Brash led them toward the largest central booth. What made the room peculiar? Doors lined the walls. They alternated between obvious and hidden, presumably to prevent the place from looking cluttered.

Judging from the spacing and her peek at where the back wall would be, she'd guess there were ten on the right wall and five on the right. That would mean there were five at the back given Ophelia had said there were twenty rooms off the main floor.

"Darlings! You found us!"

Ophelia's voice vibrated through the air. It took Harlow a minute to locate her coming from the other side of the walled-off area.

Lydia was with their hostess. The four women reached the central booth at the same time. Nibbles were laid out on the table with flutes of champagne ready for them too. Ophelia had catered this meeting like it was some sort of happy social event.

"Hello, Harlow," Lydia said, a quiver in the words.

So the woman was still wary of her, maybe smart.

"I don't think you know each other," Ophelia said to Lydia and looked at Anwen. After the way things had gone at the last meeting, Harlow didn't expect to feel Ophelia put an arm around her waist. Stepping out of the embrace, Harlow was too aware of Brash behind her to relax. She didn't like feeling closed in. Ophelia didn't acknowledge the retreat. "Lydia, this is Anwen. She was engaged to my brother before his demise."

Before was a loose term. Anwen hadn't been involved with Jarvis Hagan immediately before his death. Lydia didn't ask questions, which was probably wise on her part. Ophelia didn't appreciate being questioned.

"What are we doing here, Ophe?" Harlow asked. "And why is it that the only penis allowed to be present is commanded by you?"

Tipping her chin toward her shoulder, Harlow made it clear she was referring to Brash. Ophelia laughed and waved the henchman away. Good. Target one eliminated. Getting him out of the room subtracted one threat from her periphery.

"I don't think Ryske would appreciate the implication that his penis can be commanded," Ophelia said. "That is who you would choose to be here, isn't it?"

"He is not the only penis I know," Harlow said.

"I'm sure he'll be sorry to hear that," Ophelia said and stepped back to open her arms, presenting the room. "What do you think? This is our kingdom."

"Ophelia was showing me around," Lydia said. "It has all sorts of… things."

"Yes," Ophelia said, putting an arm around the shorter Lydia's shoulders. "We can try out any of the toys and games you like the look of later. I want to give all of you a full tour. Once we're finished with that, we can sit down and talk… What do we think?"

Harlow nodded once and presumed Anwen gave the same kind of permission. Ophelia whirled around the room, giving the sales speech.

The men could gamble and drink on the main floor. The rooms were decorated in different ways and given different names. Some were basic, just a bed and a sink. Others contained devices and apparatus that Harlow could only begin to guess about. She didn't ask questions and maintained the demeanor of being unimpressed throughout the tour. Each room had access to a restroom and a panic button, as Ryske requested.

One room was specifically designed for dispensing Pothos. Although it did contain a bed, a curtain could be pulled across the full width of the room to conceal it. The half of the room in front of the curtain had a seating area, coffee table, and television. It offered the dispenser a comfortable place to wait between customers.

On the upper floor, Ophelia spoke of building a playground for women as men had had their day for too long. The décor upstairs was a little brighter. There was a stage too. Everything was just a little more delicate. The rooms upstairs hadn't been decorated or equipped yet, though Ophelia implied she wanted them all to have a hand in developing the strategy.

For her, this operation was ever-expansive. She had all sorts of plans. One about a full BDSM dungeon in the basement. Another for a separate romantic space above where couples could enjoy a more typical, vanilla experience.

This wasn't just a straightforward way to make money. Ophelia spoke with a real passion and exuded joy over what she'd accomplished. Maybe her optimism was premature. Ophelia had sold off much of her brother's business to fund it. As of yet, there was no consistent revenue stream. The hostess seemed to have forgotten that its future depended on an illegal operation.

"Where do people park?" Harlow asked as they were returning to the central booth on the main floor. "People don't want their license plates on show in a place they're not proud of being. And if there's a gathering of cars, especially of city officials or prominent people, someone might ask questions."

"Oh, so practical," Ophelia asked, gesturing them into the booth. It was a curved C-shape, so Harlow let Lydia and Anwen slide in first before going in last, ensuring an out if she needed it. "We offer a chauffeur service. Our drivers will pick up clients anywhere and bring them here and then return them home at the end of the evening." Which lessened the chances of DUIs. Smart. "But we do have a private parking level for those who choose to bring their own vehicle. Entry is by password only. If someone doesn't have the password, they don't get in. If we suspect anyone has shared the password, they will be denied entry forever more."

The women settled in their seats and Ophelia handed out the champagne.

Or tried to.

"If you think we're going to drink that, you're insane," Harlow said, taking Anwen's glass from her and putting it aside before she could drink anything.

Lydia had been about to drink, but her eyes crossed to the glass on her lips and she put it back down.

Wearing condescending sympathy, Ophelia folded her hands on the table. "I remember a time when you weren't like this, Harlow... Do you remember the night we met? The night you were on that date with Jarvis?"

"It wasn't a date," Harlow said.

"You weren't so cynical then."

"Why don't you cut the crap and tell us why we're here."

Ophelia looked at each of them. "It's simple. We're here to make friends. To get closer... We're going to have to rely on each other, to trust each other." Softening her tone, she turned her focus to Anwen. "On that note, I have to start with an apology to you, my sweet friend. It's so silly to get bogged down by the past. I let my emotions get the better of me. I was hurt and jealous. It was ridiculous. I hope you can forgive my abominable behavior."

"I…"

"Ryske wouldn't want us fighting, would he?" Ophelia spread her smile. "It makes his life so much easier if his women get along, doesn't it? So what do you say? Fresh start? Let's start from today. Everything else is forgotten."

"I…"

"Excellent," Ophelia said. "I hope we can embrace this as a fresh start for all of us." She drew in a breath. "Now, the next thing we have to discuss are the details. On Friday night, this place will be filled with horny, rich men, and beautiful women willing to accommodate them. We know Parratt and Yarker are going to do the schmoozing, whispering to clients about what's on offer. Ryske will take care of dispensing the product and allocating resources." Doing the actual exchange of Pothos and matching clients with hookers. "I think it would be best if each of us supported one man. With the fourth acting as a go-between. You know, passing messages, ensuring the men have what they need."

"Let me guess, you want to support Ryske," Harlow said.

Ophelia laughed like it was a joke, but it hadn't been. "I think it would be best to rotate probably by hour or we could do it by night."

"By hour sounds great," Harlow said. "Why aren't the men present for this?"

"Simply put, I wanted to talk to you about what we'd have to do beyond the basic operation."

"We can't support the men if we're banging the clients," Harlow said.

Ophelia drank some champagne. "Oh no, I don't mean that," she said, screwing up her face and shaking her head. "We're not prostitutes, are we?"

She hadn't minded using sex as a manipulation tool. Underhanded manipulation was probably worse than a consensual, informed exchange, where everyone knew what they were getting into.

"So, what is required beyond the basic operation?" Anwen asked.

"Each of our men will have different needs," Ophelia said. "We have to ensure they keep their eyes on the task they've been assigned."

"And off the women prancing around in their underwear," Anwen said, seeming to relax.

"And the product," Ophelia said. "If they want to sample it themselves for fun, and they can afford it, then they can do it on their own time. It may be tempting for them to try the experience for themselves after they see others enjoying it."

TWENTY-ONE

"YOU TALK ABOUT trust, but you're admitting you don't trust them," Harlow said. What was really going on? "Is that fair?"

Ophelia had called the women-only meeting. Though her points were valid, there was more going on. There had to be. Nothing said so far was urgent, or really necessary to be singled out in a specific meet. Was it a test to see who would show up and who would refuse? Could be it was a power trip, or that Ophelia had nothing else in her life and wanted company?

Harlow couldn't figure it out. The whole situation was too genial. She'd come to learn Ophelia was far more devious than she first appeared.

"It's not about fair," Ophelia said. "The men have more trust in us than we have in each other." Pointing between them, she gestured to Lydia. "Think about it. You three don't know each other well. Why should you trust each other?"

"Harlow and I know each other," Anwen said.

Ophelia's condescending smirk was almost ironic. "Sweetie, sharing Ryske's dick doesn't mean you're acquainted."

"We're not here to talk about that," Anwen said. "I thought you said you were over that." Conquering her nerves, Anwen was becoming bolder. "This is so typical of you, Fi. Everything circles back to what you want. If you want him, go ahead, take him." She folded her arms and slumped back. "We don't care."

"What Ryske and I do is our business," Ophelia said. "I apologize if my relationship with him causes this tension between us. I know you care for him deeply."

"None of this is Ryske's fault," Harlow said. "He doesn't cause this tension."

"Of course he does," Ophelia said, refilling her champagne flute. "Playing women off each other is one of his specialties. He wants us to fight over him."

Restraining her laugh wasn't easy. "No," Harlow said. "He really doesn't. You give yourself too much credit. You really don't enter his thoughts that much."

"Clearly I enter yours if you've come to that conclusion," she said. "Look, ladies, I don't want us to fight. I want us to bond. We have to know we will support each other if the men act inappropriately. Preventing them from making fools of themselves, or our operation, will fall to us."

"It can't be us against them," Lydia said. "They are our men."

Harlow wasn't sure about Lydia and resolved to ask Ryske for her story later. Lydia was Parratt's mistress, not his wife. To her knowledge, Lydia hadn't ponied up any cash. That left a question mark over her attendance. Though, Anwen hadn't invested either and Ophelia wanted her around, so green wasn't a prerequisite.

Having women involved softened the process and provided the men another avenue of negotiation. Although it hadn't been discussed, she'd like to think if Ryske was involved with an operation and asked to select a woman to speak on his behalf, he'd pick her. No, she didn't like to think, she knew.

That put a new slant on Lydia's presence. She'd dismissed her as just a woman who slept with Parratt. Maybe that's what she was supposed to think. If Lydia was there acting on Parratt's behalf, as Harlow would act for Ryske, maybe there was a deeper connection there. Maybe even love.

Except how could Parratt love her and not leave his wife for her? How could he be sleeping with Ophelia? How could Lydia be okay with any of that?

"Yes, they are," Ophelia said. "It's our job to protect them too. They have money invested in this and want credibility. It's our job to make sure they are conscious of both. It's important for us to nurture our male partners. We're going to be bonded and working together for a long time… It wouldn't hurt for us to socialize. It's easier to discuss business when everyone is relaxed… Perhaps we should have dinner later in the week? Thursday?"

Lydia and Anwen both nodded in agreement.

Harlow was more reserved. "I don't make Ryske's schedule."

If she told him to be at dinner, he'd be at dinner. But she wasn't going to make it seem like he was the kind of guy who could be kowtowed, because, well, he wasn't.

"I'll talk to him," Anwen butted in.

Ophelia's smile was feline in its pleasure. "I'm sure you'll find a way to persuade him, Anwen… You were always good at that."

The two enjoyed a laugh that even Lydia seemed to relish.

"Ryske prefers a game of cards," Harlow said, doing her best not to focus on Anwen's proclivity for blackmail. "My suggestion, if you're interested, he'll come to dinner if you give him something in return."

"Cards?" Ophelia said and nodded. "You're right. He played cards here with Jarvis."

Nostalgia might be nice for her. For Harlow, it was less tasteful. Windsor's was a crime scene, Ryske was stabbed within these walls on the night they met. It was no wonder that he'd been bleeding out and on the verge of death by the time he collapsed on her.

The distance he'd had to cover on foot between Windsor's and where they'd met, was considerable. On top of that, he'd led Animal and his minions in circles; he hadn't taken a direct route.

"Harlow?"

Harlow snapped from her trance. Each of the other women were peering at her with curiosity, probably wondering why she'd spaced.

"What?"

"Cards. After hours," Ophelia said. "That would be a good time to bond in private."

"There's booze and bedrooms on the premises," Anwen said, picking up the glass of champagne Harlow had taken from her.

Anwen's confidence was rising. Harlow grew dubious of the affinity these women were building. Was it fake or genuine?

"Yes," Ophelia said, raising her glass to Anwen. "Anything goes after hours!"

Anwen drank from the glass in time with Ophelia. That was the moment Harlow grabbed the reins and got out of the booth.

"It's time to go."

The women just blinked at her. If Anwen refused to leave, Harlow would face a difficult dilemma.

Ophelia was the one to come to her aid. "Yes," she said, sliding out of the booth. "I have taken up enough of your time today… We'll meet at my favorite restaurant nine p.m., Thursday."

"Nine is late," Lydia said, shimmying out of the booth after Anwen.

Ophelia retrieved her champagne. "Ryske is more comfortable in the dark."

Harlow didn't like that their hostess' attention dropped to her bracelet. She did her best not to react, even though impulse wanted to cover it up, to protect it from view.

"Nine is fine," Anwen said. "Demar always keeps his place open for you."

"It's one of the reasons he's my favorite," Ophelia said.

Demar's was just a couple of blocks from Windsor's. That restaurant was elite, beyond five star, and had a dress code. Ryske would hate it and its likely dainty portions… To satisfy his appetite, they'd have to pick up something else on the way home. If they didn't, he'd be hungry again before bed. But Harlow would use the steak to sell it to him. These premier places usually had good steak.

In contrast to their tense greeting on arrival, Anwen and Ophelia shared a double cheek kiss in farewell. Lydia did the same, just as Brash came back in. Ophelia must have summoned him somehow; there was probably a secreted button. Either that or they'd been watched on camera the whole time.

Though they were subtle, cameras were visible in various places dotted around the club. She didn't see any in the bedrooms, only in the public areas. Still, she'd warn the crew that there was always a chance of being watched.

She was thinking about getting home and asking Maze if he could hack the system when Ophelia spoke again.

"Harlow, could we have a moment alone?"

Everyone else was preparing to walk away.

Harlow hung back, and after a quick moment of eye contact with Ophelia, she turned to Anwen. "Meet me out back."

Anwen nodded.

"Tell Ryske I say hello," Ophelia said to Anwen and then watched the group leave.

Only after they were gone did Harlow turn back to Ophelia. When Ophelia tried to touch her arm, Harlow swung her upper body out of the way.

"What do you want, Ophe?"

"Nothing bad," Ophelia said, all innocence. "I meant what I said about being friends. We used to be friends. We trusted each other."

"And then I went to jail for a crime you committed," Harlow said, folding her arms. "It's been downhill from there, wouldn't you say?"

Harlow didn't like this soft, fake sympathetic Ophelia. It made her queasy. "That's forgotten now, isn't it? It's in the past," Ophelia said. "I think you're taking what happened very well."

"It helps that Ryske told me not to rip your head off with my bare hands," she said and arched a brow. "Not even Brash knows the truth, does he? You have him working for you and you can't even be honest with him."

"Like I said, sweetie, it's all in the past. We're about moving forward," she said. "But when I heard about that poor man…"

Ophelia was trying to lead her into a trap. Harlow saw it up ahead and didn't want to fall into it. Damn. What choice did she have? Walking away meant never finding out what Ophelia was talking about.

Taking a deep breath, she gave in. "Man?"

"Yes," Ophelia said. Harlow didn't buy her surprise for a minute. Ophelia put down the glass and picked up her hand, faking sincere concern. "Oh, I'm sorry. I thought you'd heard. I got the call last week… He died."

"Ophe," she said, extracting her hand. "I don't have a damn clue what you're talking about. I don't—"

"The officer guarding the evidence locker," Ophelia said. "The one attacked when your evidence was taken… You do know it was Ryske who arranged that, don't you?"

At the time, a fleeting thought on whether Ryske or her crew could be involved in her liberation hadn't stuck. One drama led to another; she hadn't dwelled on the brief suspicion.

Looking at Ophelia almost drew her in. "That he arranged for the locker to be ransacked."

"For your evidence to go missing, yes," Ophelia said, nodding, picking up her champagne again. "The man in charge of the evidence fought. He was subdued and had been in a coma… until he died."

An innocent man had died so she could be free. Harlow couldn't believe it. Even though she hadn't been the one to pull the proverbial trigger, if it hadn't been for her predicament, Ryske would never have sent anyone in.

"I…"

"They made it look like a juvenile prank, of course," Ophelia said. "They were very clever… Six people have had their charges dropped. I suppose those people have a lot to thank you for."

"Six?" she asked. Her nausea returned, creeping deeper into her bones. "Murderers?"

"Alleged," Ophelia said with a shrug. "At least three of them. Yes… One murdered his wife and children… Though, he didn't really, did he? He won't be convicted."

Slowly, Harlow's eyes closed. This was what Ophelia wanted. She wanted Harlow to be sickened by what had been done in her name. As much as Harlow didn't want to give her the satisfaction, it was impossible not to have a reaction to finding out that although justice had been done for her, it wouldn't be done for the victims of others.

"I really thought you knew," Ophelia said.

Anger burst out. "You knew I didn't know."

"My advice? If you spent less time screwing and more time listening to anything he has to say, you might be more aware of his capabilities…" Her once warm, friendly eyes cooled. "How can you claim to love a man you don't even know? You make him what you want him to be in your head. You don't accept what he truly is."

"You don't know a damn thing about my relationship with Ryske," Harlow said, backing away. "And you should know better than to screw with me."

Not intimidated, Ophelia matched her retreat by advancing. "Do you think I fear you, Harlow? How many times must I extend the olive branch? I try with you. I try and I try. Why can't you see we'd be great allies?"

The woman stalking toward her had a purpose and it was nothing to do with keeping the peace.

"You think you can fuck with me?"

"Do you think because you got the better of me once that I'm afraid of you?" Ophelia said. "Why don't you go to wherever you've got that weapon hidden and remind yourself what I'm capable of?"

Harlow stopped. "Is this where we are, Ophelia? Caught in a race to see who can murder the other first?"

Shrugging, Ophelia checked her manicure. "I just want you to think long and hard about whether you want me to be your ally or your enemy. I can be either. I'm willing. But if you choose the latter, don't fool yourself. You'll lose."

Proud as she was of herself, Ophelia seemed to forget there was one unchangeable thing; one thing she'd never win.

"You could slaughter me right here," Harlow said. "He'll never come to your bed."

Her hand fell to her side, yet there was a glimmer of a smile on Ophelia's face. "Oh, don't worry about that… He swore he'd never return to Anwen's bed and he spent six months of his life at her sexual beck and call… You may think I regret not having what you and she have, but I don't. Because I know you're temporary and she was a fool. I will outlast both of you."

"That's it, isn't it? It's all about him. You've got yourself stuck in this mire. You warn against it, pretend to give a crap, but who's the one who doesn't listen to him now? Ryske knows a vendetta can ruin a person… I'm not sure you even know what you want from him. Is it sex? Love? Or do you just want to take down women like me who have broken through to him? You couldn't do it. You're inept and can't handle your own incompetence."

Ophelia lunged at her. Harlow leaped out of her way, smirking at her attempt before spinning around and exiting through the door they'd entered. Running down the stairs, she didn't want Ophelia on her tail or to come across Brash.

Neither happened and she got to the alley where Noon's car was waiting. Anwen was in the back already. Harlow didn't get in. Instead, she stuck her head in Ryske's window again.

"Go home," she said. "I'll catch the next one."

Before she could stand up, Ryske grabbed the loop on her necklace. "What the fuck, Trink? What the hell did she want you alone for?"

Anwen must have told them about Ophelia's request. Ryske wouldn't have liked that she'd been in there by herself, but she was pleased he'd trusted her enough not to storm the place.

"Doesn't matter," Harlow said, grabbing his chin to pull him around for a kiss. "I've got something I need to do."

"We'll give you a ride," Ryske said, nodding

backward. "Get in."

She shook her head. "I can walk. I want to walk."

"Babe—"

"Don't sound so worried," she said and smiled. "Anwen told you about dinner Thursday?"

"Yeah," Ryske said. "Wait a fucking second, that's Thursday. This is only Tuesday. You're talking about not—"

"Don't wait up," she said and kissed him again.

Drawing his hand away from her necklace, she made short work of leaving the alley, choosing to go out the back way where a car couldn't follow. She didn't want them creeping after her trying to decipher her route.

Harlow didn't plan on going straight to her destination. She wanted to walk a while and knew there was a park close by. Wrapping her head around Ophelia's news would take time. To get some perspective, there was one ideal location. After her walk, she'd need to vent.

TWENTY-TWO

"WHAT DID RYSKE do now?" Clyde asked on a sigh when he opened his apartment door.

Her friend stepped aside and gestured her inside.

"I do not only come to see you when Ryske does something to…" Harlow stopped walking and looked over her shoulder at him as he closed the door. "That's exactly what I do, isn't it?"

Laughing, he slipped an arm around her shoulders. "Yeah, it is," he said. "But it's okay. I'm just happy to see you. So spill it."

Clyde guided her to the couch and sat her down.

"I don't know that he did anything…" she started. "I mean, I guess I do, but… I haven't asked him because…"

"Because…"

Slipping her finger from her pointed ring, she set it on the table and slid her shoes off to curl her legs under herself. Made sense to get comfortable before making an uncomfortable confession.

Propping an elbow on the back of her couch, she let the truth out. "I think I killed someone."

Losing his ease, Clyde twisted to face her. Searching her with concern, he seemed to be trying to judge her veracity.

"Well, if that's true, I think Ryske is a better guy to talk to than me."

"I would but… I think he killed him too."

That just confused her poor friend. "I don't get it. You both killed a guy, but you're not sure that he killed him? Were you blindfolded?"

"No," she said, glancing over her shoulder. "You got booze?"

Breathing out, he presented a hand to the kitchen. "You know where it is."

Harlow headed into the kitchen and opened the cabinet to retrieve the alcohol and glasses. "Remember I was in jail?"

"Uh, yeah, it hasn't slipped my mind."

"And then, remember I was out of jail?" she asked, bringing everything back into the living room.

"After house arrest, yeah. I came to visit you at your parents."

She sat on the floor between the couch and coffee table. "They dropped the charges because evidence was lost."

"Yeah, I heard about that at work," Clyde said. "A bunch of people got away with murder…" He trailed off, putting the pieces together much faster than she had. In her defense, he had more information in quicker succession. Harlow offered him the liquor she'd poured. "Oh."

Picking up her own glass by the rim, she slumped against the couch, curling an arm on the seat to toss back her measure. "Yeah."

"But you weren't guilty, right? So it's a good thing for you. You can't look a gift horse in the mouth. It wasn't your fault that…" His words faded. Probably something to do with the way she looked at him over the rim of her glass. "You think it is your fault?"

Maybe he hadn't been so quick to figure it out. "I think I know some people who believed in my innocence. People who were tired of seeing me locked up…"

"People like… men you may have slept with recently?"

"Maybe," she said, being vague was more for his

benefit than hers.

Harlow trusted him, but if the shit hit the fan, Clyde could find himself in his own interrogation room. Keeping details vague gave him plausible deniability. If she didn't name names, he could swear she hadn't named names.

"Shit, Har, that's… a lot."

"I know," she said, topping off her glass. "I know that nobody meant for anyone to be hurt… or killed. When you're not in the room, you can't control what's going on, can you?"

"And he wasn't in the room?"

"No," she said, shaking her head. "That would've been stupid. We never talked about it. I never asked for details. I did have a thought that maybe someone I knew might have had a hand in it, but I was so grateful to be free that I let it go." Sipping her drink, she ran a hand through her hair. "Like I always let things go… God, Clyde, when did I get like this? When did I let myself have selective memory? I knew it. I mean, I did. I had to, right? I had to know it was him. It was too convenient. He's antsy about me being inside for months. We find out there's no end in sight because the trial will be months away. I'm telling him that I'm going away for it anyway… He was annoyed." Slurping her liquid, she slammed the glass onto the coffee table and then pounced around onto her knees, laying both arms on the seat of the couch. "My boyfriend doesn't do well with sitting on his hands. He takes action when something isn't going the way he wants it to."

Just like he didn't pout, or sulk, Ryske marched on regardless. If there was a problem, he addressed it. If something needed to be done, he did it. She'd been locked in a cage and he'd resolved to do everything in his power to free her.

Harlow should've known from the exact second she looked up into Floyd's window and witnessed Maze and Noon holding him back that Ryske wouldn't just accept her fate as lost.

Clyde was figuring it out. "You think he wanted you out and arranged for someone to make that happen." She shrugged; he frowned. "But killing a guy I…"

She licked her lips and laid her head down on her

crooked arms. "There was an officer guarding the evidence locker."

Clyde's mouth opened in understanding. "Oh, I heard about that… yeah… Oh…"

At work, no doubt. Everything was at work. Those at children and family services were clued in because they worked with a lot of cops and officials.

"I don't know what happened. If it was an accident, maybe the guy was already weak, or maybe they beat the bejeezus out of him, I don't know… It's bad enough that he died. I mean, it's truly awful. But then, I hear six other people got their charges dropped. Six, Clyde. What if they were guilty?"

"What if they weren't?"

"We'll never know, will we? There will never be a trial. We'll never know. They could go out and hurt other people and whose fault would that be?"

"That's a lot to have on your conscience…" Peering at her, he leaned down. "Give yourself a break. You had no idea he was capable of something like this."

She pointed a finger. "I didn't say that, I… He's capable of anything. I just never sat down and considered specifics, you know? And now it's real. Someone has actually died. It's all cause and effect."

Clyde wasn't done trying to ease her conscience. "Surely it's not his fault then. It's the fault of the person who did kill Jarvis Hagan."

She scoffed. "You think? If the guilty party had been in jail, he-who-shall-not-be-named wouldn't have done anything, would he?"

Shifting around, Clyde slouched. "Guess not…" They both sat considering the situation for a minute. "Whatever happened, it's not on you. You didn't ask anyone to get you out or ask anyone to act on your behalf, did you? You're not like some mob boss who can pull the strings from the inside."

"No, but…" Sitting slowly, she faced the truth she'd kept coming back to in her hours wandering around the park. "That makes it worse."

Tilting his head, he frowned again. "How so?"

"Because he loves me that much, Clyde. I bring out the worst in him. Do you know what that's like? To know that the person you love did the worst thing they've ever done because they thought it was what you wanted? He did it because he loved me so much; he couldn't be without me. I told him to give up and move on, and that was the catalyst. That pushed him to make the decision he couldn't leave me in there anymore... If it wasn't for our love, people wouldn't have died... Our love killed people."

The grim understanding on his face said it all. "Shit, that's heavy, Har."

Inhaling as she twisted around to put her shoulder blades against the front of the couch cushion, she sighed as she relaxed. "I don't know what to do about any of this... I can't say it's okay. I can't say I agree with it. Even if I tried, he'd know I was bullshitting because if he'd believed I would condone this, he would've told me before it went down."

"He couldn't have told you, you were in jail. Someone would've heard him."

"He'd have told me," she said, stretching her legs out under the coffee table. "He wouldn't have been explicit or he'd have done it at visitation... He can tell me things without saying them out loud."

"So, even knowing you wouldn't approve, he did it anyway?"

"Yeah." In spite of everything, she couldn't let Ryske be painted as a villain. "I know why he did it. I love him for loving me that much, but... it's a lot, you know?"

"Yeah."

More silence followed. When he didn't say anything else, she smiled over her shoulder. "You're supposed to be giving me advice."

Seeing her friend at such a loss made her feel bad. Given that she felt the same way, she couldn't begrudge him his astonishment.

"Babe, I... I wish I could, but... The guy is already dead. You didn't kill him and neither did, you know, anyone you might have slept with... As for the people who are out...

I don't know. Short of tracking them all down and checking them out for yourself, I don't see what you can do… You might not even find evidence that you can corroborate either way. Even if you do, there's no chain of custody. You can't con them all into confessions."

"No," she said. "I can't."

"But then there's the…"

"The what?"

He put his glass on the table. "You can't tolerate this kind of thing, Harlow. You have to… Shit, he'd put me through a wall for saying this, but… You can't have this kind of thing done in your name. What if it happens again? You can't do anything about what's done. But you can let him know that this kind of behavior isn't acceptable."

Harlow shook her head. "You don't understand the life we live."

It sounded like she was making excuses and that just made her sick. She'd had the same thought. Her love was capable of anything. She even believed him capable of murder if the moment called for it.

But he'd stopped her from killing Hagan once and knew the danger of crusades. Her love might be capable, but he was smart too. Frivolous killing didn't make sense to him; he knew what it could cost him. That was the reason he'd given for not killing Ophelia. Good as it might feel to watch the life seep out of her, they'd have to pay the price, and it wasn't worth any of them giving up their freedom.

Ryske wouldn't have ordered whoever went into the evidence locker to kill the guard. Yet, he must have forgiven the act. He'd have heard through his contacts that the man had died. If the victim had been in a coma, then he'd been in hospital. Whoever put him there must've been paying attention, at least through back channels.

"Maybe I don't understand your lifestyle or the choices that you make," Clyde said. "But I still remember the Harlow Sweeting who started in my department. You worked hard, kept your head down. You had a mission. Even though you didn't share it with anyone else, it was clear you wouldn't be moved if you didn't want to move. You were tenacious."

"I've changed," she said, picking up his glass to sip the liquor.

"Changed? Yes. But you're still as headstrong. You still have the determination that always burned from you." Slipping his fingers onto her jaw, he guided her eyes to his. "You've always been so in control, Harlow... You're no pushover and you don't need anyone to save you."

The texture of his thumb moving across her jaw was nice. Clyde was such an upright guy. He was reliable and always around when she needed support, no matter what.

"Can I stay tonight?" His eyelid twitched. She pushed his hand away from her face. "Not like that, Clyde. On the couch. Come on."

"I knew that," he said. Getting up, she went into the kitchen seeking takeout menus. "I knew that. I did."

He made her laugh, he always did. In future, she shouldn't take him so much for granted.

Clyde gave her a safe haven, away from the madness, and a place for her to make decisions. He was right. She couldn't pardon what Ryske had done. Accepting it once would leave the door open for it to happen again. Harlow didn't need to be saved. Although it wasn't a happy life choice, it had been her decision to accept the rest of her life was going to be lived in jail.

No surprise Ryske thought he knew better. He must have known the mission came with risks. Still, she wouldn't believe he'd sanctioned what happened to the guard. No way had the job been arranged to end with another murder. Accidents did happen.

The evidence that was taken from the other cases was another story. As a cover for her evidence going missing, other evidence had to be corrupted or stolen too. Were those cases vetted?

If the police were convinced it was a gang prank or initiation, the perpetrators couldn't have appeared to be searching for specific case numbers. Hers would've been hard enough to locate discreetly. To avert suspicion, it had to appear the evidence was lost in the melee rather than hunted down.

What should she say to Ryske? What did this mean for their relationship? She needed some downtime to absorb and process so she didn't do anything rash. Her feelings often overwhelmed her sense. That was why, at times like this, she had to put distance between her and Ryske.

All he'd have to do was kiss her or say something that reached her… Hell, he could erase her doubts with a look if he wanted to. Harlow loved him, no doubt about that. Accepting this truth was going to be difficult. Their love now came with a body count. Could she take the risk that it might keep climbing?

TWENTY-THREE

WHEN MAZE HAD insisted she memorize specific credit card numbers, Harlow hadn't thought she'd ever need them. She may have even accused him of being pedantic. But her unscheduled stay at Clyde's left her with nothing to wear suitable for a fancy restaurant. So she had to stretch her memory and do some online shopping. Having to eventually put up with Maze's mocking was a more appealing option than returning to Floyd's while her mind was still screwed up.

Harlow could've gone back on the Wednesday, except she found herself enjoying the peace. After spending some time walking in the park, she'd cooked for Clyde. The normality was such a novelty that she'd stayed to watch a movie and fallen asleep at his apartment again.

When the time for her dinner date rolled around, it just made sense to get ready at his place given it was closer to the restaurant. Clyde gave her a hug on her way out and a look that said be careful.

She hoped her expression conveyed gratitude. He didn't have to accept her into his home to disrupt his life whenever she was selfish enough to feel like showing up, but he did. She couldn't put a price on his generosity.

Ryske would be late to dinner, Ophelia would know

it too. Given he was bringing Anwen, she wouldn't be on time either. Still, that didn't prevent either of *them* from being on time.

Ophelia was just getting out a stretch limo at the same moment Harlow came around the corner. They spotted each other, and Ophelia surprised her by waiting on the sidewalk. Before Harlow reached her, another car pulled up. Parratt, Yarker, and Lydia got out.

The group were just finishing their greetings when Harlow joined them.

"Where is he?" Parratt barked.

"Hello to you too, Gil," Harlow said.

Ophelia looped an arm through hers. "Oh, Gil you know Ryske is never on time. The man missed his own funeral."

The joke fell flat. Maybe because it was an actual fact.

"Let's go inside," Yarker said.

"Yes, yes. Of course," Ophelia said, leading the way with Harlow still attached to her side. "Demar always has a private dining space for me."

The owner was right inside the entrance waiting to greet Ophelia. He fell over himself welcoming their group and getting them seated. Obviously, Demar had done the math and noticed the whole party wasn't present. Still sucking up, he promised to go and wait for the last couple personally.

Ryske wouldn't like the brown-noser, but that made Harlow smile. Chances were high that her love would have to restrain himself or risk getting kicked out before being shown to his seat.

Lydia sat between Parratt and Yarker at their circular table. Ophelia guided Harlow into the seat next to Yarker and then sat at her side, leaving two empty chairs between herself and Parratt.

"It's rude," Parratt said. "Being late for a meal is rude."

Their personal server came and took the drinks order. "Bring an extra bourbon," Harlow said and the server looked to Ophelia as though that request needed sanction.

"For Ryske?" Ophelia asked and laughed. "You

shouldn't order for him. You don't have any right to—"

"She has every right," Ryske said.

Everyone whirled around to that voice.

Typical that he wouldn't come in the main door of the restaurant. He'd come through a service door at the back of the room, from behind a screen that was supposed to disguise it. He moseyed over to stand next to the table, at the first empty seat by Ophelia.

How did he know this was the room they'd be in? Being it was Ophelia's favorite restaurant, he may have been there before.

"Bring wine and bourbon for everyone," Ophelia said and waved at the server. "Shoo. Shoo."

The server did as told and scurried out of the room. Ophelia stood up to slide a hand onto Ryske's shoulder, rising to her tiptoes. But when she tried to kiss his mouth, Ryske leaned past her and snagged a finger through the loop of Harlow's necklace.

He stole her attention from Anwen hanging back by the screen. Harlow's curiosity snagged there, why wasn't the woman coming over to join them? She'd had no intention of standing up to greet her love. Ryske, it seemed, had other ideas. He drew her onto her feet and bowed to take her mouth, leaving Ophelia in the awkward position of almost being caught between them.

Having not been kissed by him for two days, Harlow wasn't prepared for the impact. All the melancholy and confusion of the last couple of days faded into the abyss of her love for him.

When her tongue beckoned his for more, he eased back. "Let's bug out," he murmured, brushing his lips back and forth on hers. "Hmm?"

Without really thinking, she felt herself nodding and his fingers slipping between hers. The reaction of the others didn't even enter her mind.

Ophelia was forced to move when Ryske pulled Harlow away from the table. "Wait, what?" Ophelia blustered. "You just arrived. You can't leave! Why did you come if you were just going to leave?"

Ryske kept on going toward the screen and pushed open the service door to urge Harlow out. "I came to get my girl, Fi," he said. "Your ride will wait for you, Annie."

He didn't pause for a response, but Harlow could hear Ophelia squawking as they departed. Ryske took her hips and pushed her down a narrow corridor past the employee restroom and out the propped open fire escape.

"Can we leave Anwen with—"

Ryske spun her around and thrust her against the hard wall of the restaurant building. He planted his forearm on the wall above her head and leaned in. "I don't give a fuck about anything 'cept you right now," he growled and lunged lower to steal a hard kiss. "What's going on?"

"Take me to dinner; we have to talk."

His hand moved from her side to her stomach.

Smiling at his presumption, she pushed his hand down. "No, not that," she said and cupped her hands around his face, arching her body toward him. "No matter what, I love you, okay?"

His frown intensified, implying that might not have been the right thing to say. "Trink, if you tell me someone hurt you, I'll raze the city."

Dropping her hands, she sank deeper against the wall. "You love me too much."

"You say that like it's a bad thing."

Seeking his hand, she laced their fingers together and took him from the wall. A few steps later, she spotted Noon parked in the shadows. She waved and he reciprocated, but she and Ryske kept on going out of the alley and onto the street.

"Did Anwen know you were going to abandon her at the dinner?"

"I didn't say anything," he said, picking up his arm that was joined to hers and looping it around her neck.

"Noon knew."

"How do you know he knew?"

She peeked up at him. "I know my crew. If he hadn't expected to see us walking away, you'd have said something to him or there would've been a question in his expression.

And you told Anwen her ride would wait."

"Noon always waits."

"Is he going to wait for us?" she asked.

"He knows we can find our own way home," Ryske said and kissed the top of her head. "You are coming home tonight, aren't you?"

"Is there space for me?"

Stopping, he turned her around to examine her. "Baby, where there's you, there's me. If you think it's too crowded at home—"

"I didn't say that," she said and took his hand off her shoulder to pull him along. "Come on, we're never going to find a good Chinese place around here. We have to move fast."

They walked about five blocks in the direction of home and found exactly the kind of Chinese place she loved. Not too upmarket, it had plastic tablecloths, paper lanterns and pagoda prints on the walls.

Harlow ordered more than she'd eat figuring whatever they didn't finish would be well-received at home.

Leaning over the table, her eyes slunk around the room. "Don't look now, but I think we're on our first date."

Ryske put down his beer and thought for a second. "Damn, baby, you might be right."

Sitting up straighter, she touched her paper wrapped chopsticks. "Shame for you I have a rule against giving it up on the first date."

Confident as ever, Ryske raised his beer bottle to his lips again. "You will for me," he said. "Why'd you think I picked this place? There's a dark dead-end alley right next to here. Perfect for what I plan to do to you."

Smiling at him, Harlow admired the cut of his jaw, the roughness of his stubble, his finger-combed hair. Ryske was a whole package on the outside. With a ripped body and menacing tattoos, he was every bit the bad boy.

Her smile wilted. But without boundaries, without rules, he was capable of anything. His love for her would drive him beyond any limits he might try to set for himself. There wasn't an atom in her body that doubted it. He'd do anything within his power to keep her safe, to make her happy. Nothing was too much.

"I bring out the worst in you," she whispered.

His gaze drifted from the window to her. "What?"

"I think we have to stop."

Just saying the words threatened her throat to close. They wedged themselves in her voice box and battled not to be said. Harlow forced them out, though they scratched at her, cutting at the sensitive flesh within her vulnerable neck.

Tension and anger seized his body. As the words slithered into him, he became rigid. "Stop what?"

"Being... being together."

A desperate gasp punctuated that sentence, which was exactly what she didn't need. Harlow should be strong for this, because any chink he'd wedge open until he tore her resolve away.

Bounding around the square table, he inverted his chair, bringing it to the corner of the position perpendicular to hers. Straddling it, he hunkered down, resting his torso against the chair back and grabbing up her hand in both of his.

"Listen to me," he said, imprisoning her hand on the back of his chair. "Look at me, Trinket. Look at me!"

Shaking her hand, he tugged her closer, forcing her dazed eyes to his. It was ending. Harlow couldn't quite believe they'd come so close to bliss and now she had to sacrifice it.

"Crash," she whispered.

"You are the best thing in my world, in any world, goddamnit. Whatever it is, whatever happened..." He smiled and pressed her hand flat to his chest, holding it over his heart with one hand. The other snatched the side of her head, beneath her ear, in his powerful grip. "It doesn't matter. Baby, don't you get it? Nothing matters more than this. You and me, we're gonna own the world."

He'd said that to her before, so long ago that it felt like an illusion. "What we feel, it killed people, Crash. People died so we could be together."

His optimism faded into concern. "You're talking about the guard."

Loose, because she was a little out of it, Harlow nodded. She was aware enough to be grateful he wasn't lying or playing ignorant. But she had to know how far his honesty went or if he'd try to cover his tracks.

"Was it us?" she murmured. "Did we arrange it?"

A beat of silence passed before he answered, "Yes."

TWENTY-FOUR

SUCKING IN A SHAKY breath, relief came with knowledge, but there was a deluge of guilt too.

"Goddamnit, Ryske," Harlow said, pulling her hand away. "Why didn't you tell me?"

"Because it was my burden. It didn't go down like it was supposed to. A bunch of stuff went wrong, but we got the result… And I know you're not an idiot; I thought you'd figured it out. 'Cept you didn't ask, so I thought you were protecting yourself. If you didn't want the details, I wasn't going to force them on you."

"Protecting myself?" Harlow was so offended that she wanted to punch him. Instead, she clenched her jaw and huffed out her words. "Protecting myself? You asshole." She socked his shoulder. "When have I ever put myself above us, above our crew, above the truth? Huh? Protect myself, fuck you."

"You didn't need to know. At first, it was plausible deniability. I was protecting you."

"And after? I asked you when we were in bed at my parents' if there were any other secrets and you said no. How can I ever trust you, Ryske? Clearly, you don't trust me."

"Don't trust—where the hell did you come up with

that?"

"Plausible deniability? So what? If the cops asked what I knew, I might just spill everything in exchange for a deal, is that what you think? I was willing to rot in jail so you and the guys didn't have to answer for Pothos and your pasts. I was willing to do that for you. Why wouldn't I have kept this secret too?"

"I don't want you to resent what we do," he said, matching her anger. Having this kind of discussion in a public place meant a lot of hissing and mumbling. Still, it was better to draw attention to themselves with the odd raised word and obvious tension than to have this conversation at home where there would be all out war. "Me and the guys have connections all over. We're used to making a plan and getting things done."

"And killing people? You didn't tell me you're used to that."

"Non-lethal force was the instruction, but the guy kept coming. Idiot wouldn't stay down. He got up and lost his footing, he fell and hit his head. That was the injury that put him in a coma. No one beat him to a pulp or used a weapon."

"It wouldn't have happened if our people weren't in there."

"They weren't our people. These things happen with six degrees of separation. Everybody knows something; no one knows it all."

"And what about the others who got out, huh? Killers back on the street. How do we live with ourselves if they kill again?"

Shaking his head, he balled his fists on the table, pushing deeper against the back of the chair. "We did our homework. Why do you think it took us three months to get it done? If we didn't care what we were doing, it would've happened overnight."

"I don't understand what you're…"

"We weren't the only interested parties. We matched people to those who had evidence in that locker. We weren't the only ones with people inside we wanted to get out."

"So you had another consortium? Nice. A consortium of killers."

"We did our homework. Those people were either innocent or victims of circumstance."

"What about the guy who killed his wife and kids?"

He scowled and pushed back. "Vehicular manslaughter. That guy has to live with what he did for the rest of his life. The State's Attorney says it was deliberate, but we looked at the details, there's no way… We checked everyone out. Then Maze went into the system and made sure that gradually, as we vetted and approved someone, that all the evidence was moved to the same area. He had a map of the whole place. There wasn't a sheet of paper in there he couldn't account for. We made up replicas, so they would know exactly what was in each box. They memorized it, so they wouldn't come out with a thing they shouldn't have. They didn't touch anything they weren't supposed to. Evidence that wasn't vetted wasn't touched. The stuff they smashed up was window dressing, cop stuff that meant nothing. The graffiti was in the hallways and outside. It was a performance, theater… Baby, you have to believe me, we were thorough."

So that was how the perpetrators had known where to go and what to look for.

"Until the last step," she said, raising her gaze from the table. "Until it came to telling me."

"I won't apologize for what we did," he said, sitting up straight. "To get you out, I'd do it again."

"That's what worries me, Crash," she said, beseeching him.

"I would do anything to keep you safe. Anything for us to be together. There are no limits. I'd have slit the guy's throat myself to keep you safe."

"I know and that's why I said you love me too much. You love me so much that it blinds you to any sense of right and wrong. Your love for me is so powerful, it's intense and now it has cost lives."

He swept up her hand again and leaned closer. "Do you love me, Trink?"

"You know I do—"

"And when I died, you wanted to hurt the people who hurt me," he said. "You were ready to tear out Hagan's throat.”

“Because he attacked me.”

“Is that the only reason?” he asked and she squirmed. “You say our love costs lives because I’m willing to go to any level for you, to pass every boundary and limit. But, baby, if I was in need, or I was hurting, would you do anything less for me?”

No, she wouldn’t. Harlow had completely reinvented herself to avenge him; she’d embraced her cynicism. But that didn’t make it better. It didn’t make it right.

“Ryske—”

“Why did you ask me for that gun?” he asked. “When you came to Floyd’s and demanded the weapon, why did you want it? It was for Hagan, right?”

Everyday taught her something new about herself, but this was pushing her limit. “He told me he was the one who arranged for Felipe to be hurt.”

“And you saw red.”

“It wasn’t like that,” she said, though it was. Harlow had been incensed and motivated. “I didn’t go over there to kill him. I wanted the gun for protection. After the way he’d treated me before, it made sense. He’d imprisoned me at his apartment. Assaulted me. I didn’t want that to happen again. No one knew where I was, it seemed like a sensible precaution.”

His brow arched. “Trink, you were switched on. You weren’t making a calm, rational decision when you asked me for the weapon.”

Flattening both hands on the table, her head was spun. It wasn’t great to have all the negative sensations of being drunk without the happy buzz, and that was how she felt. Like she’d had one too many and might throw up. Except she feared if she stood that her legs wouldn’t be stable enough to hold her.

“I wanted the recording, something in his own words. I hated that he could imply he was the instigator with Felipe and we didn’t have a shred of proof. I knew he was still mad at you; he’d already made two attempts on your life…”

“And if it happened again, or it was successful, you

wanted something you could dangle in front of him… Because if I'd been dead or out of action, you wouldn't have cared what happened to you or anyone else, right?" Like a naughty child, she kept her eyes on the table and shrugged her shoulders one after the other. "It wasn't just self-defense, was it? The gun."

Truth time.

She made eye contact. "I wanted to use it. If he'd given me the chance…"

"You wanted something final. Any hint he was gonna put his hands on you or hurt you… you'd have used it."

She nodded. "I wanted him to give me the excuse."

"Because killing him would protect me from his agenda." Again, she nodded. "So, baby, tell me, how is that any different from what I did?"

"Maybe it's not different," she said. "But that doesn't mean it's okay… Our love would've endured no matter what and that man would still be alive. If I had stayed in jail, no one would've died."

"No?" he asked, his expression opening. "You don't think I thought about putting a gun to my head?"

Horror parted her lips in a gasp. "Crash!"

"I love you, Har. There's nothing without you."

"That's not true," she said, grabbing hold of his chair to pull herself closer to the corner of the table. "You have the guys. You have your work. You have Floyd's and the neighborhood. You have Felipe, and Anwen, and—"

"Don't say her name like that," he spat as though the suggestion offended him. "Don't say her name like she's any kind of substitute for you."

Trailing a fingertip down his arm resting on the back of his chair, she drew her nail around the shapes on his wristband tattoo. "Have you been sleeping with her?"

Touching the underside of her chin, his fingertip glided down the front of her throat to snag the loop of her necklace so he could guide her mouth forward to meet his. "You're my girl, Trinket… If you want to put me in the doghouse for a few days or a few weeks, go ahead. But don't ever kid yourself this is over. There's no such thing as over where us is concerned."

"We can't hurt people," she whispered, her mouth on his. "We can't love each other so much that we're willing to destroy other people's lives."

Easing back, he met her eye. "I don't give a damn about anyone else, Trink. To keep you, I'll destroy anything that gets in my way."

There was such conviction in him that she could almost feel it bleeding from his pores. He would do anything to have her, to keep her. The notion was so seductive that she couldn't deny being aroused by it.

But that only made it more wrong. She wanted him to love her as much as he did, but it was selfish to prioritize her desire over other people's lives.

Their food came. Ryske did his usual flirtation with the waitress, giving Harlow some time to regroup. He put noodles on each of their plates and was scooping her food from the serving dish when he spoke again.

"We've got a plan for tomorrow night, you want in?"

"Hmm?" she asked and then closed her eyes and shook her head, trying to reorient herself. "A plan, yes. I… I want to know the plan."

"You did a good job getting Ophelia to think the after-hours poker game was her idea."

She opened her chopsticks and selected a piece of her chicken to feed between Ryske's lips as he scooped out his own dish onto his noodles. They always sampled each other's food. Food in Floyd's was community food anyway. It was impossible to claim ownership of anything in a home full of hungry, healthy men.

"How do you know I did that?"

He swallowed. "Anwen gave us the rundown," he said and nodded at her plate. "That's good."

She opened his chopsticks for him. "She told you I let Ophelia think it was her idea? I didn't know Anwen knew we wanted after-hours poker."

"She didn't," he said, taking his chopsticks and picking out a vegetable for her to try. "But she told us what happened and we know you, babe."

Chewing on the carrot he'd given her, she moaned at the pleasure of the taste. "That's amazing," Harlow said, and dipped her finger into his sauce.

"Want to trade?" he asked, enjoying her enjoying it.

"No, mine's good too," she said and swayed closer. "But you will have to bring me back here."

"Not a bad start for a first date," he said, and picked up some food in his chopsticks. His eyes slunk away from her when he murmured a melody. "I'm so getting laid tonight."

She poked his wrist with her chopsticks and then ate some more. "Did Anwen tell you about the rotation of women?"

"And that I'll be dispensing the drugs," he said. "Yeah, she did… I don't mind so much. I prefer to know which guy is with which girl, you know? Svetlana is good at looking after her girls, but if she's working, someone has to be watching over them."

"Is she pretty?"

He popped more food in his mouth. "Who?"

"Svetlana," she said. "I was thinking, I'm going to be in a building with fifty of your ex's tomorrow…" Sitting straighter, what they'd just been discussing altered her perspective. "Or maybe I'm one of them now."

"There won't be fifty; tomorrow will be like a soft opening. I haven't slept with all of Svetlana's girls. They rotate a lot. She has high turnover and I haven't seen her for a while. Doesn't mean I don't want Parratt to think I've been with them. I can be more credible in protecting them if he thinks I have personal history with them." Made sense. "And you are not my ex."

TWENTY-FIVE

SKIMMING OVER THE topic of the state of their relationship, Harlow put down her chopsticks to pick up her beer. "What's it like sleeping with a prostitute?"

"That's really your question?"

"I'm curious," she said. "Do you know any male prostitutes?"

"Yeah," he said with food in his cheek. "Haven't slept with them though."

He was looking at her like she was crazy, but she just rolled her eyes. "Straight male prostitutes."

His chin bobbed when he swallowed to clear his mouth. "Sex with a hooker still counts," he said, and flicked her necklace. "You're mine. Even if you dump my ass, you don't get to screw around with gigolos and then tell me it doesn't count."

"Not for me," she said. "Didn't Anwen tell you about Ophelia's big plan to have a space for women? She thinks we deserve the same opportunities as you men, and she's not wrong, you know."

"Equal opportunity fucking."

"I like sex," she said.

He snickered but kept eating. "I know."

"So if I like it, other women can like it too… I know plenty of women who can't get what they need from their husband or boyfriend… I'm not condoning cheating, but I'm saying, if those relationships end, women aren't always comfortable bringing up their curiosities or their needs with their guy."

Frowning, he chewed. "What do you want that I don't give you?"

"Not us," she said. "You… well, you're different. You make sex a safe and happy place. Some men can make it awkward or be closed off to things." She thought for a minute. "I'm trying to think if there would be anything I'd be embarrassed to ask you…"

"Long as it's not pegging or CBT, I'll do it," he said, washing down his food with a drink.

She didn't know what either of those things were, but him expressing his boundaries sort of proved her point. Even if she was to ask for them, he'd be comfortable enough to tell her no.

"But I'm me, I haven't changed." She scoffed. "I mean, my basic threshold hasn't changed. I have fantasies now that I've always used when pleasuring myself—"

"Keep talking," he said and winked before feeding her another carrot.

"The way we are in bed is a pretty good representation," she said. "But I would never have dreamed of telling Rupert that." Just the notion of bringing it up was enough to shake her bones. "How do you think he would've reacted if I told him to squeeze my throat or spank me?"

"You didn't ask me to spank you."

"No, but you knew I'd like it. Your sexual instincts are spot on. You have them honed." She grinned. "I've been lucky enough to be on the receiving end of them… Why do you think so many women want you?"

His mouth was still full, but that didn't prevent him from responding to the rhetorical question. "Because I'm ultra-hot… It's my super power."

Just giving him a look, she ignored his swagger and his wink. "You know how to treat each female, and you don't treat any two the same."

He stopped playing. "It's nothing to do with sex. I haven't slept with Ophelia and you keep telling me she wants me."

"The mess you're in with Ophelia, Anwen, and me is all interwoven. It's about way more than sex."

"Yeah, the guys have some theory about how me falling in love with you started all this crap."

"Dover told me," she said. "Ophelia is the one who feels most aggrieved. You were hers first."

"I was never hers."

"That's not the way she saw it. She had this whole marathon plan for seduction and pictured a future with you. She developed real feelings based on actual time you spent together. She thought you were starting a relationship."

"It was never like that."

"Not to you because you were used to having flirtations with women. Used to taking up with them, teasing, kissing, and moving on. Ophelia wasn't used to that. She saw a relationship as a man and woman who like each other, they court, they get together. You showed her a whole other way."

"Just how much time did you two spend talking about me?"

"I don't have to ask her how you made her feel. I was that woman too. I didn't have a damn clue what I was getting into when I met you."

"You haven't ended up as a mad psycho intent on getting your way."

"Haven't I?" she asked, making momentary eye contact. "Isn't that what we were just talking about? How we'd go to any lengths for each other?"

"We're actually in love. Your feelings are reciprocated," he said and waved his chopsticks at her. "No, I take that back. *My* feelings are reciprocated. I fell for you a damn sight longer before you fell for me."

She smiled and leaned in to tease. "Dover says you fell in love with me the night you fell over me."

"With the woman who put herself in front of me and didn't flinch at Animal's intimidation? I think you kept me alive that night by diverting blood to my cock and keeping it in my body. Fuck, I wanted you then and I haven't stopped a minute since."

"You were bleeding out. Maybe I should put your feelings down to your brain being oxygen deprived. All this time I thought it was love, but it's actually brain damage."

"Keep your cure because I want my disease," he said, picking up her hand to kiss her palm.

Admiring him as he adored her, Harlow didn't want to ever think of a day when she'd have to walk away from him. But if they couldn't control their ability to be rational because of each other, how could they head into the future together?

"You didn't finish telling me the plan," she said, tearing her attention from him. "Are we agreeable to Ophelia's setup and role allocation?"

"We want to be as agreeable with Ophelia as we can be through the night to make sure we get what we want at the end of it."

"Then you better apologize to her for tonight," she said. "Instead of kissing her, you kissed me. You embarrassed her by walking out on the meal she'd arranged… She agreed to poker after hours as an exchange for you coming to dinner."

"I don't want to apologize."

Harlow grinned. "You'll have to kiss her."

"Oh, man," he groaned like a child being told to go to bed. "I don't even want to be nice to her."

"I don't know how you'll do it in the space of one night, but you'll have to convince her you're into her, or at least intrigued."

"Convincing her of that has never been a problem," he said. "It will be even easier in her sex club that she's so proud of."

"You're not allowed to have sex tomorrow night."

"Uh, we'll be having sex."

"No," she said. "Sex between investors is not allowed."

"And I say again. I haven't invested dick."

She laid a hand on her upper chest. "As the woman

who's been calling herself your girlfriend until very recently, I'm happy about you not investing your dick into a sex club." He smirked. "But you have invested. You've invested time and personnel… It's better if we don't anyway."

"Why?"

"Because with all the sexy ladies around… the mood… the atmosphere, it won't be difficult to get turned on."

He frowned. "You don't want me to have sex with you because you'll be too easily turned on? Trink, you're always easy to turn on. All I have to do is look at you."

Almost fearing he'd do it right there, when their eyes met, she slapped a hand over his. "I didn't mean me. I meant you can be turned on with Ophelia. Attention will seduce her. But it's against the rules, so you can't have sex with her. Apologize, kiss her, get hard if you have to, she'll like it, but you can't do anything with it."

Her hand dropped to find his brow low beneath. "You think I flip a switch and it dances? I can't get hard with her."

She groaned at him. "Of course you can."

"Anwen gave it a damn good shot and I had nothing for her."

Swallowing her feelings of nausea, she didn't want to ask when he was referring to. "You got hard for her on Monday after we got back from my folks."

"When?" he asked and then scowled. "You mean the threesome thing when it was your hand doing the rubbing?"

Harlow pointed her chopsticks at him. "My hand, her direction."

"Your hand," he said like that was enough. "That's what my cock does when it gets your attention. Think you'd be used to it by now."

Intrigued, her head tilted. "Even around other women?"

"Hey, it happens when the guys are around," he said, raising his chopsticks high to pull out a noodle from the pile on his plate. "If my hard-on can survive Noon and Maze jabbering about intake manifolds on the other side of the shower screen, I can fuck you through anything."

"Well, we thank you," she said, licking sauce from her finger.

"We?"

Dragging her finger through her sauce, she offered it to his mouth and he sucked it clean. "My pussy and I," she said. He groaned around her finger and sucked it harder. "I've never had a lover more incredible, Ryske, and you know I never will again."

He pulled her finger from his mouth. "Stop saying goodbye to me," he said. "All this past tense shit pisses me off."

"We just have to breathe," she said, brushing her thumb across his lip and yielding a smile. "And I'm not going anywhere. I'll be on your crew as long as you'll have me."

"Which will be forever," he said. "You'll be on my crew longer than anyone… You and our babies."

"I'm not pregnant," she said, doing her best to stay calm. "I'm starting to think I look fat… I need to get back to Costello."

"Had an interesting conversation with him yesterday."

That piqued her suspicion. He must have known it would because he got a kind of distant look while inspecting his food. Though he masked his triumph with a smile, she saw it.

"Were you talking about sex?" she asked. "Don't tell me you—"

"I don't walk up to guys and say, 'Hey, would you like to fuck my girlfriend?' It's not a good icebreaker, you know? He was helping out with the bar, and we got to talking about the empty building next to Floyd's. He needs more space for the gym; Noon wants to open a garage."

"A legitimate garage or a return to his roots?"

Ryske shrugged. "Maybe a bit of both."

"So, you want to buy a new building? What do you know about running a gym or a garage?"

"Me? I can turn my hand to anything," he said and winked at her. "But Maze and me were talking about if we extended the second floor over the alley into our stairwell, we could run a pool hall with access to Floyd's. So, you know, we all feed into each other."

"I think that's a great idea," she said. "Where will you get the money?"

"Money?" he asked, slurping a noodle. "We'll figure that out. The gym would be on the first floor with the garage, both would have space in the basement. Then we'd have the whole second floor for the pool hall. It's a huge building."

"Will you show me?" she asked. As he was nodding, a thought struck her. "You're not pissed I told Lena to keep that money from mine and Rupert's wedding fund, are you? If we need it for Floyd's—"

"I'm not pissed, baby," he said, picking up a curled section of her hair. "Better than a blender… It's not like we need it for our wedding."

That was sort of a sad truth. If they couldn't be together, they couldn't get married. She'd told her family they could rely on Ryske and she stood by that. She didn't think he'd ever be bitter enough to hurt the people she loved.

Suddenly, her left hand looked depressingly bare.

Ryske slid his hand over hers, his fingertips grazing her ring finger. "In a heartbeat, baby," he said and she looked up. "You know that, don't you?"

She nodded. Their whole lives were riding on her decisions. Ryske let her call the shots. He didn't rush or coerce her… Well, maybe he coerced a little, but she didn't mind him being led by his passion for her.

They'd had so much turmoil that when she turned her hand and his fingers laced through hers, she was ready to play.

"You do know the number one reason we could never get married," she said. "Before all the other bullshit, there's one major reason."

"What's that?" he asked, prepared for her to tease.

"You'd have to pick a best man. Whoever you didn't choose could fall out with you."

"Nah," he said. "They'll draw straws. Whoever isn't best man can be bridesmaid."

The image of them trying to convince any of the guys

manicures and massages were a good idea was funny enough without even beginning to think about dresses and shoes.

They couldn't let them coast in their teasing for long. Releasing his hand, she slipped hers under the table onto her knee. "Tell me the plan."

"Tomorrow," he said and cleared his throat. "Like I said, we keep Ophelia sweet… If I have to, I'll apologize…" Not that he seemed happy about it. "I'll make nice with her. We need that game after."

"What do we want?"

Pushing his plate away, the first thing she thought about was the waste of food. Though, that wasn't exactly important in relation to what they were discussing.

He pushed her plate away too. "There's a reason I wanted to talk to you alone about this," he said, scooping up her hand.

Harlow wasn't finished eating but knew better than to argue when he got serious. "You're going to do it, aren't you?"

It didn't take him long to admit it. "Yes."

"Goddamn," she said under her breath. After their discussion, their relationship, their future was back in flux. And there he was, telling her that he was going to be with another woman. "Goddamn."

Stealing her hand away from his grip, pushing her chair further from him was instinct. Her hand went up through her hair and came back to her forehead to hold the weight of her skull as her elbow landed on the table.

"Baby, if you say no—"

"I don't say no," she said, her eyes closed. "I would never say no. I would never tell you not to do what you had to do."

"I know what jealousy is like, how it gnaws at you. I won't put you through that."

With her hand still on her forehead, she rolled her gaze to him. "I'm not jealous," she murmured. "We've discussed this."

One of his eyes narrowed. "It turns you on to think of me with her? You don't look turned on."

"I'm not turned on. I'm not jealous… I feel sick."

"I'm not going to have sex with her," he said. "There's something we need. I need to win a hand to get it."

"What?"

"We want the deed to the club."

Her head rolled further around. "We do? Why?"

"There's no reason for her not to put it on the table. She has plenty of money. Other than its worth as the Pothos venue, Windsor's means nothing to her. We're in on that, so who owns the club isn't the problem."

"I don't think she'll mind you having it," she said. "Remember, Ophelia's ultimate prize is to be with you. If you own the club, and you're together, it doesn't really matter whose name is on the piece of paper."

"What's mine is yours."

"Exactly," she said. "Why do we want it?"

"Control," he said. "Because if it's ours, we can control structural changes… Ultimately, we'll strip it and sell it."

Though she'd kind of known it, getting confirmation inspired happiness. "Pothos isn't a permanent plan for you?"

"I'm not telling our kids that daddy's a drug dealer."

"Much better that he be a grifter," she said, warming her lips with a smile.

"Haven't done much of that this year either."

"You were dead," she said. "That's got to be your biggest con yet. You're entitled to a little time off after that performance… I tell you, I don't mind admitting it, you really sold it to me."

TWENTY-SIX

SOMETHING CHANGED in Ryske's demeanor. He sat up straighter, his hands slid to his spread thighs. "Do you still think about it?"

"Think about what? The day you died? Living every minute without you? Reminding myself to breathe when my throat wanted to close to cut off the oxygen… I despised every breath I took in that world without you."

"But you want to walk away from me now."

"I don't want to," she said. "I can't. I just told you I'm on your crew. Nothing will change that… I love you, Ryske, but… Bale told me I had power over you and I didn't understand it. I saw glimpses of it, but I didn't get it until I found out someone died for us… I don't know, I'm just… I'm just upset by it, that's all… I *know* I'm the same way. I don't think you're some evil Big Bad Wolf. We just need some perspective."

"What if I don't want perspective?"

"I think living with Ophelia will give you it," she said.

"I don't know what she'll want, but she'll ask me to give her something."

"I know. I agree. She told me as much."

Resting his forearms on the back of his chair again,

he relaxed. "When you talked alone at Windsor's?" She nodded. "What did she say?"

Anwen could only have told the guys what happened up until the moment Ophelia dismissed her. "She tried to get in my head," Harlow said. "It was her who told me about the guard... She said I was temporary in your life and that Anwen was a fool... Though she did also seem impressed that Anwen had seduced you in the way she did."

"Seduced me? She blackmailed me into screwing her."

"Ophelia said you spent six months of your life at Anwen's sexual beck and call," Harlow said, picking up her beer. "Lucky Anwen."

He exhaled a snicker. "I've been at your sexual beck and call since the minute we met."

"Since the minute you regained consciousness, maybe."

They shared a smile. "Hey, I told you to take advantage of me, and that's an open-ended offer... Any time you see a chance to ride me... whether I'm conscious or not, you take it."

Her lips curled. "You think I don't know you're waiting for me to reciprocate?"

"You don't have to reciprocate, Trink," he said, tipping some beer into his mouth. "I know you want it from me every minute... I'm not even worried."

For her, with him, there was no disconnect between sex and love. Harlow did want to have sex with him, all the time. But she'd never be able to have that physical connection without losing herself in the emotional one.

"Do you think you could have sex with me without loving me?"

"Yes," he said. "Do I think that will ever happen? No. I've told you before, there's nothing that could make me stop loving you."

"What if I fucked Bale?"

Ryske's brows rose and his beer lowered. "You came up with that one fast," he said and she grinned. "Did you... fuck Bale?" The ease with which he asked the question betrayed he didn't really suspect she had. Harlow didn't answer right away and gave him a chance to narrow his eyes in suspicion. "What?"

"Nothing, just… he is a doctor and I have been under sedation in his care, so… I wouldn't really know, would I?"

Ryske put down his beer. The scowl set on his face looked permanent. "That fucker…"

She laughed. "I don't think he has sex with the patients he sedates."

"No, but fuck knows what he's seen… I'm getting your medical records."

"You mean you're going to tell Maze to hack my medical records," she said. "I don't think doctors who violate their patients write it on their chart… Maybe they have little secret codes… Like… a big O stands for unnecessary enema, and a little one is digital vaginal probing or something."

He sneered. "Do you really have to put that into my head?"

She laughed. "Maybe hyphen figure-8 means cock gag reflex test."

"You don't stop talking, and I'll give you one of those right here."

"This is fun," she said, pinching some food from his plate. "And, hey, if he did it to me… you were under his care for a while too."

"Yeah," he said. "Why do you think I'm so worried? It's nothing to do with you, I'm just sitting over here feeling violated."

"I watched them strip you that first day," she said. "Those guys looked like pros… I'd say it's something they do for fun on a slow weekend."

"Drug me and take my clothes off?"

"You never know," she said and grabbed her bottle. "I would." Sliding back a little, he pulled at the knot on his tie and unfolded his collar to take it off. "What are you doing?"

He lassoed the tie around her neck and began to unbutton his shirt. "As you wish, Trink," he said. "I'm taking my clothes off."

Leaping up, she grabbed his hands to stop him going

past the third button. "Can you ask them to pack up the food first? I don't want to be kicked out before we have something to take back for Noon."

She sat back down, relieved he'd desisted.

"You spoil him," Ryske said, twisting to gesture at the server.

"He loves Chinese food almost as much as I do, and this is the best I've had so far."

Ryske charmed the server into packing up their food and then handed over a card that she guessed he'd gotten from Maze. "Want to get a cab or walk?"

"I don't know," she said, thinking about the rest of the night. "Maybe I should go back to Clyde's."

"Figured that's where you were staying… You didn't share a bed with him, did you?"

"This from the man who's been sleeping with Anwen."

"That's different."

"Why? Because you've fucked her before?" she asked. "That makes it worse. Especially since your morning wood can be persistent."

"That's me who's persistent," he said. "Not the wood."

"Oh," she said, accepting his help to stand. He moved behind her to drape his jacket over her shoulders. "Shame. I always liked the idea that you were powerless to stop your cock from taking what it wanted from me."

"Well, there's that too."

The server came to return Ryske's card and handed over a bag of food. With her prize in one hand and Ryske's fingers between hers, they went out into the night air.

"You didn't tell me what the other space would be for," she said.

"Hmm?"

"The building next to Floyd's, if it's the one I'm thinking of, has that big flat roof and the sort of little cabin on top. It's like a third floor, but it's only a third of the size… Am I thinking of the wrong building?"

She couldn't imagine that she was. He'd spoken about

connecting the second floor of Floyd's to the new building over the current narrow alley. There was no building at the other side that could be connected. That was the way Noon drove his car around back. It was a wider lane than the dead end alley.

"No," he said. "That's where we'd live… It's just a shell up there at the moment. The flat roof gives outdoor space and I'd bet there's space for two, maybe three bedrooms up there." She stopped to look at him. "What?"

"Where we'd live?"

"Yeah, I know you love Floyd's, but we couldn't have kids there. There's not enough room. We'd be connected to Floyd's, so you could hang out there whenever you wanted. The kids can run back and forth to their uncles… After the extension across the alley, they can walk right across the roof from our door to Floyd's. We'll have a door or a hatch or something put in to Floyd's roof so they can get straight into Dover's… They wouldn't have to go through any bars or past any people."

The corners of her lips rose. "You've really thought about this."

"About our future? Yeah. I was making plans. I do have a deal with Bale after all… Always thought it was BS, that it wouldn't matter, 'cause I never planned on settling down. You changed that and I thought we were on the same page… until tonight."

"I said I didn't know if I wanted kids."

Smiling, he drew a finger down her cheek. "And that works just fine for me. We still need to invest in something for the future… Maze will probably move with us if there aren't any nippers running around."

Flabbergasted, Harlow was shocked and awed that he'd put so much thought into it. "I don't know what to say."

"It's okay," he said. "Nothing is set in stone. You said yourself you'll always be on the crew. So you'd be a part of the designing and setting up either way."

"You continue to amaze me, you know that?" she said, looping her arm through his and starting to walk again. "You just… you set a goal, figure out what you want, and you do whatever you have to."

"That's me," he said and leaned over to kiss her head. "Never thought it would cost me this though."

Big picture future aside, there was one topic they hadn't discussed. "You said we have to play nice tomorrow night? You'll play nice with Ophelia. I won't."

"You won't?"

"If I play nice, she'll know something's up. We both pretty much admitted that the only way this ends is with one of us dying, so…"

"What?" Now it was his turn to pull them to a halt. "She said what?"

"She said we could be allies or enemies, and if I chose the latter, she'd win…" She sighed. "It's all about context. I'm not worried."

"I am," he said and pulled her back. "Or have you forgotten that Animal is working for her?"

That reminded her of something else and she raised a finger. "No, but did Anwen tell you what Brash said to me when we first went inside?"

He thought for a second, then shook his head. "No."

"He basically threatened to kill me."

Ryske wasn't impressed. "And you're happy about that?"

"Yes," she said, grabbing his upper arm. "Because he said it in reference to how I was responsible for killing Jarvis Hagan. We both know I wasn't. He doesn't. Ophelia has their loyalty, but she must have known she'd never get it with honesty… She told them I killed him, or at least she didn't correct the assumption that I did. We can't let the cops hear the recording, but…"

"If we need to flip Brash and Animal…" he said, catching on to her thinking. "That's good, baby. That could be useful."

"Do we still have the recording?" she asked. "With the fire…"

"Maze has it. You'd have to ask him where."

They started walking again.

By the time they got to the end of the block, her

thoughts had moved on to the following night. "What should I wear tomorrow?"

"You want to know if you should wear panties?" he asked. "We have rules, but if you don't trust me to keep you safe..."

Harlow dug her nails into his upper arm through his shirt. "No, I mean, should I wear a cocktail dress? Maybe just a slip? Should I go slutty? What are you going to wear?"

"Animal print thong probably," he said, delivering the reply with sincerity. Harlow didn't contain her laughter. "I don't know, baby. Wear whatever you want. What about that beige dress you wore to Bale's that time?"

"It was blush pink," she said, not that the color mattered. "You spend a lot of time thinking about that dress, don't you?"

Ryske didn't even hide the truth. "An inordinate amount of time."

"I could wear that. It's tight... It's sort of demure though, isn't it? I have a white halter that goes to about my knee, but shows a lot of side boob."

"Works for me."

"Or I have a loose fitting shift dress that's backless... I have an LBD with a plunge neckline and mesh panels and... You're not really listening to me, are you?"

"No, not really," he said. "I'm thinking about what will be under the dress."

She squeezed herself closer and returned to the plan. "So you're making nice. Maybe I'm acting a little jealous."

"Maybe."

"At the end of the night, you'll make sure she goes ahead with the card game. Everybody's in, and..."

"We play a few hands, keep it friendly," he said. "Then up the stakes. When it's appropriate, I ask for the deed to the club."

"You going to spend the night complimenting it?"

"Probably... Not hard to compliment a place with a hundred bedrooms in it, stacked high with hookers." She tightened her grip on his arm. "And the gorgeous woman I love in there too of course."

Her smile fell to the sidewalk. Her love never forgot to toss in a compliment. That was why he was so good at what he did. Even though he was sort of sassing her, he still managed to make her feel good.

"I don't come with the deed."

"No," he said and took his arm from her embrace to coil it around her shoulders so he could snag his thumb into her necklace. "But if I ever write one up for you, I won't be signing it away."

That was sweet. Harlow slid her arm around his waist, hooking her finger into his belt loop. "You said you were going to give yourself to her. Are you thinking of doing an exchange?"

"It's typical that I should offer her the chance of a rematch, so I have to play another hand."

"To let her win the deed back?"

"She can request anything she wants," he said. "She might ask for that, but Maze will be there, looking unimpressed, as he does. He'll goad her into asking for something else… if she doesn't ask for it straight away."

"You."

"Right."

"She asks for you, you lose. I have to walk out of there without you. She'll want sex."

He held her tighter. "Don't underestimate my skills, baby," he said. "Yeah, she might try to go for gold, but it won't be hard to put her off."

"What are you going to do? Be a slob? Pick your nose?"

The question was genuine, but he laughed. "No… I didn't fall in love with you because you opened your legs for me. Anwen did and I didn't fall in love with her."

The man was a pro.

Harlow was impressed. "You'll talk her out of it… Make her think she needs to do more if her goal is keeping you for good."

"Yep."

"And so, what? You'll just be her slave following her around? Beating people up or intimidating them… Doing what Brash and Animal do?" She shivered. "God, you'll have to spend time with them too… What if Animal tries to hurt you?"

The petrifying idea didn't slow Ryske down.

She was shocked to hear the smile in his words. "Best part is, Ophelia won't let them. I'll be golden, cock of the walk, ruler of the roost, the big kahuna—"

"I understand, baby," she said. "She'll give you the authority to control them because she loves you. You're not afraid because you'll be their superior…" Harlow drew in a breath. It wasn't so easy for her to rely on Ophelia's logic. "The point is, you want to be close to her. You'll get the inside scoop on what she's up to and what's important to her."

"And we can sabotage from the inside."

"She'll know it's you."

"Doesn't matter," he said. "We know she loves me… I won't be obvious. Initially, we won't take action. It will be eyes and ears only. All we need is a crack, a way in. Something that will help us take her down… It could be a side deal or a maybe she's in deep with the wrong person, who knows. But I'll find something."

"What will you do with it? Take it to the cops?"

"Depends what it is," he said. "We need her out of our lives. That's the ultimate goal."

"She threatened to pin Hagan's murder on you. Don't forget that. If she doesn't think she's getting what she wants, she'll take you, and everyone else, down with her."

His swagger was undeniable. "I know how to keep a woman happy…" His confidence dwindled. "Every woman but you."

Turning her face up, she gave him more of her weight. "You keep me happy, Crash… Hey, if I was a straight forward woman who always said and did the right thing, you'd be bored with me already."

He inhaled and blew out the breath in a sigh. "Yeah," he said. "You're probably right."

"Let's just get home, heat up some of this food, have a drink, and go over the plan with everyone one more time. Will Noon be outside Windsor's tomorrow night?"

"All night."

They went a few more steps before she got curious. "What do you think he does when he's stuck sitting in the car all night? He never seems frustrated or fed up. He's always quite chilled."

"Baby, take a lesson from me… don't ask," he said. "I've never met a man so close to his vehicle in my life… I don't like to think how he might get personal in there."

Laughing, she nodded. "Fair enough."

Noon was a great guy with a kind nature, she didn't think he got intimate with his car. Even if that was how he passed his alone time, she wouldn't judge him. He was who he was, and she loved him. Harlow loved them all.

Despite what he thought, she loved Ryske too. She was happier with him than she had ever been. His plan for the future was appealing, but… Could the universe stand to lose what them being together might cost it?

TWENTY-SEVEN

THE ELECTRICIANS HAD been in to rewire Floyd's. Harlow hated they'd left a mess. Seemed crazy given that the whole place was being remodeled. But she'd spent the better part of the morning putting the apartment back together because she was ready for the upheaval to be over… Not that it would be any time soon.

Coming down the spiral stairs on another mission, Harlow was delighted to find a friend. "Felipe!" she said and ran over to pull the boy into a hug.

"Nightingale," he said, squeezing her in return, though he didn't seem too happy to see her.

"What's wrong?" she asked, pushing his hair away from his face to examine his expression.

"Nothing," he grumbled but moved away from her to kick at the ground.

The stroller in the middle of the room drew her over to say hello to Tiffy, happy chewing on her teething ring.

"Oh, sweetie, are those nasty teeth coming in?" The baby seemed happy and flashed her a gummy grin. "None through yet, huh?"

"She is always awake," Felipe said. "Always. All the time."

"Oh, honey, I know it's not a lot of fun," Harlow said, going over to put an arm around him. "Soon, it will be much easier. She'll start sleeping through the night and then she'll be running around. When she's a little bigger, you'll be able to play real games with her."

"I don't want to play stupid games with a stupid baby."

The teenage years never failed to turn perfectly pleasant children into moody terrors. "You don't mean that. She's your cousin."

"She's my stupid cousin."

"Come on now, this isn't you. What's wrong? Is your mom still talking to your dad?"

Felipe nodded, though he stayed fixated on the floor. "He's getting out soon."

"Is he coming back to yours?" Felipe shrugged. "You only have two bedrooms, right?"

He nodded. "He won't like the stupid baby crying all the time."

If Felipe's dad went home, it wouldn't be to sleep on the couch. At the moment, Felipe was on the couch. If his father came home, he wouldn't be asked to vacate.

"She's not stupid," she said, but had concerns of her own.

Felipe's father was violent. The youngster's reticence made sense for his own sake, but also for that of his mother, aunt, and little cousin. From what Harlow knew of Pablo Soto, he wasn't a patient man. It wouldn't hurt to get another look at his files, just to see if there were any real concerns.

"I'm always looking after her," Felipe said, throwing his hands up at the baby. "Always me! I should be out there... with the men, doing the men's work... This baby stuff is for women!"

Though she knew he'd been raised a certain way, Felipe wasn't an intolerant kid. His attitude made her smile.

"How about," Harlow said, curving an arm around his shoulders again. "I take Tiffy to the store with me and Ryske will find you something manly to do, huh?"

He nodded but didn't seem a whole lot happier.

Something else was on his mind. She would need to spend more time with him to get to the bottom of what it was.

Guiding Felipe out of the den while pushing the stroller, they found Ryske up a ladder in the corner of the main bar. Already the room was starting to look a lot cleaner than it had a few days ago. Ryske noticed Harlow wheeling the stroller with Felipe at her side. Sticking his screwdriver into his tool belt, he descended the ladder to meet them.

"Where have you been?" he asked, using her necklace to pull her in for a kiss.

"Upstairs," she said while he smudged the baby's cheek.

"She's getting big, huh?" Ryske said, smiling at Felipe who barely tried to reciprocate. "What's wrong with your mug?"

Ryske gave the kid a shove. Felipe slipped his hands in his pockets and dipped his focus.

Harlow rested her shoulder on Ryske to lean in and stage whisper. "He feels left out," she said. "Wants to do man's work."

"Man's work?" Ryske asked. "It's a man's work to keep the women happy."

"I said I'd take Tiffy to the store. He's been left on baby duty a lot." She liked that Ryske was concerned in his observation of the quiet kid. "Will you find him something to do? I'm going to make lunch for everyone; Tiffy won't be a bother to me."

"Okay," Ryske said and whistled, drawing the attention of the half dozen people around the room doing various jobs. Noon was the one in his focus. "Felipe's gonna show you how to do that right."

The men exchanged a look of understanding and Noon held up a spare mask. Felipe perked up some and darted over to see what he could learn about sanding.

"Keep an eye on him," Harlow said. "Looks like Pablo might be coming back home after all."

"Shit," he said. "Why does Martina do that to herself?"

Tipping her head back, Harlow smiled up at him.

"Love does strange things to otherwise sane people," she said. "Maybe when you're all grown up some nice girl will catch your eye."

"My girl caught more than my eye," he said, trying to turn her into his arms, but she resisted. "Fuck, baby, when you gonna let this go…? Will you relax?"

"Relax? You want to get laid, Ryske. Call it what it is. You want to fuck."

Glancing at the baby, he checked Tiffy wasn't watching them before he spoke. "I want us to get back to normal. Nothing's different than when we were at your parents. You were happy to tell your mom I was gonna be a permanent feature. Since we've got back, you've done nothing but push me away."

"I think some distance is smart given your plan to give your life over to another woman," she said. "I trust your skills; you'll hold her off for a while. But this is about more than sex. I'm protecting myself, Ryske. Tonight, I'm coming home without you… I don't know when I'll see you again—"

Her voice broke, so she averted her gaze, pissed at herself for showing weakness in such a ridiculous way.

Dipping down, he buried his face in her hair. "Trink," he said, sliding a hand flat onto her belly. "You know that no matter what happens, I'll always be yours."

"You don't know what it's like," she whispered, not responding to his caresses, but not pulling away either. "To be powerless to protect the person you love. I feel useless and pathetic and weak… I should be able to protect you."

"From what? Fi? She doesn't want to hurt me. We talked about this. I'll command her minions; I don't fear them."

"You don't understand."

"I do," he said, rubbing her stomach and coiling his other arm around her to stroke one hip while her other rested against him. "Because it's exactly how I felt when you were in jail." Her eyes darted up to his. "I didn't know what was happening to you in there. They were keeping you from me and I was stuck out here, powerless."

Except he'd taken action to free her. Maybe that was

why. Ryske didn't do well with being told no.

"That's why you arranged the..."

"Yeah," he said, nodding, though he started to frown. "They weren't going to keep my girl caged. Nothing keeps us apart." Letting himself smile, he touched her lips. "That's how you can be sure that this isn't forever. Trinket, I don't care if I have to climb out the window like a teenager sneaking out, I'll find a way to visit you."

"It's not the same," she said, shaking her head.

Sinking a hand into her hair, he cradled the side of her head, bringing it upward to join their lips. "Pulling away from me isn't protecting yourself. It's punishing us both. We're strongest when we're a unit."

"How can you say that, then give yourself to her? How will I walk out of there tonight?"

The pain that hung in her gut grew into a tight ball of anxiety. Ryske would be alone. Yes, he was capable, but she didn't want another wall between them.

"Whatever she wants me to do," he said. "We'll still have Pothos every week. We'll see each other then."

Opening her fingers on his on her hip, she welcomed his digits coiling between hers. "Do you remember what it was like at visitation?" she asked. "When you'd come to me in jail and that guard would make noises at us if you tried to touch me?"

"Yeah, I fucking remember." His quick scowl suggested he still wasn't over it. "I should track that fucker down..."

Harlow grazed her thumb across his lips and let her hand move to his jaw. "Ophelia will be ten times worse," she said. "Watching us every minute. The first thing she'll do is make you promise never to touch me again."

He snorted out a laugh. "You think I'll agree to that? Even if I do, you think it'll stop me?"

"She despises me and wants you to despise me too."

Combing her hair from her face, he kept stroking. "How do you think she'll do that?"

"I don't know... She'll find a way."

Maybe that was her real fear. Ophelia wanted to drive

a wedge between her and Ryske. She'd go to any lengths to do it.

"Baby, it's not possible," he said, confident and relaxed in his smile. "There's nothing she could do or say that would make me care less about you; that could make me love you less. You *know* that." Squeezing her closer, he kissed her hair. "She doesn't have the power to change this."

Trying to think of what Ophelia might use, Harlow searched her memory, and made eye contact. "I haven't been with another man," she said, feeling a sudden urgency to clear up any misconceptions. "Since I met you, you've been the only—"

He laughed and pressed a finger to her mouth. "Would you relax? She could tell me you fucked the whole neighborhood; do you think that would make me not love you? You think I'd believe her?"

Anything else awful, Harlow was sure he already knew. He'd heard the recording of what happened on the night Hagan died. He'd been eavesdropping when Ophelia discussed them sleeping with Parratt and Yarker. Everything from the past, Ryske knew.

"I love you," he murmured into her hair and opened his hand on the side of her head to bring her focus up to him. "Whatever happens, Trinket. I love you." She nodded. He winked and smacked her ass. "Now go get the food, we're starved. It's not a good idea to have the baby in here with all the dust."

He kissed her and gave her a nudge toward the door. Nothing would erase her worries of what was to come that night. Ryske was going to be Ophelia's. It didn't matter that it was the plan; Harlow couldn't console herself to the idea of being parted from him.

Any obstacle between them was unwelcome. She resented barriers. Especially those erected by others. Given her existing feelings for Ophelia Hagan, this night wasn't going to mend any rifts between the women.

Ryske might be hers in his heart, but what difference did that make when they were being attacked, manipulated, and kept away from each other?

TWENTY-EIGHT

GETTING READY FOR their first Pothos night had been a somber experience. During that time, Harlow existed in her own head. Her crew seemed to respect her need for distance, so hadn't pushed her to get out of her zone.

Anwen was high as a kite, which was understandable. She'd been locked away from the world for so long. This was her chance to be social again.

Harlow, Ryske, Maze, and Anwen arrived at Windsor's together. Noon parked in the back alley and no one said anything as they got out and went into the building.

In a strategic move, Harlow took Maze's arm, and Anwen didn't hesitate to take Ryske's. As soon as they'd entered the main floor and spotted Ophelia at one side of the room, Ryske split away and went to her.

Maze seemed to understand what Harlow was doing when she steered them in the opposite direction, toward the bar. Left alone, Anwen loitered for a moment, then went over to join Parratt, Yarker, and Lydia in the central booth.

Harlow slid onto a bar stool.

Maze stepped in close, resting a hand on her hip. "You okay?" She nodded and kept her head down. Maze called the bartender over to order drinks. "I've never seen you quiet and hunched like this."

Forcing herself to straighten her back, Harlow plastered on a glittering smile. "Better?"

"No," he said, pushing her curls from her shoulder. "Don't give me that false shit. This is me. You know he doesn't want her. Making up with her is a—"

She touched his lips. Focusing on him meant ignoring the mirror behind the bar. In her peripheral vision, she could see the reflection of Ryske doing his thing with Ophelia.

"Do you think I'm threatened by her, Maze?" she purred, pushing her chest out, against him.

Taking the hand he had on her hip, she slid it further around to her lower back, bringing them even closer to each other.

"I think you shouldn't be," he said, playing on her flirtation by projecting interest and drawing a fingertip down her temple. "So why did I need to tell you to turn on the sparkle… You haven't been yourself tonight."

"We'll have to go home without him," she said. "It doesn't feel right to leave him behind."

"He knows what he's doing. He won't fuck her."

"If it's that or lose him, I don't care what he does with his dick. Don't you get it? Animal shot him. Brash stabbed him. These men are at her beck and call… and both of them are erratic. I don't trust them with his life. I don't trust her with his life."

Putting together her own experience of Ophelia, Hagan and Anwen's tales, and her knowledge of the beating Ophelia ordered on her friend… No matter which way she sliced it, Harlow couldn't be at ease with leaving the love of her life at the mercy of a maniac.

Her gaze dropped again, but she didn't notice until Maze touched her chin to bring it back up to his.

"Trust him, Nightingale. He won't stray from the plan, especially when that plan is to come home to you."

"You'll marry me if he dies, right?" she asked, drawing a coy finger up and down the edge of his lapel. "I don't want to die a spinster… We won't be able to have sex because you'll never be able to match up—"

"Ha," he said and shoved her. Laughing, Harlow grabbed for him, wrapping her arms around his waist under his jacket. "You keep that up, I'll make you marry Noon."

"That wouldn't be so bad. I'd never have to drive anywhere again and he'd keep me in Chinese food."

"Yeah, but you'd have to live with his snoring."

Bobbing her head, she agreed. "So it'll have to be you then… Good news is, I've already met your mom."

They'd told Maze about running into his mother. During that conversation, there had been a brooding exchange of scowls between him and Ryske, but she didn't probe into his family business. Harlow had enough of her own family drama and didn't want to involve herself in anyone else's.

If Maze needed her, she'd be there for him. Without a doubt, she'd play any role he needed her to.

"Do blowjobs count as sex?" Maze asked, stroking her back.

He was an idiot in the most wonderful way.

Flirting with her was his way of distracting her. "I don't know. Are you going to eat my pussy?"

Taking her shoulders, he pushed her back. "God, that's disgusting," he said and picked up her glass to put it in her hand. "I'll marry you if you never suggest that again."

Filling her mouth with liquor, Harlow let her head fall back and smiled.

Maze ducked and pressed his mouth to her forehead. "You're gonna be fine, Nightingale. Until we're dirt in the ground."

Circling his thumb and forefinger around her wrist, he raised her arm and kissed the star that represented him. As he brushed his lips against it, their eyes met. She felt it, his absolute conviction that he would always be by her side. Her crew loved her and she loved them.

A noise at the other side of the room attracted their attention. The lights dimmed and the first group of men were escorted in by a trio of scantily-clad women. Like being on stage, the show was on.

"Let's get to it," Harlow said, chugging her drink and

hopping off her stool.

Snatching his hand, she pulled Maze toward the booth where Yarker and Parratt were perched. This was real and it was starting now.

Men continued to come in and women appeared from the private rooms to court them. Games began and practiced croupiers appeared. Pothos might be new, but game night wasn't.

Ophelia was glowing, happy to be on Ryske's arm. "Gil, do you want to move to the back and you can stay here," Ophelia said the latter to Yarker, directing the men.

"I'm going to find myself a game," Maze said and touched Harlow's jaw to raise her focus. "Want to come, Princess?"

Harlow tilted toward him. "Come? You'll have to put in a lot more effort if that's the outcome you're looking for, Sugar."

When she flicked her tongue at him, he covered her mouth with a curved hand. "Didn't we just talk about this?"

Ophelia laughed. "I'm sorry, sweetie, but Harlow is needed with Gil," she said and pouted, pressing herself against Ryske.

The hostess' input wasn't required. Her goal was probably to draw attention to how close she was to Ryske.

Sighing, Harlow resigned herself to work and not play. Letting her head fall back, she gazed up at Maze. "Go have fun, honey. But don't leave without me. I'll probably be pretty drunk by the end of the night."

Maze bowed to kiss her lips. "Be a good girl."

"Doesn't seem likely," she said as he drifted away.

"Anwen you stay here. Lydia, you float," Ophelia said. "You all know what we're doing… I'll get Ryske up to speed."

Everyone began to move in the directions Ophelia sent them, including Ryske. Just before she walked away, Ophelia cast a satisfied smile over her shoulder.

The woman might think she'd made progress. She believed Ryske liked to play women off each other. If that were true, it was credible he'd be all over Harlow one night and then move onto Ophelia the next.

Ryske was good. With his talents, he could convince a woman of anything. The fact that Ophelia wanted to believe the seduction made his job easier.

Ryske belonged to her, but that didn't allay her fears. He was vulnerable with Animal and Brash nearby. Both men were still loyal to Hagan's vendetta. Anwen might be alive, but Harlow doubted that made a difference. They'd been cultivated to hate Ryske, to want to hurt him. And after the card game tonight, Harlow and Maze would walk away and leave him alone in the viper's nest.

TWENTY-NINE

PARRATT TREATED HER like she was invisible, but Harlow was at peace with that. Just sitting at a table with him was enough to bore her. The last thing she wanted to do was pretend she gave a crap about anything he said. Once or twice, he tried sliding a hand up her thigh. Icky as it was, at least he was smart enough not to persist after she removed it.

In some ways, he reminded her of Edgar Charnock. He had that same kind of pompous attitude when with an audience of his peers. Gilbert Parratt liked to talk a lot about his own success and others failings.

Yarker was more interesting to sit with. He wasn't quite as lecherous as Parratt. More of a gentleman, Yarker actually made sure she had drinks and was comfortable… Although she didn't discount his attentiveness may be a direct consequence of her threats of violence at their last meeting in the hotel. Sitting with him did give her an advantage. He preferred to play cards than chatter, so she got a glimpse at his style.

Someone touched her shoulder. She turned to find Lydia behind her, giving her the nod to switch stations.

Sliding out of the booth, Harlow didn't interrupt Yarker's concentration, and let Lydia take her place. Ryske would be her assignment for the next hour. After her position with him, it would be onto the job of floating between the men.

How was Pothos doing? Ryske would be able to give her the numbers. From there, maybe they could work out how long it would take to get their investments back. She spotted a familiar face. At the same time her attention landed on him, he noticed her too.

Adjusting her trajectory to meet him, he did the same, moving away from the card game he'd been observing.

"The night just got interesting," he said as they met.

Harlow smiled. "Aren't you involved, Mr. Vane?" she asked. "Or do you prefer Penzance. Does your fiancée know you're here?"

"Alas, she has broken my heart," he said, flattening a hand on his chest. His grim look of heartache quickly became a sly grin. "How else you think I can afford to be here?" She appreciated that truth with a smile. "You know, it's funny, I actually thought for a minute that Ryske was really into you. Guess he's better at the con than I give him credit for."

She didn't follow. "For a minute?"

"Sure," he said, sipping the brown liquid from the glass in his hand. "If he was, he wouldn't let you turn tricks in a place like this…" He drew a fingertip up her arm. "You got a suitor?"

"You're a good bet. I know you just got a payday," she said. "But you do know what's going on here, right? You have to pay for the kick before you get the bang."

"With a pretty like you, I don't think I'd need it."

Harlow leaned in. "But I might," she whispered. "Come on, I'll set you up."

Even though she'd been honest about her intention, Penzance went with her anyway. He wrapped an arm around her and fondled her ass as he pulled her closer.

Ryske's position was in the central room. The door was open, though a curtain over it acted as a veil for what was going on inside.

Bowing to nuzzle her hair, Penzance wasn't shy with his hands. Harlow led him through the curtain and into Ryske's room, set up like he was hosting a private party. A TV played porn on mute, and a laptop was balanced on the high arm of the couch next to her love. Behind said couch was a bed. It was semi-concealed by a half-closed curtain stretching the width of the room between the end of the bed and the back of the couch.

Penzance didn't even look up when she approached Ryske, but he did.

Projecting childlike innocence, Harlow pouted. "This man says he wants to put his pee-pee in my twinkle and play with my tatas," she said, following her words with a smile. "I said he has to pay you first."

"Yeah, pay with his life for thinking about it."

As soon as Ryske spoke, Penzance looked up and groaned. Ryske lifted a hand; she took it to let him pull her onto the couch at his side. She rested on her knees and linked her fingers to drape them across his shoulder.

"What?" Harlow asked Penzance's glare. "I told you I was setting you up and you followed me anyway."

"If you think I was listening, you haven't seen you in that dress," Penzance said.

Ryske nodded at a perpendicular armchair and Penzance sat. "What are you doing here, Zance? I thought you were running an op."

"Over," Penzance said, opening his arms. "Her old man paid me to leave… so I left."

"You out of work?" Harlow asked, recognizing an opening. "You should get a job here."

"Sorry, sweetheart, I don't sling cards."

"Not that, with Ophelia," Harlow said and patted Ryske's chest. "He's protection. You can tell Ophelia he approached you about a job. You guys are friends, right?" She frowned at Penzance. "What do you know about the Hagans?"

Penzance laughed.

Ryske bobbed his head in Penzance's direction. "Penzance is the guy I was helping out the night of the auction."

"With the switch," she said and he nodded. "The night you met…"

Ryske was still nodding.

Harlow wasn't paying much attention to the other man in the room until he said, "You told her about that?"

"I don't lie to Harlow," Ryske said.

She hit his chest harder, then pointed to his mouth. "That there is a lie, right there."

Penzance laughed and sank deeper into his chair. "Her I believe… If you trust her that much, I'm in for whatever you need…" He scanned the room. "You have to be making a mint out of this."

The door at the bottom of the room opened. All the rooms adjoined, for emergency purposes. The long, sleek blonde who sashayed in didn't seem to be in need of assistance.

"I am bored, Ryskey," the blonde said, stopping to check her nails before running them into her glossy hair. "These men had no skills."

The silver dress she wore, while only a scrap of material, managed to make her look sexual, sophisticated, and expensive all at once.

"What you gonna do, sweetheart? I can't coach them before you ride them. What do you want from me?" Ryske asked and slid his arm further around her, pulling her closer. "Baby, this is Svetlana… Svet, meet Harlow."

The blonde's smile burst wide. "Ah, yes, we speak on the phone," Svetlana said, extending a hand to Harlow. "It's okay, I wash them." Pleased to hear that, she took Svetlana's hand expecting to shake. Instead, Harlow was yanked onto her feet into a hug. "I could do wonderful things for your career."

"She works for me," Ryske said. "Exclusive contract."

Easing back, Svetlana checked her out. "She is too good for you."

"I don't doubt that," Ryske said on a distracted snicker.

Svetlana was arranging her hair when Penzance spoke up. "You gonna ignore me all night, Lala?" he said, sort of sheepish in the way he peeked up at the beauty.

The blonde seemed to be happy to do just that. "I may, you evil man."

"Yeah," Penzance said and stood up. "But you called me, that's why I'm here." Moving to her side, he presented himself to her. "What do you need, Red?"

Turning quickly, Svetlana let go of Harlow and brought her hand across Penzance's face in a harsh slap. In the silence that followed, Harlow winced at the probable sting of that slap and took a discreet step back.

This couple had issues… or a penchant for pain.

"That the best you've got?" Penzance asked, which Svetlana answered with another slap.

Grabbing Vane's wrist, Svetlana addressed Ryske. "I is going for break."

Ryske wasn't paying attention at all when Svetlana dragged Penzance from the room and slammed the door.

When they were gone, Harlow sank onto the couch and took a second before leaning back to peek at the laptop screen.

"Solitaire?" she said, getting closer. "Is that the best you can do?"

"It's better than that," he said, side-nodding to the silent porn.

"I've never seen you watch porn."

"I'm not watching it," he said. "It's there for ambience."

She watched for a minute, then tilted her head. "I like the way they're doing that."

When she turned, his eyes slunk to her, the screen, and back again. Harlow bobbed her brows and bit her lip.

Relaxed as ever, his attention slid back to the computer. "Get on the bed and I'll do it better."

Nudging him, she reminded herself it wasn't a good idea to tease him. "Has it been a good night?"

Breathing out a groan, he tilted the computer lid down and stretched his back before taking her by surprise and scooping her into his lap. "It's about to be."

Even though his actions were presumptuous, it was impossible not to be flattered when he leaned in to kiss her neck. She ran her fingers up through his hair. Ryske obviously hadn't gotten the memo about teasing being a bad idea. Though this wasn't really teasing, he was being direct.

"For Pothos," she said, dipping to kiss his thick locks. "Has it been moving?"

"Yeah. It's been good for Svetlana too."

"That's good. Have you tried it?"

"Zance is right," he said, licking the notch of her throat through her necklace ring. "You haven't seen you in that dress if you think I need a drug to be hot for you."

Hmm, curious prospect. "I don't think it's possible to enhance what we have when we're together," she said. "We'd probably both drop down dead if it got any better."

Sounds from next door carried through the wall; pounding and moaning that could only be one thing.

Grinning, she touched her mouth to his. "Listen to Penzance go."

He sighed. "I've been listening to that shit all night, in stereo."

Slipping a finger under the strap of her dress, Ryske drew it down and cupped her exposed breast. Squeezing and fondling, he dipped his head to suckle her nipple.

"Is that why you're like this?"

"I'm like this because we haven't had sex since you ditched me to go to the sap," he said, scooping a forearm under her ass to pick her up and carry her around the armchair.

Harlow held his shoulders when he climbed onto the bed on his knees. She clung tighter when he dropped forward, putting her on her back and laying down over her.

"You know we can't," she murmured into his hair when his lips descended from hers to head for her cleavage. Ryske hooked the back of her knee on his wrist and guided her leg around him, putting her knee to his ribs. He held it there with an elbow.

"What's the story with you and Penzance?" Harlow asked, running her fingers through his hair as he liberated her other breast to pay it the same attention as the first.

"Used to run with us when we were kids," Ryske said.

"He's from the neighborhood. He dabbled with us." He rose to flash her a feral smile. "He and me had a great system… Best wingman on the crew when it came to picking up girls."

He ducked back down and dragged his teeth on the swell of her breast.

"What happened?"

"Don't know," he said. "Floyd did, I guess. Don't know what he told Dover. Vane fell for a girl, it was all good. He ditched her and then he was gone. His aunt too. Don't know why. Don't know what happened. Always figured he'd be back."

"He never was?"

"Nope," he said, shaking his head in her cleavage.

Scrunching his hair, Harlow tried to drag his head away from her flesh. Ryske grumbled and resisted. His amour was flattering, but this wasn't the place for them to be making decisions about their relationship.

"Baby, we can't do it here," she said, running her calves up and down his sides. "If you fuck me here, you'll have to fuck everyone. You can't break the rules for me and not them."

"You were designed for breaking rules."

Harlow wasn't really sure what that meant, but it sounded hot. "Let me go on top," she said, trying to turn him over.

Again, he resisted. "No," he said and lifted his hips just enough to open his slacks. "This is my rodeo."

Was she the bull in this scenario? Didn't matter because a delighted squeal interrupted them.

Ryske took his mouth from her breast to look over his shoulder. That gave Harlow the chance to push onto her elbows to see who'd come in.

A brunette in a bustier on the arm of a pot-bellied banker Harlow was sure she'd met at one of her father's functions. Given her position and situation, she forgave him for not recognizing her. She couldn't remember his name either.

"Should we come back later?" the brunette giggled, leaning to the side to address her while Ryske climbed off the bed. "I'm sorry, I hate to interrupt a girl while she's working."

Sitting up, Harlow scooped her breasts back into her dress and smiled. Ryske was stomping around doing something in the concealed corner of the room.

"Hey, it's his nickel," Harlow said. "I get paid either way."

The girl laughed again, but Harlow was more amused by the glare on Ryske's face. He tramped around the end of the bed, past the curtain and completed the transaction with the pot-bellied banker.

After, Ryske bowed to murmur something in the brunette's ear and then kissed her cheek. It was nice the brunette remembered she was there. They waved farewell as the brunette trotted her client out.

Ryske turned to her. "It's my nickel?"

"I suppose technically," she said, pushing her fists into the mattress to slide off the bed. "Since I invested money and you didn't…" Sashaying to him, Harlow took hold of his hips and guided him down onto the couch. Putting her hands on his shoulders, she bent at the waist to get her face close to his. "You work for me, big boy."

His amused smirk tried to play down his enjoyment of the idea, though it was an epic failure. "Oh, do I? And what are you gonna do with that power, boss?"

"I can do whatever I goddamn like to you, any time I want."

Skimming her hands down his torso, she sank to her knees and slid her hands down his thighs to his knees. Pushing them apart, her eyes drifted up to his. She wasn't surprised to see the drowsy heat he had pinned on her.

"Yes, you can," he purred.

He'd already begun to open his pants on the bed, so she finished what he started. Freeing his cock, she worked his shaft in her fist.

"This doesn't mean anything," she said, leaning in to circle his head with her tongue.

"You think I give a damn?" he asked. "Suck it."

Opening her mouth wide, she sucked him into her throat and lost some of her anxiety when he released a hiss of satisfaction. She'd go down in the annals of history as the best boss ever after this. Even knowing they could be caught any time didn't slow her down. People did come in, but they didn't distract her.

Harlow maybe had one more chance to enjoy him before Ophelia took him away from her, possibly for good. If Brash or Animal got their way, it would definitely be for good.

News of what she'd done would travel to Ophelia and probably infuriate her. But Harlow was supposed to want to aggravate her, so this could be sold as a maneuver. Although Ryske was supposed to be charming Ophelia tonight, it wouldn't be hard to convince her that he'd been suckered in by the allure of a blowjob.

After tonight, life was going to get messier for all of them, and Harlow wouldn't have Ryske to ground her. So she resolved to do this and enjoy it. To hell with the plan and the complications and the uncertainty of what they were. She wanted to comfort him, and take his comfort, and she couldn't think of a better way to do it.

THIRTY

HARLOW HAD TO ABANDON Ryske when Lydia came to relieve her. In the floating position, she was in and out of his room with customers who wanted to purchase Pothos, female companionship, or both.

Before that hour was out, Penzance returned to the armchair he'd left to screw Svetlana. The next time Harlow went in, Maze was there, and the trio were playing cards.

Her last couple of rotations were just going through the motions. Although the sun would be rising soon, there was no sense that the night was over. If anything, her own sense of anticipation had risen; the card game was pending.

When the time came to shut it down, Brash and Animal checked out the rooms and busied themselves ushering people out of Windsor's. Other than the select few still being entertained by Parratt and Yarker, everyone else was clearing out.

Harlow was probably off the clock, but she left her post to move to the next one anyway. Anwen was still with Ryske when Harlow got there. She didn't comment or shoo the woman away. Everything was winding down after all.

"You guys got stamina," Penzance said when she climbed onto Maze's lap.

The porn was off and a table had been brought in for the men to play poker. Positioned in front of the couch with a chair at either end, it held the piles of chips in front of each of the guys. The pot looked to be a large one.

"Want in?" Ryske asked her.

Moving Maze's wrist, she peeked at his cards. "No, his hand's too good."

"Nightingale!" Maze protested.

The other men laughed at her apparent fatal error.

"Guess I'm out then," Penzance said.

Ryske winked at her and tossed his cards down. "You're a good girl," he said. "Take it, Maze."

Snaking an arm around her, Maze pulled her down to smack a kiss to her cheekbone. "Yes, you are, Nightingale," he said and threw his cards to the table.

Ryske's face dropped and Penzance swore. "Nine high, are you kidding?"

"I think the expression is read 'em and weep," Harlow said.

Maze leaned over her lap to scoop the chips toward them.

"You conned me," Ryske said. "Trinket… you conned me?"

She was still laughing when the curtain moved and Ophelia came in.

Although the hostess smiled, the laughter died. With a widening stance and her arms folded across her chest, it wasn't difficult to see that Ophelia wasn't amused. There was a party going on and she wasn't invited. Everyone was enjoying themselves. Without her. Anwen was draped against Ryske. Harlow was on Maze. By all appearances, this seemed to be a close-knit group.

Ophelia wasn't welcome; at least she wasn't trusted by them. In other rooms, there were so many misconceptions and half-truths that it was difficult to remember who had loyalty to whom and what everyone's motivations were. But in this space, there were bonds so strong they wouldn't ever be shaken; no matter how much Ophelia wanted to damage them.

Gliding toward Penzance, Ophelia stretched a hand toward him. "Mr. Vane," she said, singling out the only man in the room who wasn't occupied by a woman. "I must welcome you aboard properly. Dinner? Tomorrow?"

"Sure thing," he said, taking her hand when she put it in front of his face.

He had been stacking chips. Ophelia gave him little choice except to kiss her knuckles, since that was clearly what she wanted.

"These guys will clear this up. I'll pack up the product, and we'll all chill next door for a while. Sound good, Fi?"

Smiling, Ophelia nodded once and slid her hand away from Vane. It pleased her that Ryske ignored Anwen and Harlow, and deferred to her. The woman thought she was breaking through.

"Yes," Ophelia said. "Although I have to steal Harlow away."

"Take her," Ryske said, sweeping the cards together to pile them into a deck.

Harlow rose.

Maze held onto her hand. "Maybe I'm not done with her."

His attempt to give her a sense of importance while Ophelia tried to diminish it was sweet.

Ophelia just laughed. "Oh, Mr. Rowe, you can have her back in just a jiff."

Retreating to the edge of the room, Ophelia held open the curtain with an extended arm and gestured for Harlow to join her.

Curious about what Ophelia might want, Harlow went, and reached the main floor first. Parratt and Yarker were by the door saying goodbye to the last of their friends as the servers cleared tables. Women moved in and out of the private rooms, wearing street clothes, many with wet hair piled on their heads. Harlow didn't blame them for wanting to wash the night off their bodies. In their position, she'd be eager to do the same.

Ophelia guided her toward the back of the room,

where there were no patrons and few employees.

She huddled close. "Are you playing?"

"Cards?" Harlow asked. "Yes. I was planning on it."

Although she was no shark, Harlow had picked up quite a lot since she'd started dabbling in poker. She wouldn't win big, but she could make up numbers. She was an investor, like anyone else. To be treated like an equal, she had to act like one. After the night she'd had, being sidelined, especially by Parratt, she needed to assert herself.

"Oh," Ophelia said, surprised. "I… I thought you might refrain."

Sensing this was going somewhere, Harlow lacked patience, but folded her arms. "Why would I do that?"

"Just because you have so much to lose," Ophelia said and narrowed her eyes. "You do understand that these games are rarely about money. Most of us have little interest in monetary stakes. We have plenty of that."

Most of them, meaning not her.

Harlow understood the attempt at an insult. "What do you think I have to lose?"

"Your virtue, for one," Ophelia said. "You have no property to offer, no assets. I can't think what you will be able to put on the table that isn't…"

The way she trailed off made Harlow feel like she was being setup. It was funny. Being so used to Ryske and the guys, who were much more subtle in their manipulation, she began to think of Ophelia as the graceless elephant of the game. The hostess was too desperate and obvious to disguise what she wanted.

"What?"

"Nothing," Ophelia said and picked up a section of Harlow's hair. "Nothing, honey… You should play. You're right… Did you have fun tonight?"

"I wouldn't exactly call it fun."

"No?" Ophelia said. "Word was you had a special kind of fun on one particular rotation…" Harlow didn't know what to say. She didn't flinch and certainly wasn't going to apologize. Ophelia laughed. "Oh, don't worry, honey. I'm sure you were easily persuaded. Some women are designed for that kind of work."

Harlow wanted to state that she was designed for Ryske but wasn't going to rock the boat this close to the finale. "Is that all you wanted?"

"No," Ophelia said, dropping her arm and becoming all business. "You stated that once you got your buy-in back, you would hand over your Pothos interest to Ryske. Is that still accurate?"

Why would Ophelia want this confirmation? And what would Ryske want her to say? Yes or no? If he had her shares, and Ophelia took possession of him in the card game—which the woman thought would lead to them becoming a power couple—then they would have a stronger position in the consortium.

But it would also mean Harlow would be cut out. If she was given back her buy-in, she could return the money to Rupert. That was an important factor to consider. Her ex would need the money for his wedding and for his child.

Harlow assumed Rupert would be selling the apartment they'd lived in together. He'd need more room when the baby came. Her sister needed Rupert to get that money back.

That wasn't the only consideration. No matter what, Ophelia needed Ryske. Parratt and Yarker did too. If they tried to swindle Ryske out of anything, he'd pull Svetlana and her girls from their deal. That would lead to Pothos being available without any outlet for its effects.

"I can write you a check," Ophelia said.

Just knowing that cutting her out was so important to Ophelia, she wanted to push back. "I think I want to stick around for a while, see how this plays out."

Ophelia's lips narrowed; she didn't do a great job of holding back her irritation. "If you're sure," she said. "But you know we won't see any return for quite some time."

There was probably money tonight. Except money made at the bar was kept for Ophelia's overheads. The money made by Svetlana's girls was kept by them. The only profit Harlow was entitled to was the Pothos money. Given the consortium had agreed to expand both in terms of physical space and client base, they'd need something to invest in the restructure.

Ryske's plan started to make more sense.

Ophelia would be entitled to a cut for structural changes and remodeling needed for the accommodation of Pothos. But if Ryske took the deed for the club, he would have to approve those changes, and it would become their ballgame. If he refused to make the changes—which, of course, he wouldn't do until after everything was made legal—then there would be nothing the others could do. They'd have to be happy with the status quo, look for new premises, or follow whatever plan Ryske fed them.

"I can live with that," Harlow said. "Ryske won't mind covering my bills if I barter with blowjobs."

Ophelia's jaw ticked and her attention faltered. Harlow turned around. About twenty feet away, the group who'd been in Ryske's room were exiting, spreading out on the main floor.

"Crash," she called over her shoulder, grabbing his focus. He started to come toward them, but stopped when she held up a hand. "No, it's okay, you don't have to come over. Just a quick question. Will you pay my cellphone bill if I suck you off?"

His brows rose. Penzance laughed and slapped his buddy between the shoulder blades. He then walked away from Ryske, sliding an arm around Anwen as he went.

"Try it, see what happens," Ryske said and sauntered off after Penzance.

Harlow was enjoying her own audacity when Ophelia leaned in to whisper in her ear. "I suppose the hooker label my brother gave you was accurate," she hissed. "He pays you for sex. You just admitted it."

Tipping her chin toward her shoulder, it didn't matter that Harlow couldn't see Ophelia when she replied. "And he won't even fuck you for free… What does that tell you?"

Walking away from Ophelia, she wasn't ashamed of what she had with Ryske. Ophelia obviously couldn't understand it if she thought money had any bearing on their relationship.

Despite her certainty, whatever happened tonight, no matter how it sickened her, Harlow had to go with it. This was a night when going all in would mean going all out. Being back there where Ryske had been stabbed on the very night they met, there was no denying their lives had gone full circle.

When Ryske had sat down at the card table on the night he'd been stabbed, he'd had no idea who she was. They'd been oblivious to each other. Tonight, by the time he got up again, he'd have to be oblivious of her once more. If he didn't block her out, if he didn't forget her, he'd never be able to do what he had to do.

THIRTY-ONE

THE FIRST HOUR involved silly stakes. Chips were thrown in the pot and small amounts of money were bet to get the night started. Things began to get more interesting when Parratt and Yarker made bets on each other's holiday homes and yachts. Harlow got the sense that was more about bragging than either of them having a genuine interest in using each others' facilities.

Maze had been allowed to play; he sat next to Ophelia who had Ryske at her other side. Anwen was next around the circular table. Then it was Parratt, Harlow, and Yarker completed the set.

Parratt, Ryske, and Ophelia were the only three left in this hand. Everyone else had folded. They were waiting for Parratt to decide if he wanted to match Ryske's bet of the Lamborghini he'd apparently been gifted by a model. Harlow didn't know if he really had access to such a car. Probably not. She'd never seen a Lamborghini but had no worries about their crew following through if needed. Noon would take care of acquisitions.

Lydia wasn't playing. Her role was to stay perched behind Parratt, keeping a note of all the bets and agreements. As they went along, each note was signed by all parties to form a rudimentary contract. They were thorough if nothing else. At the start of the game, a declaration by each individual required they state they'd honor all bets and agreements.

Fidelity to their claims wasn't a leap. If someone reneged on a deal, they'd lose credibility, and forfeit their right to collect on their own winnings.

"I'm out," Parratt said and tossed down his cards.

All eyes fell to Ophelia who shifted to get a better look at Ryske at her side. As per usual, his expression gave nothing away. Ophelia, on the other hand, was wearing a smile. It wasn't difficult to see that the hostess was enjoying this game. The game or being seated in close proximity to Ryske, could go either way.

"What have you got, Fi?" Ryske asked. "Want to see me?"

"With what?" Ophelia asked, pressing her cards to her chest. Everyone else liked to leave their cards on the table and just peek at them. Ophelia insisted on holding hers in her hand. "One car for another? The only cars I own are limos."

Shaking his head, Ryske turned out his lip. "You've got to have something I want."

Ophelia's cards descended to her stomach. She squashed them against her to better slant toward him. "What would you like?"

Giving her what she wanted, Ryske admired her chest, and the rest of her figure. His deep, admiring eyes remained alight with intrigue. Yet, they were subdued like he was hiding an interest in more than her cards.

"I can have anything?" he asked.

Licking her lips, Ophelia dropped her register. "Anything."

After thinking about it as his attention floated around the room, he nodded. "Okay," Ryske said. "This place."

Ophelia blinked while Parratt sat up straighter. "You… you want my club?"

"Yeah," Ryske said. "Why not?"

"You can't give him the club," Parratt blustered. "We need Windsor's. It's a perfect location, discreet, and close enough to the nicer part of town without being a main hub."

"I don't think you need to list its attributes," Anwen said. "Ophelia knows how important Windsor's is to Pothos… We don't have to worry. Ryske is an integral part of the operation."

"Right," Ryske said. "I'm not screwing around. All I'm looking for is an even playing field with you rich fucks."

Good, his interest seemed genuine. That came off as a credible reason for him to desire ownership. Ophelia, Parratt, and Yarker weren't shy about waving their assets around, or making her, Ryske, and anyone without it, feel less than they were.

Keeping her eyes on Ryske, Ophelia called over her shoulder to the man who'd been on the periphery throughout. "Brash, be a sweetheart and run up to the office. Grab the deeds for the club."

Tightening his lips until they thinned, Brash hesitated. He could be as irritated as he liked. At the end of the day, he had no choice in present company except to march off and do as commanded.

"Are you sure you want to do this?" Yarker asked Ophelia who was basking in Ryske's focus.

"Oh, please," Ophelia spat over her shoulder. "What does this hovel matter to me? It doesn't matter who owns the building, we all profit from it. My Ryske wouldn't do anything rash… Besides…" She raised a finger to Ryske's jaw and drew a line around its angle. "I have notions of my own… When I win…" Ryske's expression loosened. "I want to make an amendment to your offer."

"What's that?" he asked, turning his mouth to graze the base of her thumb with his lips.

"I'll need someone to drive me around in my new car… Will you take me for a spin?"

"You win, and I'll do that. If I win, you get a lawyer here first thing to transfer ownership to me."

Putting her cards face-down on the table, Ophelia wriggled closer. Harlow didn't need to see to know the beauty was sliding a hand up Ryske's thigh.

"Hmm, transfer of ownership…" Ophelia drawled. "Is there anything else you'd like to own, Mr. Ryske?"

On impulse, Harlow touched the chain around her neck. The one Ryske padlocked onto her while whispering in her ear that as long as she wore it, she belonged to him. Whether she liked it or not.

Knowing that her heart was his, Harlow would never consider taking it off. The connection it gave her to him was powerful. Only they knew it existed, much like the depth of their relationship.

Ophelia continued to tease. Her mouth came within a tantalizing inch of Ryske's. She didn't get to make contact though. Brash returned and broke the moment by tossing the papers onto the table.

"Well," Ophelia said. "I call… What have you got, handsome?" Although she asked, she didn't wait for a response. Ophelia picked up her cards and turned them over. "Does it beat my flush?"

All eyes moved from her cards to Ryske assessing the revealed cards. He didn't need to verify the hand, it was there for all to see. But her love knew how to build suspense. Even Harlow—who knew he'd have this—was on the edge of her seat, holding her breath to see if he'd won.

"I don't know, sweetheart," he said and put down his cards. "How does a straight flush do?"

The table erupted with noise, some happy, some not so.

Ophelia slapped a hand off the edge of the table, everything bounced. "Damnit."

Although she wore a frown, the hostess didn't really seem all that disappointed.

Harlow suspected Ophelia didn't care who won, her or Ryske, because she believed they were going to get together. Ryske took a pen from his pocket and offered it to Ophelia. Without much reluctance, she grabbed both the pen and the deed to begin filling it out.

From what Harlow had seen of the document on the table, it was a warranty deed. Her father said they were used as proof there were no encumbrances on a property, such as a mortgage, or others with a claim to ownership. Ophelia must have had the document prepared after her brother's death.

Smart. No one would want others to have ties to a business used for illegal dealings.

"Wait a minute, we should give her a chance to win it back," Yarker said. "One more hand."

Ophelia finished filling in the deed. Though it would probably need to be recorded by a lawyer and witnessed by a notary to make it official. Harlow didn't know for sure, but she doubted signing over a building was that easy.

"Yes," Ophelia said, throwing the deed at Ryske and sitting up poker straight. "I do want to play one more… I get to call the stakes this time… I want to pick my opponent too. Play head to head."

Ryske was the one who'd lost and the one who she wanted, so Harlow waited to hear his name.

"Go for it," Ryske said, no doubt expecting the same.

"Harlow," Ophelia said, pointing across the table. "I want to play her."

"You lost to me," Ryske said.

A new wariness shimmered around him. Compared to Ryske, Harlow was a rookie. Ophelia was no pro, but this was a helluva risk for them to take. While Ryske was trying to talk Ophelia out of her choice, Harlow was more interested in what Ophelia wanted from her.

The point of this hand was to lose. Harlow knew that from the numerous times they'd gone over the plan. Ryske was supposed to lose to Ophelia who would pick him as her prize. It seemed Ophelia was up to something far more devious. Her prize would still be Ryske, but she wanted Harlow to be the one to give him up. Maybe as a way to drive that wedge between them.

Putting Ryske on the table could be seen as disrespectful or emasculating. Ophelia might believe Ryske would resent Harlow for handing him over like he was her possession. Except he'd already promised that he wouldn't let Ophelia put a wedge between them. Harlow couldn't screw this up, she couldn't. It was literally impossible because the point was to lose.

"I'll do it," Harlow said, shirking her wondering and ignoring all the shocked, intrigued faces to fixate only on

Ophelia.

The hostess' smile spread like the cat who'd caught the mouse and the fish and sautéed them in thick fresh cream.

"Excellent," the beauty said, shuffling the cards. "Are we ready?"

All but Ryske apparently. "Wait a second—"

"You don't trust me to play in your stead?" Harlow asked.

There wasn't even a comparison between her skills and Ryske's. He'd been playing cards since he was a kid; she hadn't even been playing for a year.

"Trinket, I—"

"I promise we won't stake your precious new building," Harlow said and looked at Ophelia. "Fair?"

Ophelia nodded once. "Agreed."

Both tossed in their blinds, the measly amounts meant to get the game started. Ophelia dealt them five cards each, and placed down the draw pile.

The game went on in almost silence, with only the players muttering as required. Harlow kept her focus on Ophelia's. Even though neither of them were expressive, Harlow felt a cool serenity in her gut. This stage of the plan was easy. It was easy to lose a game of cards. What came next would be harder, but it wasn't the time to be thinking about next. If Harlow thought too much about that, she'd lose her ability to project the cool confidence needed to play this game.

"So, Miss Sweeting," Ophelia said. "I suppose it's time to negotiate." Harlow nodded once. "Why don't you tell me what you are so eager to have?"

"What we were talking about earlier," Harlow said without being explicit. Theirs had been a deal within a deal when it came to the money invested. She wasn't sure what Parratt and Yarker knew about it. "But I maintain my stake."

"You want me to write you a check," Ophelia said and cracked a pitying smile. "Oh, money. It is so precious to those who don't have it, and so meaningless to those of us who do."

"It's only meaningless because you do have it," Maze said, defending her, but remaining cool.

His family was loaded, so most would believe he was in that category too. Only a select few knew how completely he'd shunned that part of his life.

"I will agree," Ophelia said. "You get your check and your stake."

It didn't really matter what Harlow said. She could've asked for a unicorn Frisbee and left it at that. She didn't have a winning hand. Three of a kind wasn't going to win her much, and she'd bluffed it well, but that was okay. Her goal wasn't to win.

Glancing at Ryske, she let herself see him for the first time. All through the hand, she'd felt his eyes on her and had refused to look his way. With each breath, his chest moved shallow and slow. Harlow couldn't imagine he was mad. It worked out better this way. Her losing was more credible than him losing. Everyone knew he was a shark. He would never put himself in a position to lose; especially something as valuable as his own freedom.

"When we lay these cards down," Ophelia said, bringing Harlow's attention back. "One of us will be the victor."

"Yes," Harlow said. "Now why don't you declare to the table what it is you want from me? What do I have that you want?"

"Oh, it's simple really," Ophelia said, sitting back and draping an arm across Ryske's lap. "One little thing… It's something you shouldn't have any trouble giving me at all… It won't bankrupt you and it is yours to give… I could ask for so much more—"

"Spit it out, Ophelia," Harlow said. "What do you want?"

Something about the way Ophelia angled her head from one side to the other, and curled the corner of her mouth, piqued Harlow's anxiety.

Moving forward, away from Ryske, Ophelia leaned across the table. "You."

Anwen gasped, but it was Ryske's nasal intake of breath that Harlow heard over the shift of others.

"Me?" Harlow asked, trying to act like she hadn't

expected a different response.

"Yes," Ophelia said. "Simply put, you'll be mine… until I say otherwise or am convinced to put your freedom back on the table." The smug smile on her face betrayed how unlikely that was. "I'd say my bet matches yours given how much you're requesting I hand over."

Which was Ophelia's way of telling Harlow it would take her a decade to make a half million dollars. Except maintaining her stake in Pothos in addition to the payout meant Harlow could make ten times that amount. So, in truth, her request totaled more than just a half million dollars.

The tension at the table was palpable. Everyone seemed to be holding their breath, but Harlow kept her cool. None of this mattered. She'd promised herself that no matter what happened tonight, she would go with it. The point was to lose and collect intelligence on Ophelia. It didn't matter which of them was on the inside, so long as one of them was.

"Done," Harlow said.

Both Ryske and Maze sat straighter; Harlow didn't let herself look at them. Lydia was scribbling behind her, but it didn't matter. Everyone heard their agreement.

Harlow revealed her cards. Ryske immediately sagged as Ophelia whooped and turned hers to show a full house. The hostess had won, but that was no surprise.

Trying her best to appear downtrodden and beaten, Harlow was doing a dance inside.

Whatever Ophelia wanted her to do, she'd do it with bells on. Her fear had been leaving Ryske behind, and now she wouldn't have to.

Almost everyone was rising from the table and Ophelia was calling for champagne. Ryske hadn't moved. Their eyes found each other through the melee. She didn't need him to speak; he was furious. Mad as all hell. Harlow smiled.

This might not have been what she meant by distance, but they were going to be parted. Ryske would be worried, the way she was at the thought of leaving him behind. Ophelia wasn't going to make this easy. Her new boss would probably have all sorts of demeaning tasks lined up. Harlow would do them and wouldn't complain.

From here on out, Harlow belonged to Ophelia. Her belief in her earlier claim to Ryske remained true. No doubt Ophelia's first requirement would be no contact between her and Ryske. But she was going to be on the inside. Someone from their crew had to be, and this was the way it worked out.

She wouldn't let her crew down. Whatever the price for triumph, Harlow would pay it. Even if it meant never having his heart, or his body, again.

TO BE CONCLUDED...

Thank you for reading this tale!
If you can, please take the time to review.

~

Ask your local library for more Scarlett Finn novels!

~

For all things Scarlett Finn
check out:

www.scarlettfinn.com

www.ingramcontent.com/pod-product-compliance
Lightning Source LLC
Chambersburg PA
CBHW010539170726
48285CB00008B/2683